A DECLARATION OF LOVE

Grinning a challenge, Standen leaned a hand against the doorframe over her shoulder and enquired, "Is that why you like me so well?"

Tucking her papers like a shield against her bosom, Grace blushed involuntarily, then stammered, "Y-you are too sure of yourself." She dropped her gaze self-consciously.

Lowering his hand from the wall to cup her chin, Standen raised her face and smiled down at her. She fairly glowed in the half light of the hallway, and he found it difficult to speak. His mouth felt dry of a sudden, as it had done when he was called to recite sums he had forgotten. Running the tip of his tongue across his lips, he said, "I have never had reason to doubt myself before."

Mesmerized by the motion of his tongue over his lips, Grace laid a hand upon his lapel, saying, "You are a rare man."

"Yes, I am," he said proudly, yet lightly. "Would you like to know me better?"

His voice drew her toward him, and she shivered in his tender grasp, wanting him with a shameless longing that betrayed her upbringing. With their disparate backgrounds, she knew better than to throw herself at him. Still, she could not help but confess what they both wanted to hear: "I wish it above all things."

ZEBRA'S REGENCY ROMANCES
DAZZLE AND DELIGHT

A BEGUILING INTRIGUE   (4441, $3.99)
by Olivia Sumner

Pretty as a picture Justine Riggs cared nothing for propriety. She dressed as a boy, sat on her horse like a jockey, and pondered the stars like a scientist. But when she tried to best the handsome Quenton Fletcher, Marquess of Devon, by proving that she was the better equestrian, he would try to prove Justine's antics were pure folly. The game he had in mind was seduction—never imagining that he might lose his heart in the process!

AN INCONVENIENT ENGAGEMENT   (4442, $3.99)
by Joy Reed

Rebecca Wentworth was furious when she saw her betrothed waltzing with another. So she decides to make him jealous by flirting with the handsomest man at the ball, John Collinwood, Earl of Stanford. The "wicked" nobleman knew exactly what the enticing miss was up to—and he was only too happy to play along. But as Rebecca gazed into his magnificent eyes, her errant fiancé was soon utterly forgotten!

SCANDAL'S LADY   (4472, $3.99)
by Mary Kingsley

Cassandra was shocked to learn that the new Earl of Lynton was her childhood friend, Nicholas St. John. After years at sea and mixed feelings Nicholas had come home to take the family title. And although Cassandra knew her place as a governess, she could not help the thrill that went through her each time he was near. Nicholas was pleased to find that his old friend Cassandra was his new next door neighbor, but after being near her, he wondered if mere friendship would be enough . . .

HIS LORDSHIP'S REWARD   (4473, $3.99)
by Carola Dunn

As the daughter of a seasoned soldier, Fanny Ingram was accustomed to the vagaries of military life and cared not a whit about matters of rank and social standing. So she certainly never foresaw her *tendre* for handsome Viscount Roworth of Kent with whom she was forced to share lodgings, while he carried out his clandestine activities on behalf of the British Army. And though good sense told Roworth to keep his distance, he couldn't stop from taking Fanny in his arms for a kiss that made all hearts equal!

Available wherever paperbacks are sold, or order direct from the Publisher. Send cover price plus 50¢ per copy for mailing and handling to Penguin USA, P.O. Box 999, c/o Dept. 17109, Bergenfield, NJ 07621. Residents of New York and Tennessee must include sales tax. DO NOT SEND CASH.

The Secret Scribbler

Cynthia Richey

ZEBRA BOOKS
KENSINGTON PUBLISHING CORP.

For my husband Lou with love,
because he never minded that I was
a Scribbling Woman.

One

For the fourth time in less than an hour, Letitia Penworth pulled aside the curtain of the window in the vicarage parlor in Cherhill and peered out toward the London Road. After a moment, she let the white starched curtain fall in place and turned to frown at her daughter. Grace was sitting quietly as if she were at her last prayers.

Indeed, it seemed she may well be. Letitia did not account Grace a pretty girl, for her pale hair and colorless eyes tended to gaze off in a distracted manner that lent her an otherworldly appearance and reminded one of a martyred saint. Grace often had to be jarred out of self-absorbed daydreams, but Letitia believed that if her daughter would repress the tendency to dream long enough to accept an offer of marriage, she would soon find herself too busy to indulge foolish thoughts.

Alas, Grace seemed destined to remain upon the shelf. At three-and-twenty, she was still unwed. And if the coach did not come to deliver her to London, she would never meet an eligible male willing to marry her. Glancing once more toward the unaccommodating road, Letitia demanded, "Will the coach never come?" on the end of an impatient sigh.

The object of maternal concern, sitting very straight

on a hard-backed settee, wondered did her parent despair for the dilatory coach or for having been burdened with an unmarriageable daughter on a parson's living? Turning a compassionate smile toward her mother, Grace concealed all signs that she believed marriage was not the only means of keeping body and soul together. Unlike her elder sister Amity, she possessed a talent which would allow her to live independently. However, if she said anything in that vein, Grace knew her mother would rehearse the tired refrain, beginning with "Women were not meant to live independently," and ending with the warning that she had disappointed everyone last spring when she turned down a very kind offer of marriage by the Reverend Thomas Gladstone.

A shudder rasped down her spine as she recalled what a cold fish her hopeful suitor had been. Yet, rather than call attention to herself, Grace kept her tongue between her teeth.

However, her mother seemed to think she needed one more lesson on "Woman's Place" before her daughter left for London. While she heard another rendition of the "Duty of Woman," including such Capital Topics as "Submission" and "Sacrifice," Grace schooled her expressive face to affect a respectful, but distant mask as she allowed herself to think about the Rights of Women.

The younger daughter of the Reverend Mr. Penworth had not been given permission to fill her head with such radical ideas, but Grace had long ago decided true Christianity was far more revolutionary than the views espoused by Mary Wollstonecraft or William Cobbett. Her faith had led her in equally dangerous paths, having compelled her to write a series of heartfelt articles decrying an aristocratic indifference to the poor that bordered on oppression.

Grace was careful to let no one in her family know of her dangerous opinions or to reveal the fact that several of her more volatile social commentaries had been accepted for publication and compiled into one slim volume which had been entitled *Cock and Bull Stories.* Furthermore, her publisher, Mr. DuBarry, had expressed an interest in meeting her. As soon as she had read his flattering letter, she began to hope she might support herself by her scribblings.

Grace knew her parents would forbid her to step out their door if they realized she harbored such unladylike and dangerous ambitions. Her parents were sending her to her sister in London, to accept an offer of marriage—*any* offer of marriage. Grace wondered who would take as his bride a woman possessed of no ability to paint, sing, or embroider.

It was all for the best she did not pin her hopes on marriage. No husband would allow her to express her extreme social views.

But that need not concern her. She was launching a career that could possibly be of great benefit to her countrymen and women. That possibility invading her thoughts, Grace found it nearly impossible to rein in feelings of mounting excitement.

She did not know how, but this visit to town was going to change her life. It took all her hard-won self-control to keep from exclaiming her hopes.

Fortunately her silver-haired mother seemed not to notice her inattention, as she was completing her harangue with the final admonition, "I hope you will do your sister the courtesy of being a helpful guest."

Jolted out of her meditation, Grace mumbled a guilty "Yes, Mama." She was relieved at last to hear the clatter of iron wheels on gravel and the blast of the coachman's horn as their neighbor's coach halted in front of the vicarage gate.

Grace's father, the Reverend Andrew Penworth, wandered from his study with a drowsy look on his well-fed countenance. "Are you going now?" he enquired.

"Yes, Papa," Grace replied as he moved to the window. "Mama has been reminding me of my duty."

"Do not begrudge her the lessons," he said kindly as he returned to his daughter's side. "She means well." He kissed her forehead as he said, "Be a good girl." He spoke in an indulgent manner, as if his youngest daughter were only going upstairs to bed, not on a trip of nearly one hundred miles, then handed her into a warm pelisse of violet-colored cashmere. The richly hued, dark fabric miraculously tinged her pale complexion with a delicate blush of life that made the parson look at her more closely. He was accustomed to having an almost invisible younger daughter. "Do say your prayers," he concluded, nervously patting her arm.

"I will, Papa," she replied, tying bonnet strings into a severe bow beneath her chin.

He retied the bow into a more becoming knot alongside her left ear. "My dear, I cannot understand how such pretty fingers can tie such an inelegant tangle."

Letitia exhaled another great sigh before she said, "Nor can I, Andrew. Was there ever such a graceless girl?" She refastened two frogs which Grace had misaligned in her haste to be away. Frowning, Letitia added, "Now you'll do. But keep a level head, daughter, and look no higher than you ought."

Recalled to her duty, Grace's self-confidence slipped a notch, as did her hopeful smile. "I shall do my best, Mama."

Her father gently pinched her cheek to pluck up her courage. "If those fools in London fail to come up to scratch, daughter, you will always be welcome back home," he said in a half whisper, as his wife swept to the front door in a flurry of somber gray skirts and crisp white apron. "I have always been grateful for your diligence in parish relief." He seemed to reconsider, then said in determined tones, "Not what I will, however; the Lord's will be done."

Grace buried her face in her father's shoulder before lifting wet, shining eyes to his gentle brown ones. As a child there had been nothing she could not tell him. How she wished she might confide her hopes to him before she took her leave. But six years ago when she came out into local society, he had commanded her to put away the foolish things of her youth. As far as he was concerned, her stubborn idealism had gone with her chapbooks into the box which had been placed in the dusty attic.

A pang of guilt that she had disobeyed her parent made her cling tightly to him and say, "I hope I will make you proud of me."

He rubbed her shoulder. "I *am* proud of you. And so, if you asked her, is your mother. Only Mrs. Matthews has married off all of her daughters, one to a baronet; and your mother cannot stand to be outdone on anything."

Grace raised a tremulous smile to his benign countenance. His brown eyes were twinkling with mischief as he added, "So you see she is pinning all her hopes on your marrying at least a baron."

Realizing the vanity of such hopes, Grace still was able to smile. She longed to believe the best in others, but she had developed a swordlike understanding of people that cut to the true reason behind their actions. She knew her mother was considering not the romantic, but the more practical side of marrying her into the nobility: she hoped to secure a lucrative preferment for her husband so they might be rid of the meager living provided by his currently disinterested benefactor, Mr. Edmund Davies.

Mr. Davies was a middle-aged and childless widower who had fortunately been content to leave his vast wealth to a nephew rather than embarrass Grace by proposing to her so that he might set up his own nursery. But thankfully he felt some sense of duty to her family. After enduring Letitia's many complaints about the expense of purchasing a ticket on the stage and the dangers incumbent on a young lady traveling alone in a public conveyance, he offered his coach to convey the vicar's younger daughter to London.

As her mother opened the door, Grace was struck with the thought that the burden of sending a daughter into the World must not weigh as heavily when others bore it.

A footman, clad in maroon and gold livery, stepped inside, hauled Grace's trunk upon his broad shoulder, and carried it to the maroon-painted conveyance. Carrying her portmanteau, Grace followed her parents down the flower-decked stone walk and kissed them both goodbye. The footman handed her into the flyer, then folded up the ladder and took his place on the box as the coachman gave his high-spirited team the office to start.

Grace lowered the window and leaned out to wave a final farewell to her parents. But they had seen her off on too many hopeful journeys and witnessed too many dismal returns to share her excitement in leaving this time. They had turned back to the house, as if, out of their sight, she was already out of their minds.

Two

Having refreshed himself in the taproom while his groom saw to the change of horses, Alan Perry Faulkner, the Duke of Standen, pulled his curricle out of the cobbled yard of the Swan and Bell in Newbury, just as a lumbering maroon traveling coach made a wide turn into the yard. Despite his best efforts to avoid the mobile obstruction, the near wheel of his curricle became locked with the right rear wheel of the unwieldy vehicle. As the driver of the other conveyance seemed unaware he was transporting a very expensive vehicle into the yard against its driver's will, the duke cried out, "Stop, you blasted fool! Where did you learn to herd cattle?"

Immediately the coach ground to a halt, whereupon its driver heaved himself unsteadily to the pavement. By the way he returned the duke's scowl with an ingenuous grin, it seemed he believed he was not at fault for the wreck. "Did ye not hear m' trumpet, m'lor?" he enquired rather thickly as he raised his broad-brimmed hat and scratched his head in a befuddled manner.

"I think the dead must have heard it," remarked the irate peer as he took a step away. The jehu's alcoholic breath was in danger of catching fire from the lanterns being lit in the twilight. "I wonder you could keep your seat."

Drawing himself into a more erect, but still rubbery posture, the bleary-eyed man asserted, "Can drive wi' me eyes shut."

"I think you must have been," Standen muttered. He glanced toward the wheels which his groom Tat and the coach's footman were attempting to unlock, when his attention was recalled by an anxious female calling from within the coach, "I cannot open the door!"

Immediately the duke turned from his impatient examination of the rough operation to regard the owner of that melodious voice.

A pale face appeared at the window. Standen wondered whether she meant to faint.

Normally he had no pity for such missish tricks. However, the young lady's unstudied concern struck a sudden chord of sympathy in the duke's cynical heart. Against his pragmatic nature, he felt a manly impulse to protect this young woman from whatever future disasters her elevated coachman might drive her into.

"Pray, calm yourself, miss," he said in a quietly reassuring tone. "Our carriages are wedged within the gate." This information caused her to recoil from the window as she emitted a gasp of alarm. He strove again to ease her fears. "You are in no danger."

"No, of course not," Grace agreed, attempting to extricate herself from the coil John Coachman had driven her into. She pushed ineffectively against the door, which was wedged tightly against the curricle. Peering once more out the lowered window, she said in a surprisingly commanding tone, "Do have to goodness to move the coach, John. Then you may remove the obstruction."

She said the last word in a manner that convinced Standen she believed him at fault for the collision. Determined to set her straight and regain some of his dignity, he said in faintly offended tones, "That . . . obstruction is a very expensive curricle, ma'am. Which your coachman has foolishly wrecked with his tippling ways."

Grace leaned farther outside the window to get a better view of the tangle. The right wheel of the racing vehicle was locked between her coach and its right rear wheel. A yellow fender crumpled like a paper fan alongside the window nearly cut her cheek as she drew back inside, saying, "Oh John. I thought you had sworn off the bottle."

"A man can't help his thirst, miss," said the guilty coachman, dropping his head and fumbling with the brim of his hat.

"I suppose not," Grace said in disappointed tones. She thought she had finally convinced him rum would do him no good. Perhaps the experience would sober him. The last thing he needed was her criticism. Clasping her hands together to control their sudden, inexplicable tendency to shake, she said in an equally tremulous voice, "Well, it pains me to confess it, but I cannot help myself either. Kindly hurry."

While he was too worldly-wise to be unduly affected by such feminine wiles as trembling voices and tearful entreaties, Standen could not but understand her predicament. Though he meant to tell her in the most detached manner he could assume, he was surprised by the sincerity in his voice as he said, "I daresay I should be uneasy were I in your place."

Grace pulled herself together to regard the man standing outside the coach. In her customary style, she sized him up at a glance, but to her amazement the sight caused her heart to flutter even though she deemed him nothing more than a dandy who lacked the manners even to remove his hat in the presence of a lady. She suppressed the urge to tell him that she was only eager to be away. Instead she was struck by an uncharacteristic breathlessness affecting her ability to think. Smiling giddily, she said, "How kind of you to understand, sir. But I believe you would not allow yourself to remain a prisoner. It would be no trick for you to climb out the window." As soon as the words had left her mouth, she wanted to bite her tongue. She sounded as silly as Amity did when complimenting a certain gentleman's skill with the ribbons or in the dance.

Her smile, having disturbed the duke's natural cool detachment, left him determined to single-handedly dislodge the wreckage from the gate. Indeed, the same amount of strength coursed through his veins as had enabled him to perform near-impossible feats on behalf of fallen comrades at Waterloo.

Then, his heroics had been accompanied by an overpowering rage. Now, however, the impulse was tempered by a gentleness that flummoxed him. But his reflexes suffered nothing from his unaccustomed reaction.

The inn's groom was leading the hired team from the traces of his ruined curricle. Tat was directing the dislodgment of the expensive trap from the heavy wheel of the coach. A terrible sound of grinding metal and popping spokes filled the air.

"Oh, do stop," Grace snapped, appearing once more at the dark window to survey the proceedings. As usual, the men ignored her suggestion, thinking they could do very well on their own. All their efforts did was damage the smaller vehicle more. "Why do you not move the coach?"

"Can't, miss," said the coachman, blowing his red, vein-laced nose into an oversized handkerchief. "Wheels're twined tighter'n two lovers' legs."

Though most ladies would have been shocked by such indelicate language, Grace was not. She did not like it, of course, but could scarcely complain without sounding missish.

The nobleman spluttered, "I say, such language is hardly suited to a lady's ears. Mind your tongue," as the curricle was dragged free of its obstruction. Immediately he edged out the footman's attempt to yank open the jammed door. Letting down the steps and reaching forth a hand, he said, "If you will allow me, miss?"

Grace was of a mind to step down alone, but a passing glance at his face arrested her declaration. Awed by the stare of the most commanding blue eyes she had ever seen, she placed her gloved fingers in his strong grasp and hesitantly began her descent.

As she lay her hand in his, Standen was stunned by the protective instinct surging through him. Her weight as she leaned upon his arm was slight. He was unprepared when the lower step gave way with a groan, tumbling the girl headlong into his arms.

She gave a startled cry as she fell. Once more he

was captured by protective instincts as he gathered her tenderly in his arms. And though he was ready to catch her, he was in no way prepared for the shock holding her occasioned. When their bodies came into contact, the duke felt he had been singed with a firebrand.

Grace grasped his arms and stared at him. Stunned by the look of utter surprise on her rescuer's face, she dragged her gaze from his, hiding her face beneath the brim of her bonnet, knowing a furious blush heated her cheeks. What wanton feelings had coursed through her body as he supported her! She had been surprised by the fall, of course, but that in no way excused her wish to remain folded against his broad chest or the unlady-like sensations that continued to throb through her veins.

It was a good thing she had decided against marriage, she told herself, for a husband would only be shocked by her free response to his touch. "Pray, let me go," she murmured, hoping her rescuer would not obey.

Immediately he set her on her feet and ushered her to the fat landlady who had begun making her way through the unruly crowd in her yard.

Placing an arm around Grace's shoulders, the land-lady said, "You poor lamb. Come with Mrs. Tibbits, dear."

"Just a moment," Grace said, attempting to gather her wits about herself. There was something she must do, but what? A moment's thought recalled her to her manners. She must thank her benefactor and introduce herself. "I haven't—"

"No buts, miss," said Mrs. Tibbits in commanding but kind tones. "Ye'll not be wishin' to expose yourself

to any more impolite stares." And with that, she swept
a forbidding glare around the yard.

Confident that he had left his lovely nemesis in capable hands, Standen turned to make arrangements for
the repair of his curricle. But he hadn't reckoned on
the lady's persistence. Or her forwardness. His progress
was halted by a hand on his sleeve.

"I beg your pardon, sir," she said, surprising Standen
with her air of gentle authority. "But since my coachman has ruined your vehicle, I wish you would allow
me to offer you a ride to wherever it is you are bound."

The suggestion was entirely improper, but judging
from the lady's modest attire, the duke guessed it had
been innocently made. He smiled an apology. "I am
sorry, I must decline your kind offer. It would not be
at all the thing for you to travel in my company." His
elbow being jostled by an impatient traveler who was
hustling into the taproom, he drew her out of the doorway before she could be trampled.

"I realize it is not in the usual way of things, my
lord," Grace said. "But certainly, under the circumstances, there could be no objection." Once again, she
engaged his gaze directly, hoping to show him she was
no shrinking violet who feared Society's censure. "I was
taught to do the charitable thing."

"And I was taught never to compromise a lady," he
responded with a quelling frown. "Even if she did throw
herself at my head."

"Oh," she said in a surprised voice. Her remarkable,
transparent eyes widened innocently before she said,
"That never occurred to me."

"But the thought would cross several thousand other

minds," Standen said. A trace of amusement softened his warning.

"Yes," she sighed agreement. "It is the way of the world to think the worst of good intentions."

Standen could not restrain himself from laughing at this innocent assertion. "What a child you are," he said at last. "Has no one explained to you that only the worst of intentions exist between men and women?"

The landlady intruded herself between the nobleman and the bemused lady. " 'Ere now, my lord, you oughtn't to be talkin' to Miss that way," she chided, trying to hasten her charge within the public room. After ordering a maid to see to the lady's luggage, she added, "T'ain't proper. And for the same reason 'e can't ride wi' ye to Londontown, miss. Now, you 'ave a rest while your coachman dries out, then tomorra ye can be on your way."

"Tomorrow?" Grace exclaimed, clutching her reticule to herself. "But I am expected in Thatcham . . ."

Despite her appointment, Standen did not wish to let this outspoken lady go. But he was suddenly as tongue-tied as if he were an unlicked cub, and blurted, "You cannot go until we have discussed the payment of damages," for want of anything more tactful to say. With a gasp of offended dignity, the landlady snatched her charge by the arm and began to haul her abovestairs. The duke stumbled over an apology. "Mind, I do not hold you responsible for the damage to my curricle, but . . ."

Grace drew to a halt on the bottom step, staring at the nobleman, then said, "I can only apologize for the inconvenience my coachman and I have caused you, sir; and pledge my—"

"You don't owe him a thing, miss," said Mrs. Tibbits in forbidding tones. The landlady then directed a narrow, calculating look at the duke. "For shame, sir. A rich lord like yerself threatenin' a poor woman for money. She's trembling like an aspen leaf. Be off wi' ye now, before I get the blacksmith after ye." Then, placing a comforting but unnecessary arm around her shoulder, Mrs. Tibbits bustled Grace to a private room.

Unable to credit his blundering manner, the duke watched her retreat until her carriage boots and swaying hem disappeared to the upper story. When he returned, frustrated, to the coach yard, his curricle was being pushed, on its one remaining wheel, toward the wheelwright's shop, while the undamaged coach had been moved by the head ostler through the tangle of horsemen and vehicular traffic to the stable.

Thwarted by the delay in his travel plans and confounded by his attraction to the unknown but intriguing lady, the duke muttered, "Damn," and kicked at a stone with the toe of his highly polished Hessians. The stone flew across an open area and struck the impaired coachman on the leg above his sturdy boots.

The man yelped, then, rubbing his abused limb, mumbled, "Beggin' yer pardon, sir. Din't see 'e."

Startled out of his dark study, Standen was conscience-stricken at having done injury to a fellow who apparently could not see himself out of harm's way. He spoke an apology.

"No lastin' hurt done, me lor'," replied the driver as

he began to make his unsteady way toward the stables after his coach.

Realizing he had not determined the lady's name or her direction, Standen called out, "Wait! I need to know: to whom does your coach belong?"

"Why, Mr. Davies, sir," said the wary coachman. "Out of Cherhill."

"Thank you," Standen said, with the satisfaction of knowing that the cloth merchant resided in Holles Street when in London.

Although the named gentleman did not travel in the duke's rarified circle, Standen decided he would seek an introduction to allow him to make a formal apology for any inconvenience their accident had caused. "I shall call upon Mr. Davies to make certain your party suffered no injury," he announced. Knowing a generous boon would place him in the coachman's good stead, he placed a coin in the man's outspread hand. However, when he saw the gleam in the man's eye, he commanded, "Be careful you do not spend that on drink. You must deliver your passenger to London in one piece."

"Yes, me lor'," mumbled the disappointed driver as he pocketed the coin. "But a nip o' rum keeps a man's toes from freezin' on the box."

"An unlikely event given the warm spring we've had." Standen directed a dark frown toward the swaying coachman. "I shall be watching you, and unless you wish your employer to hear of your tippling ways, I would advise you to swear off the bottle, at least until you deliver your charge into Holles Street."

He turned on his heel in a smart about-face, reentering the public room as the befuddled driver remarked to no one but himself, "Got 'is direction all wrong. 'S Harley Street *we're* for."

After depositing her charge in a small quiet chamber overlooking the kitchen yard, the landlady removed Grace's bonnet and pelisse, then placed the battered portmanteau her harried maid had produced on a quaint, painted chest of drawers that was shoved against the outer wall of the room.

Gnawing on a corner of her lip, Grace longed to put her experience with the odious nobleman into perspective by writing. He had not asked whether she had been injured, either in the collision or her fall. It was what she had come to anticipate from the nobility, but for once, she was not satisfied to discover her expectations met. Perhaps she was more distressed by her indecorous response to his handling. Thank heaven she had behaved outwardly just as she ought. No one could be aware that she was inwardly a swirl of confusion.

When the landlady returned, bearing a bottle and a glass, Grace watched curiously as the woman poured a generous quantity of amber liquid into the heavy tumbler. " 'Ere, miss," she said, urging the glass upon Grace, "this'll stiffen your backbone."

Grace accepted the glass without question and swallowed deeply, then clasped a hand over her mouth, as it had been seared by the quantity of brandy she had gulped. Unable to get her breath, she gasped open-mouthed, "What? . . . what?" She choked, then managed to whisper, "What are you trying to do? Kill me?"

"Now that brought color back to your cheeks, didn't it?" crowed Mrs. Tibbits with a self-satisfied grin. Reaching for the half-empty tumbler, she said soothingly, "I'll take the glass now, miss, before you spill the dregs on your gown."

"Thank you, Mrs. Tibbits," Grace said, wishing her voice did not sound as breathless as it did. "You must know I had not planned to overnight at an inn. My friends, the Reverend Mr. Wiggins and his wife Amanda, expect me hourly in Thatcham."

"No need to worry them, dear," said the landlady, collecting her tray. "A boy will be sent with a note."

"No!" Grace cried, mentally counting the cost of sending a messenger to Amanda's. "I mean, you don't understand, ma'am. I . . . did not expect to have to pay for dinner and a room." She felt herself blush to confess, "My father, the Reverend Mr. Penworth of Cherhill, made arrangements for me to stay with friends on the way to London. He did not give me much money."

Mrs. Tibbits turned a considering eye upon her. Grace thought she would sink through the floor as her hostess appraised her worth. "You may have my entire fortune," Grace said, opening her reticule and drawing out several coins that totaled less than a pound. "In trust for your hospitality."

"La, Miss Penworth," said the landlady, waving away her coins. "I've a soft heart, some say a soft head, but I'll not take your money. You've an honest face, my dear. I know you'll pay me when you can."

"Oh, yes, I will," Grace said, vowing to dedicate her first royalties to Mrs. Tibbits.

But the landlady surprised her by laughing a merry,

"Nonsense, you'll get your husband to pay your debt as a lady always does. Perhaps bring him here for your honeymoon?" Then, bidding her guest to have a little rest, she left the stuffy room.

Rest was the furthermost thing from Grace's mind. Sliding her wealth within the confines of her reticule and snapping it closed, she strode to the window, where she looked down on the prospect before her. A kitchen maid was stealing out the open back door and running into the darkness beyond the pallid beams of light. Grace thought she heard muffled laughter coming from a pair of indistinct shadows that merged with the varying shapes of trees in the spinney at the far end of the yard.

Whatever the couple found to laugh about was of no concern to her. Indeed, feeling almost guilty for intruding on their private joy, Grace turned from the dark window to consider her own immediate future.

Independence was not as easily realized as hoped for. The accident which had caused her unexpected sojourn was one more stone in a path to self-sufficiency that might have reduced a less resourceful lady to tears. However, Grace was not so poor-spirited as to indulge in a fit of useless whimpering when circumstances turned against her. Recognizing an opportunity which must not be blinked at, she opened her portmanteau and withdrew from the bottom a lap desk which contained paper and a standish. Sitting on the floor beside the uninspiring window, she began to scribble furiously.

Thanks to a collision caused by my coachman's having repeatedly fortified himself with a flask of rum, I found myself compelled to overnight at a busy inn on the road to London.

Fortunately the landlady came to my rescue, even though I lacked the price of a room. For protection against the unwanted attentions of the gentleman whose racing curricle collided with my coach, I can only praise the accommodations and my hostess. In placing me above the kitchen, she has no doubt put me as far removed from that odious man as I could wish. I would much rather smell of cabbage and bacon than reek of scandal which must surround me should I encourage an acquaintance with a male whose every attitude cries "Aristocrat."

Though cooking odors did permeate the air in her own room, Grace thought the smell was not at all unpleasant. Indeed, the aroma of roasting chickens was delicious and whetted her appetite for dinner. But the condition of her purse made it necessary for her to disregard the insistent complaints her stomach had set up. Mrs. Tibbits might not begrudge her room for the night, but she should not feel compelled to feed her. Besides, Grace considered giving up one or two meals a small sacrifice which would strengthen her own character and sharpen her wit.

Dipping her pen in the ink and returning to her paper, she began to draw a verbal picture of the man whose prideful character failings were concealed by the physical virtues of nobility. He was tall, well-formed, impeccably attired, and one of the handsomest men it had been her pleasure to look upon, despite giving every appearance of blaming the world—or at least herself—for his inconvenience. She did suffer a temporary qualm of conscience in making him the villain of the piece. After all, her coachman was the one who had caused the wreck.

However, her imagination was given a boost by the recollection of how he had demanded she pay for the damage to his expensive equippage, enabling her to write:

Beneath a curly-brimmed beaver, my lord's hair was brown, but thick and wavy and looked as if it had been dressed by an affectionate breeze.

Grace's fingers fairly itched to smooth that fine head of hair, but she suppressed the uncharacteristically romantic impulse. The unusual yearning dismayed her, for she was not susceptible to the obvious charm of the Corinthian Set. Furthermore, the character sketch read as if she was writing a scurrilous novel for the Minerva Press, in which the heroine suffered a measure of maidenly confusion over an attractive, frightening gentleman.

Grace crossed out the offending line and continued writing her critical essay, denying emphatically that she was experiencing a similar inner conflict.

Intense blue eyes seemed to search the shadows of my bonnet as if looking for—what? A spark of interest?

Three

To her surprise, Grace discovered the anti-hero she had produced with her pen elicited more than a spark. She felt she was bursting into flame. The room had grown entirely too warm, and although the cooking smells had set her mouth to watering only a few moments ago; now it seemed she stood in the midst of a sun-baked desert.

What she needed was a glass of water. She learned, though, upon setting aside her writing utensils and moving to the washstand that the pitcher was empty and the glass sitting at its side was dusty.

Receiving no answer when she pulled the bell cord, Grace carried the pitcher to the stairs. A maid was scurrying toward the kitchen. "Excuse me," Grace said, not arresting the harried woman's course in the slightest. She hugged the pottery pitcher and followed in the servant's wake.

Standing in the door of the kitchen, she was jostled by several of the inn's employees racing back and forth to serve the hungry dinner crowd. None begged her pardon, although one trod upon her toes and snarled for her to take herself out of the way when he nearly lost his tray of dishes.

"You are an accident waiting to happen."

The familiar voice and gentle hold on her elbow did what previous impudent abuse had failed to accomplish. Grace dropped the empty pitcher. It shattered on the oak-plank flooring.

The crash momentarily silenced diners—except for one, who began to choke upon inhaling a portion of his meal. One of his tablemates pounded him on the back until the fit subsided, by which time the entire public room was again in an uproar.

Without glancing at the person who had startled her, Grace knelt to pick up the shards scattered around her feet.

The persistent gentleman plucked at her sleeve. "Get up, I say. Do you want to cut yourself?"

"No, there is no chance of that," Grace replied, placing the pieces on a wooden tray that was thrust into her hand. "I have had considerable practice in restoring broken pots. But seeing as how I was to blame for the loss, I ought to . . ."

The tray was drawn out of her arm, and she was lifted to her feet and steered toward an empty table by an open window. A delicate scent of lilac wafted into the overheated room along with the lazy sound of nectar-gathering bees. The necessary ingredients for a romantic tête-à-tête were at hand, but instead of delivering a tribute to her, her handsome escort was chiding her. "You ought to sit down and let the paid help earn a living."

She glared up at the infuriating gentleman, intending to deliver a stinging set-down, and felt a stab of conscience as she recognized him as the lovingly drawn villain of her essay. Curling brown hair caressed the impeccably folded starched neckcloth; piercing blue eyes glittered in a manner calculated to turn her bones to water.

Indeed, Grace was in danger of melting on the spot.

However, she told herself that he was acting in a manner that was anything but heroic. He was standing entirely too close to her, and he retained a possessive grip on her upper arm that did not allow her to place a more respectable distance between them.

"I do not think," she said, trying to affect a haughty tone, "that circumstances entitle you to take such liberties."

"No," he agreed, lowering her into the seat of a hard chair.

Immediately Grace flew out of the chair and into his arms with a shriek of shock and pain.

"What's this?" he demanded, putting her at arm's length as it had occurred to him that it was entirely possible that he had become entangled with a deranged person. She was dancing in a frantic circle, flapping the hem of her skirt, and completely oblivious to the horrified stares of everyone in the room. "Pray, calm yourself," he urged. "I meant no offense."

"Tell that to the bee!" Grace hissed, her normally pallid face infused with hot color. She gave a final frantic shake to her skirt.

The insect, freed at last from the confining folds of her skirt, buzzed a threat around their heads and rumbled angrily through the window.

He stared at her, saying stupidly, "I beg your pardon?"

"You sat me upon a hornet!" she cried, lowering herself gingerly upon the chair as she lifted the hem of her skirt to examine the injury she had suffered.

She was showing a great deal of neat ankle beneath her white muslin skirt. However, rather than being transported by the uncommon sight, the duke had the presence of mind to notice that her right limb was beginning to swell. Without regard to propriety, he swept her into his arms and hurried her into the kitchen.

"Pray, set me down!" Grace protested. She warred against the compelling desire to throw her arms about his shoulders, and this struggle made her ankle throb with a burning heat. Giving over to temptation, she blinked back tears and confessed, "You are hurting me."

"It is not my intention to hurt you, miss," he replied gently. When the landlady huffed into the steaming room, he ordered immediate treatment for the bee sting. With a dubious eye turned toward him, Mrs. Tibbits set to work.

While the landlady prepared a soothing ointment, Grace rested her forehead upon the gentleman's shoulder. It was firmly muscled, not padded with sawdust or stiffened with buckram as was the fashion among less physically perfect males such as the Reverend Mr. Gladstone. And rather than verdigris or musk, her rescuer smelled of soap, as if he took to heart Mr. Brummell's recommendation of daily washing. Quite unconsciously, she inhaled deeply of his clean essence and snuggled against him as if it were the most natural thing to do.

He did not recoil or stiffen in disgust at her forward manner, nor did he withdraw his strong, comforting arm from around her shoulder. Grace was glad of his support, for her ankle hurt very badly.

Having placed a chair in a corner where they would not attract the notice of every nosybody, the landlady said, "Put her down here, my lord."

The movement jostling her foot, Grace bit her lip to keep from crying out. It had been years since she had suffered a bee sting; she had forgotten how painful they were. "There, there, my dear," Mrs. Tibbits was saying as the young woman was eased onto the chair. "I'll soon have ye on your feet again."

The duke hovered anxiously at her side, not knowing what to do and feeling unaccountably guilty for her pain, until the innkeeper's wife, kneeling with Grace's swollen foot on her apron, glared daggers at him and said, "This is no place for you, my lord; be off with you now."

Begging pardon as the woman unlaced the half-boot on the delicate foot, Standen fled the room in a flustered manner. He would sooner endure the fire of battle than witness female tears. Especially *this* female's tears.

After the angry red welt had been bathed with a cooling solution of baking soda and her salved and bandaged ankle had ceased its rhythmic complaint, Grace was able to breathe a sigh of relief. Unfortunately her lower limb was still too swollen to accommodate the boot or even a slipper, and she felt the sting of embarrassment as she was conducted with one bare foot to a table nowhere near an open window.

However, the individuals populating the public room being too well-mannered to stare, her flutters soon settled down enough to allow her to enjoy a solitary meal of sliced chicken, potatoes, and early peas.

"You are lucky our landlady is so handy with a receipt book."

Grace raised her eyes from her dinner to meet her tormentor's concerned gaze.

He indicated with raised eyebrows his wish to be seated and, when she nodded, placed himself in the chair opposite hers.

"Yes," Grace replied, setting her fork on the edge of her plate. Her voice sounded strange to her own ears, as if she were speaking with a wooden spoon in her mouth. "I have always thought it an art to be cultivated." She stared unabashedly at the handsome, brown-haired gentleman, who was smiling in a manner calculated to set female hearts aflutter, if her own reaction was typical. Her pulse was tripping along at an exhaustive rate, and she found it increasingly difficult to catch her breath.

Grace could not understand it. No man had ever affected her in such a distressing manner. That it might be attributed to the insect bite and not his overwhelming virile presence did not once occur to her.

Priding herself as a woman who was able to control her emotions, her involuntary reaction shocked her. It was difficult to think when she was so distracted. For heaven's sake, she did not even know his name! All she knew of him from Mrs. Tibbits's address was that he was Noble, and that was not necessarily a recommendation in her experience.

He was probably a gamester or a rake who was weighing his chances of seducing her. Warning herself to guard against his obvious charms, she masked the welcoming light that had leapt into her eyes and applied herself to her meal.

Silence reigned at the table while she pushed perfectly delicious but untasted food around her plate and he nursed a glass of port. After her first, open perusal, she did not again look at him, giving Standen the opportunity to watch her. His quiet scrutiny led him to make the fanciful conclusions that the transparent muslin cap perched atop her pale hair glowing like a nimbus in the lamplight gave her the air of an angel.

In fact, the duke could have been tempted to believe her an otherworldly apparition. Only the fact that he had borne her weight across this very room made him aware she was no ghost, but a vital woman who made his blood pound like no woman he had met at the insipid *ton* parties toward which he was bound.

He wondered how to admit he had learned her surname from her top-heavy coachman. Miss Davies, out of Cherhill. Her father was a merchant, but he did not think Mr. Davies would object if a duke sought an introduction to his daughter. On the contrary, he might consider it an opportunity not to be missed.

But then, seeing Miss Davies's preoccupation with her meal, Standen was forced to consider the possibility she might not wish to continue their accidental acquaintance. He ran a finger under his elegant but constricting neckcloth. What lady could like a man—though he be a duke—who reminded her of such unpleasantnesses as collisions and bee stings?

Grace stopped stirring her meal and said in curiously matter-of-fact tones, "I have caused you much trouble."

"Nonsense," he replied in a hearty manner, the way

healthy people spoke to aged or infirm relatives. It was enough to plummet a weaker-willed lady's confidence, and indeed, Grace's normal aplomb suffered a blow when he added a cheerful, "Glad to be of help, that's what."

An unaccustomed lump in her throat made it difficult to speak, but she managed to say in breathless tones, "You are an amazing good sport, sir," as she again stirred peas into the potatoes on her plate.

Standen chuckled at her plain-spoken encomium. "Not entirely," he confessed.

Before he could reveal the depth of his wickedness, Grace dropped her gaze, demurely mumbling, "Well, you are human, sir, and must be permitted at least one failing." Then, regarding him once more in her straight-forward manner as he vented his amusement, she said, "I have been considering how to make everything right between us, my lord."

"Do not trouble yourself," Standen said with a dismissive wave of his long-fingered hand. "I will send that odious coachman for your father."

Grace felt her breath catch in her throat. That was the last thing he must do. "There is no need for that," she said in strangled tones as she struggled to form a convincing argument against informing her parents of this embarrassing turn. "Papa trusts my judgment."

The Reverend Mr. Penworth might do so, Grace knew, but she also knew her mother would jump to all the wrong conclusions and demand the nobleman marry her daughter. Catching herself before she could reveal that information, she pressed her lips together with the inward admonition that no sensible woman would make that lowering confession.

"Certainly he does," Standen replied in wry tones that infuriated Grace. "But in this I believe you ought to trust my judgment. You have done nothing improper, after all."

"Perhaps not in London circles," Grace replied. "But in Cherhill, I would be criticized for encouraging an acquaintance not sponsored by the local dragons of society." She felt a gentle pressure on her fingers and realized he had taken them in his hand.

The clasp felt right, but she knew it was all wrong. They lived in separate, opposing worlds. And she had no intention of relying upon a man to save her from the consequences of her own actions.

Regretfully she withdrew from his grasp. "I have inconvenienced you long enough, sir," she said firmly. "Tomorrow, my coachman will take me on to London, and I shall tell my sister that a bee stung me while I was arranging flowers."

He began to chuckle aloud. "How absurd," he chortled. "She will never believe you. It is a simple matter to put blooms in a vase."

Grace averted her eyes so as to deny herself the inexplicable tremble of delight his smile elicited. "Simple for Amity and every other finished lady of my acquaintance," she said, setting aside the unappetizing ragout she had made of her plate. "But I am a horse of a different color."

"No, really?" Standen enquired, tilting his head so as to look at her from several angles. "You appear quite normal."

"Well, I am not," Grace replied in defensive tones. "I cannot sing or play the pianoforte; nor can I embroider or paint."

"What a singularly unaccomplished female you are," he said, an amused smile tingeing his words with indulgence. He had never met a lady who did not revel in her accomplishments. The longer he knew her, the more refreshing he found this Miss Davies. "Surely you exaggerate."

"Yes, I do," she said without hesitation. "I tell stories. Exaggeration is my only accomplishment."

Her unadorned statement made his smile broaden.

How Grace wished she might trust this gentleman with her secret aptitude. But she supposed did he know how she indulged her talent, he would consider her a Scribbling Woman or even a Traitor. "You might well laugh, my lord," she said meekly. "It is not a ladylike talent."

"On the contrary," Standen said, still grinning. "You are too much the lady for anything you do to be considered unladylike."

Taken aback by his praise, Grace wondered if he was teasing her or flirting. Deciding he must be engaging in the latter sport, she primmed her mouth and came abruptly to her feet. "Thank you," she said, remembering too late her painful bee sting. Leaning on the table to relieve its throbbing, she added, "I must bid you a good night before you turn my head with your flattery."

As if stunned by her suddenly cold manner, the duke arose regally from his chair. Smiling in an enigmatic manner, he said, "You are mistaken, ma'am, if you think yourself entirely without accomplishment. Your ladylike set-down is capable of drawing more blood than Napoleon's legions ever did." Bowing, he promised to see her safely to London in the morning. Then he took himself stiffly above stairs.

His presumption left Grace determined never to see him again and feeling strangely disappointed in her resolve.

Early the next morning, the landlady placed a pewter tray on the table next to the duke's right elbow. On the tray was a twist of paper. Startled out of his early morning lethargy, he set his mug of coffee on the table and enquired testily, "What's this?"

Having been informed by his top-lofty groom that her inn had been honored by the presence of the Duke of Standen, who was Traveling Incognito, the landlady executed a nervous curtsey and replied, "Beggin' your pardon, Your Grace. It's from Miss."

Standen's narrow eyes slid from the untidy rouleau to the fidgeting woman as he said, "Where is she? She ought to have arisen by now. We have a lot of miles to cover if we mean to get to Town before nightfall."

"Gone, Your Grace." The landlady was twisting a corner of her apron into a knot every bit as tight as the distorted paper that sat at his elbow. "Left before light with her servants."

Although the communication disturbed him, he betrayed it only by tensing his jaw and clenching one hand. "Did she? And did you make an attempt to detain her?"

"Well, how could I, sir?" The woman spread her

hands in an attitude which said His Grace's disappointment was not of her making. "When you paid 'er shot."

The duke removed the paper twist from the tray and
spilled several shillings into his hand. "What is this?"

"She said it was to pay for the damage to your curricle."

Standen's fingers closed convulsively around the
coins. They were sticky, as if their former owner had
placed them in her reticule with unwrapped lemon
drops. The offering was every bit as innocently made
as her early, open-hearted offer that he accompany her
to London.

What a child she was. If anyone was ever in need of
protection, it was she, he mused, his heart clutching in
an overwhelming sensation of concern. He had never
met a lady quite like Miss Davies of Cherhill, who first
offered him the comfort of her coach, then ran from
him like a scared kitten.

And her offering to pay for his damaged curricle was
laughable. At this rate, he would own her soul before
she made a dent in the debt. And so he would tell her
when he returned her money. Twisting the coins in their
paper, he dropped them into his purse and demanded
the inn's fastest horse be saddled immediately. He would
soon teach the chit to trifle with him.

On the next day, he arrived in London, drenched by
constant rainfall and shaking from the afflictions of an
incipient cold and studied rage. His valet, seeing that
his master was in danger of collapsing from an inflam-
mation, put the duke straightaway to bed and tossed the
battered, damp twist of coins, which had found their

way into a pocket, onto a tray of seldom-worn fobs and seals.

On the next morning, Standen was sufficiently recovered to consider the stack of invitations that had been piled on his hall table. Finding one from Peter Ramsey, an old friend from school who had made his fortune with the East India Company, he discarded the others and ripped it open. "So Ram is bringing out his niece," he said under his breath. "Ought to go to see how time has treated him."

The thought of meeting a daughter of the merchant class recalled his accidental association with Miss Davies. While his valet was arranging the folds of his cravat, the duke said, "I was carrying several coins in my pocket when I rode in, Valmont. Might you recall where you placed them?" This was said in as nonchalant a manner as might be affected, given the fact that he had never before bothered his valet about such trifling matters.

Valmont betrayed his surprise over his master's uncharacteristic query by creasing the neckcloth. As he unwound the constrictor, he mentally counted *à dix,* then responded with a casual query of his own—"Were they twisted in a scrap of old paper?"—while winding a fresh length of linen around the duke's throat.

Standen spoiled that one before the second twist by lowering his chin and glaring at his valet. Affecting a moue of disappointment, Valmont chided, "You are not usually so careless of your appearance, Your Grace."

Ignoring the petulant complaint, the duke removed the neckcloth and demanded, "What did you do with that damned rouleau?"

Valmont strode to the jewelry chest and began sliding open drawers. "In here, Your Grace," he said. From the bottom drawer, he produced the peculiar talisman. Standen snatched them out of his valet's lily-white hand and threw himself into a chair at his desk, where he scrawled a hasty note before sealing the missive and coins together. Then he flung them into Valmont's hands. "Deliver this into Miss Davies's hands at her father's house on Holles Street."

"Your Grace?" enquired the stunned valet upon seeing his master's grimly set face. "What about your neckcloth?"

"I am perfectly capable of strangling myself," the duke snapped.

As if concerned by the sudden flush which darkened his master's face, Valmont asked, "Are you having a relapse, sir?"

"No," Standen replied as he wrapped a three-foot-long cloth around his neck. He looked down his nose at his glass in an attitude which was at once dismissive and damning. "I merely wish to have done some unfortunate business." Actually he confessed inwardly, he was furious with himself for having treated the lady with such contempt. Not to have introduced himself must have seemed to her an insult *extraordinaire*.

"Very well, Your Grace," said Valmont, wondering whether the duke had lost his heart to this Miss Davies.

Valmont returned to Standen House on Grosvenor Square with his own heart in his throat. Before he confronted His Grace with his information, he stopped by the sitting room of the duke's housekeeper. Mrs. Beemis, a comfortably plump matron who had developed a *tendre* for the elegant and compactly built Frenchman, admitted him with a smile that went a long way toward fortifying his cowardly soul. A glass of fine brandy served with effusive compliments by the besotted lady fully restored his deflated confidence. Finally, with a gallant bow and an affectionate kiss of Mrs. Beemis's pudgy red fingers, Valmont marched upstairs to confront the duke with his intelligence.

Standen received the valet's news with disbelieving ears. "What do you mean, the house is shuttered and the knocker is down?" He glared at the sealed note which reposed in Valmont's open hand with an unforgiving look.

"Your 'Miss Davies' does not exist," Valmont said, brandy swelling his courage but diminishing his perception. "She has taken you in, Your Grace."

The duke turned on his servant and saw at once the wiry man's smugness. "Did you think to enquire among the servants as to the lady's direction?"

"I did, Your Grace," Valmont replied, as if stricken that his master would question his alertness. "There resided belowstairs only one servant, an aged retainer named Winslow. He told me Mr. Davies was a childless widower." As he set about picking up the stack of ruined starchers from the floor, the valet cleverly suggested, "Could your Miss Davies be perhaps the cit's light o' love?"

The suspicion, once intruded upon Standen's mind, could not be removed. But he did not like thinking that the modest miss who had made light of her accomplishments was in the same class of women as Harriette Wilson or Julia Johnstone. And so he uttered a terse, "Bite your tongue, Valmont," as he pulled an impeccable blue morning coat with shining silver buttons over his waistcoat and buff-colored inexpressibles. "Middle Class Morality excludes that possibility. More likely, she is a neighbor benefiting from his kindness."

Valmont cringed in apprehension that his master might ruin the well-cut coat by donning it unassisted, but the duke believed a man whose clothing was so tight as to make it impossible to dress himself or move with some degree of freedom was no man, but a clothes tree. When he succeeded in donning the garment without ripping the seams, Valmont's beady black eyes narrowed jealously. He was fast learning that his employer was not as dependent upon him as he would like. He did not wish to have this unknown female intrude herself further into their lives, unless, of course, she was one of the members of the Fashionably Impure. Then, she could not interfere in the management of their household affairs. Valmont would continue to reign supreme in the duke's day-to-day life.

In as innocent a manner as he could contrive, given his oily nature, he said, "Perhaps, Your Grace. But her flight from the inn, leaving no direction, seems suspicious to say the least."

Telling himself that her innocent, confused manner was not consistent with the usually shocking comportment of the demi-reps with whom he was acquainted, Standen strode vengefully toward the door. If she were Mr. Davies's ward or a neighbor accepting his hospitality, she most likely would be Not At Home to strangers.

"I daresay she had more reason to suspect me," he said, firmly clutching the note in his tanned fist. "You have mistaken both her character and her direction, and I shall prove it."

But his search on Holles Street proved as fruitless and frustrating for himself as it was satisfying for his valet. Miss Davies was not to be found, and a frowning Duke of Standen was forced to consider the possibility that his valet had read the right of her character in her callous disappearance, without owning responsibility himself for not having enquired as to both the identity and direction of the lady in question. It was easier to salve his conscience by attributing the oversight to the likelihood, expressed unctuously by Valmont, that she had her reasons for wishing to remain anonymous.

But, he reasoned, lengthening his stride as if to distance himself from plaguing thoughts of laughing eyes and spun silver hair, if she imagined she might intrigue him into pursuing her, she had sadly miscalculated him. Ignoring the fact that he had actually chased her to London, he ordered his horse saddled to resume his habitual early morning ride. The duke vowed he would forget that angelic countenance but not her childish regard for his feelings. That memory would forever make him as wary of the fair sex as if they were stinging bees.

Four

Upon hearing Grace's confession that she preferred to forego that evening's ball because her ankle was still swollen from the bee sting, Amity exclaimed, "I cannot understand how you managed to be stung in such an unlikely location."

Grace shrugged her slender shoulders, wishing her sister would leave her in peace to recover from her unsettling encounter with Nobility. To her chagrin, she had been half-fearing, half-hoping the top-lofty, anonymous peer would pursue her—that he was even now looking for her. Telling herself he was more likely to charge her with a crime than seek a social introduction, Grace quelled her foolish longing. "You know how it is with me, Amity," she said with a self-deprecating smile. "If I am so unwise as to intrude upon the bee's domain, he has every right to defend it."

"But while arranging flowers?" Amity's voice rose on a disbelieving note as she threw up her hands. "I cannot credit it. Except," she amended, laying one thoughtful finger aside her rice-powdered cheek, "where you are concerned." Leaning forward confidentially, she offered some affectionate sisterly advice. "Really, my dear," she said, one darkened eyebrow shooting up enticingly as an encouraging smile overspread her porcelain features, "you cannot hope to please a gentleman unless you cultivate *some* womanly arts."

Grace returned her sister's smile, forbearing to justify her lack of accomplishment or betray by complaint that such comments made her more determined to set things right with her pen. No one decried a gentleman's lack of "refinement" or complained if a man's fingers were ink-stained. His occupation, whatever it may be, was allowed to be Important. Nothing a lady did was taken seriously unless she was dedicated to "doing good works" and then she was condemned as a "Methodist" or a "Meddler."

Before she allowed her unhappy ruminations to distress her, Grace allowed that she did possess one advantage over a man. People liked to talk with her. They trusted her with their troubles. And from having accompanied her father on the charitable rounds of his parish, she knew the depths of people's troubles—that soldiers could not support their families on promises of pensions, tenant farmers could not pay rents with corn prices so low, weavers were locked out of mills or forced to work for a pittance on home looms. She knew they suffered worse humiliations and felt her efforts at righting the wrongs at times were less than useless.

But Grace was determined. Somehow she would make the Aristocracy see that their responsibility to the souls placed by their Creator in weaker vessels or inferior social positions outweighed the privilege and pleasure of rank.

But, of course, she could not express such sentiments to her sister. Amity, despite her good heart and all her charitable Improving Works, completely enjoyed her position as a banker's wife. She would not understand the passion for justice that compelled Grace to expose Oppression in her essays.

Fortunately Grace was spared making any reply by the timely appearance of her sister's children. They burst through the salon door with an explosion of affectionate noise.

"Hello again, Aunt Grace!" exclaimed Hugh as he strode across the rose-colored carpet. The ten-year-old, a miniature of his dark-haired father Colin down to his very businesslike suit of clothes, stretched forth a very manly and proper hand. "I thought Miss Cornthewaite would never excuse us from our schoolwork."

Grace was rather taken aback when he bowed over her fingers rather than throwing his arms about her neck as he had done yesterday, but her disappointment was tempered somewhat by his younger sibling's exuberant greeting.

Blond Katharine, at six, was not too old to withhold a joyous exclamation or a hug. After nearly strangling and deafening her favorite aunt, she looked at her frowning mother and enquired in a strangely hesitant fashion, "Mummy, can Aunt Grace have tea with us in the nursery today?"

Amity folded her lips in a considering moue, then said, "Not today, dear one. Your aunt will not wish to climb all those stairs."

Katharine breathed a disappointed sigh, then plopped down in a heap of azure muslin skirts and ribbons at her aunt's feet. "That is too bad," she said. "We had planned a play."

"A play sounds delightful," Grace began, not wishing to dash her niece and nephew's hopes. "Perhaps you could perform it for me here."

"Not today," Amity interjected in firm but not unkind tones. "You will want to rest for the ball tonight."

At her sister's expression of concern, Grace's gray eyes opened wide as she said, "But I should like to, Amity. If I am satisfied to be Aunt Grace for the present, why do you not enjoy the peace?"

"That is not to the point," Amity replied. "One does not come to London for peace, my dear, and you did not come all this way to play nursemaid to my offspring." She glanced around the room as if she were counting children and had come up one short. Turning an indulgent gaze toward the door, she said, "Well, come forward and greet your Aunt Grace, Teddy. You are not usually so shy."

Dressed in a military-styled suit, the four-year-old was hanging back by the open door, chewing on one finger. Grace winked at him.

In the face of such encouragement, he seemed to come alive. He dashed joyfully across the room and flung himself at her. Grace's demure cornette took a tumble when he threw his arms about her neck and bestowed a smacking kiss upon her cheek.

"Never mind then," he asserted, stepping back and executing a manly little bow in a belated effort to appear as grown up as his hero Hugh. "We'll have tea here with Aunt Grace if she's too old to climb stairs."

"Teddy!" cautioned his mother. Her blue eyes opened wide in shock. "Your aunt is not old."

"*I* did not think so," he persisted, climbing into

Grace's lap as he regarded her with adoring blue eyes. Grace could not refrain from kissing his curly golden head. It smelled of Castile soap and baby sweat, and made her arms ache to hold a blessed burden of her own. Innocent of wrong intentions, Teddy was explaining to his mother, "Only I heard you tell Papa that she was too old for another season."

Grace's mouth fell open in a burst of embarrassed giggles. Controlling the giddy fit with an effort, she covered her lips with fingertips that were not quite steady and said, "Oh my."

Her sister's mouth also flew open, but she was incapable of speech just at the moment. She had not lost all her faculties, however, for she was blushing in a becoming manner that expressed regrets for her tongue far more readily than words could. When at last she found her voice, she said in disappointed tones, "Teddy, you have hurt Grace's feelings. I hope you will apologize."

The little boy turned a gaze upon Grace that wrenched her heart. "I-I'm sorry," he sniffed, linking his chubby fingers with hers. "I didn' mean to hurt your feelings. Only, I thought Mama meant you were going to die."

"That is what comes of listening at keyholes," Amity said in loving but firm tones, adding the regretful caveat, "In my infancy, such behavior must have sent me to bed without supper." Despite her dire warning, she lifted a silver bell from the table at her side and rang for tea.

While her sister was expressing to a housemaid her desire that nursery tea be served in the salon, Grace hugged Teddy when he made to slide in disgrace from her lap. "Pray, do not trouble yourself, Teddy. I do not intend to turn up my toes just yet. There are too many places to visit and too many sights to see." His face brightened at the prospect. "Furthermore, sir, I do not think you are foolish. Your honesty is refreshing."

Amity must have heard this last, for she offered the opinion, "He is very like you, Grace."

"Thank you," Grace replied as she stroked Teddy's curls. They were damp in the overheated room.

"As a matter of fact," Amity said, turning an affectionate eye on Hugh and Katharine, "I am reminded of you in each of my children."

Little Katharine, who had been content to sit at her aunt's feet, arose and draped herself over the arm of Grace's chair. Her silver-gray eyes sparkled with childish affection as she lisped, "I want to be like you in all things, Aunt Grace."

"Oh no, Kate, you must be an Original," Grace urged, recalling with horror her several unsuccessful seasons. "Take the world by storm and make your mama proud."

The little girl absently twined a lock of her aunt's pale hair around a finger. Then she gazed straight at her and said, "There is no one like you, Aunt."

Laughing, Grace agreed, "I am sure of that, sweetheart."

"It is true," Kate reiterated. "Mama said God broke the mold when he made you." Grace heard Amity's gasp and saw her embarrassed blush, and regretted Katharine's lack of tact, not for her own sake but for the reproach it must earn the little girl. "You *did* say so, Mama," Kate vowed in unrepentant tones. Then turning her gaze upon Grace, she said, "I am glad that no one else has an aunt like mine."

"You are forgetting me," said Hugh in an affronted tone.

"And me!" declared Teddy, twisting about in Grace's lap. "There is nobody I'd rather have tell me a story than you."

Despite the children's loving approbation, Grace felt the sting of her sister's unthinking comments. Kate was stroking her cheek with baby soft fingers. *"Will* you tell us a story?" she enquired.

"Plenty of time for that later," Amity interjected. "Your aunt is fatigued by her journey, and she is ill with the bee sting." Her fingers fluttered about as if she were shooing the troublesome insects. "Do not plague her for fairy tales."

Alarmed, Hugh came to his feet. "What? Are you still in pain?" he enquired, concern etched upon his brow. Placing a footstool at his aunt's disposal, he sat beside the slippered foot she gratefully rested on the needlework cushion. Completely serious, he said, *"Now* you can be comfortable while you spin yarn."

Grace laughed. How she loved her sister's children. They were like her in many respects, not the least of which was their single-minded determination to forge ahead against all possible opposition. Indulgently she suggested, "Shall I tell you about the wicked queen bee?"

"Oh, yes!" "How wonderful!" "Is that who stung you?" came three enchanted responses. A fourth boomed out quellingly, "Absolutely not!"

Four pairs of eyes in varying shades of blue and gray

turned toward Amity as she had meant them to. Without arising from the cushion of her chair, she raised herself to her most imperious maternal height and said, as the tea tray was delivered to her side, "Not another word until I have served tea."

Grace sensed a strategic withdrawal of her cherubic allies as they chorused, "Yes, Mama," amidst sparkling glances that promised mischief in the making. One by one, before each child accepted the cup of hot chocolate and the plate of cakes and jellies, they pantomimed turning a key against their tightly pressed lips. Burdened with her own cup and plate, Grace gave the children a conspiratorial wink as Amity, unseeing, filled a cup for herself.

When everyone had been served, Hugh came to his feet and lifted his cup from its saucer. "To the Best of Aunts," he intoned in a manner as studied as it was heartfelt.

Teddy shot to his feet without spilling a drop from his half-filled cup. His plate, however, tumbled from his knees, throwing sponge cakes across the carpet. "Huzza!" he roared, as if cheering conquering heroes. "Huzza!" Oblivious to the crumbs, he marched back and forth before his aunt.

As she regarded the mess her youngest was making of her expensive carpet, Amity could only gulp tea.

Grace made every attempt not to giggle, but to no avail. Finally, before she succumbed to a fit of inexcusable mirth, she exclaimed, "Huzza yourself!" and hid behind her cup.

Kate, sitting on a chair next to her aunt, with little blue shoes dangling six inches from the floor, raised her cup in a most ladylike manner to her lips and said, "I hope *your* fairy tale will come true, Aunt."

"All of them?" Grace enquired.

"Not all," Kate replied in all seriousness. She crossed her ankles and swung them in engaging arcs as she added, "That would be beyond everything wonderful." To Grace's amused eye, the little girl appeared every bit as practiced at taking scandal broth as her mother. As if to heighten the suspense, she took a dainty sip of her beverage, then directed a meaningful look at her aunt and explained, "I meant only the Happily Ever After part."

Both Teddy and Hugh snapped to attention and echoed a resounding, "Hear, hear," before tossing the lukewarm contents of their cups down their throats.

Shortly thereafter, Amity ordered Grace upstairs to rest while her children took their customary afternoon walk with their governess, Miss Cornthewaite. "They must understand you are not here for their enjoyment," she said, after she had kissed the last of her encumbrances goodbye.

As the children filed downstairs, Grace said, "But I see them so seldom, Amity; surely five more minutes will do none of us any harm."

"Five more minutes in a darkened room with cool compresses on your poor ankle will do you much better," Amity replied firmly. She directed a housemaid to take Miss Grace to her room and see to the application of a soothing poultice. "Mind, she is to rest until dinner," she concluded, as if knowing her sister must obey her direction if she made someone else responsible.

"But the story," Grace protested.

"There will be time between the children's supper and your ball," Amity assured her.

Despite her sister's assurance, Grace was possessed of barely enough time to bid the children good night before Amity summoned her downstairs. "You *will* have your story, my dears," she promised, hugging each child before turning to go downstairs.

"Oh, do not worry your head," Hugh said in a tone of light bravado. "We're all agreed you deserve your happy ending. And we mean to help you get it."

His manly confidence brought a smile to Grace's features. "Do you?" she enquired as she disposed her rose-colored shot silk shawl more becomingly about her shoulders.

"Yes!" lisped Kate. "We are going to take you to see Napoleon's carriage and to view the Elgin Marbles and to—"

"Tattersall's!" interjected Teddy.

"Can't take 'er there," Hugh corrected. "Ain't proper. But we'll engage you for our afternoon walks, and you'll take us to Hyde Park. Bound to meet an eligible bachelor there."

Grace snapped open her painted silk fan and concealed an amused smile behind it. "Goodness," she said. "I am quite fatigued with your plans."

"No, are you?" Hugh enquired, cocking an eyebrow as if wondering how sightseeing could fatigue anyone.

"A ball is just the thing for you then," Kate said, sounding very wise. "You will meet lots of gentlemen, everyone of whom is looking for a Happily Ever After. Better go before they give up."

"You are as subtle as your mother," Grace laughed as she made her way to the nursery door. Katharine leaned forward on her narrow bed, a romantic light in her shimmering eyes as she said, "I hope you will be the belle of the ball."

Sweeping back across the bare wooden floor, Grace pressed her niece against her bosom. "If you wish it, it must be so," she said.

Hugh padded in slippers to his aunt's side. "We shall *make* it come true," he vowed.

"How so?" demanded Teddy, who was bouncing on his bed.

"To prayers!" Hugh commanded as he dropped to his knees. His brother and sister knelt beside him, voicing a hearty "Amen!" to his petition that Aunt Grace "dazzle at least one gentleman at the ball and find her true love."

For all that Grace had been reared in a clergyman's home, she had never heard such a simple, practical-minded prayer. She was confident it had risen on angel wings to the Almighty Himself, and so she said as the children bid her to have a wonderful time picking a beau. But as she paused with one hand on the banister before she began to descend the stairs, her confidence wavered when she overheard Teddy's full-voiced enquiry, "What was that to the purpose?" and Hugh's incautious reply, "Only that if she is at her last prayers, as Mama says, then we must add *ours*."

Five

Grace decided not to disappoint her well-meaning young relatives. Giving her chin a confident lift, she glided downstairs and graciously received her sister's unstinting approbation in her choice of gowns—a white slip under a primrose shot silk overdress which had silver beading edging the low square neckline and diminutive puff sleeves.

"I say, Colin," Amity said, tapping her husband on the shoulder with her closed fan. "Does not my sister look becoming tonight?"

Going over a handful of financial papers, the preoccupied Colin Spencer turned an eye toward the staircase, his stolid face registering some surprise at Grace's appearance. She wondered whether she was altered so much that he did not at first recognize her, and indeed his first words confirmed her suspicion. *"This* is Grace?" he demanded. "How pretty she has grown!"

His backward compliment elicited a delightful giggle from Grace. "Hello, Brother," she said, presenting a delicately pink-tinged cheek for a salutary kiss. "Do you mean I wear my age well?"

"I do," he blurted out, then choked. "Dash it all, can't a man compliment a lady without her turning it into an insult?" Taking a lady's arm in each of his, he said, "Let us not delay, Amity. I want to see how many gentlemen fall at your sister's feet tonight."

Following Grace into the coach which awaited them at the door to their town house, Amity said, "Judging from Colin's unabashed reaction, I've no doubt you'll capture the heart of one *eligible* gentleman."

Inexplicably Grace recalled the very handsome but troublesome nobleman from the Swan and Bell. She felt the flame of embarrassment heat her cheeks as she remembered how he had laughed when she had confessed her unusual lack of feminine accomplishments. That confession was doubtless the reason he had decided she was unworthy of an introduction. For once it did not occur to her to criticize aristocracy's tendency to look down their noses at ordinary—she would not call herself common—people. She wished her oblivious nobleman could see her as the elegant lady she was tonight instead of the unfortunate waif she had seemed at the inn.

As they traveled the short distance from the town house on Harley Street to the brightly lighted home on Cavendish Square, Grace turned her eyes to the passing streets and fell silent.

While they sat awaiting their turn to disembark their coach, Colin remarked, "Why so pensive?"

Grace started from her reverie and was excused from making any reply when her sister fluttered her fan and tittered, "Judging from the butterflies in my own stomach, I daresay she is suffering an attack of nerves."

Grace saw the affectionate smile Colin turned upon his wife and heard his teasing tone as he said, "Dare I hope your nervous flutters are on my account?"

Amity lowered her gaze and touched her closed fan to her lips. Of a sudden, Grace felt completely *de trop*. To hide her embarrassment, she looked out upon the throng that was entering the large town home.

Removing the fan from Amity's fingers, Colin said, "Yes, my dear, I still understand the fan. Unfortunately, so does your sister. I fear you have put her to the blush." Grace started to excuse her missish airs, but he turned a brotherly smile on her. "Are you so surprised that we still love one another?"

"No," Grace replied, bestowing a tender smile on the happy couple. "Rather I am glad for it. One hears such abominable tales of marriage."

"Only those born of convenience or fear," Colin said thoughtfully. "Our marriage has been anything but convenient." He chuckled at his wife's gasp of dismay, then added, "But I think Amity still fears I will discover a more beautiful or fascinating creature at these balls she drags me to." He pressed his wife's fingers in a reassuring manner. "You need not worry, my dear," he said. "I am too comfortable in my choice of wives to search elsewhere for affection."

"Oh, Colin," Amity sighed romantically. Then, as if realizing exactly what it was he had confessed, she said, pouting. "What an impolite declaration."

"Yes, it was," he agreed, handing her out of the coach. After performing the same service for Grace, he conducted them through the receiving line, then said, "Now I shall be of the first respectability and leave you to sit with your friends where you may keep an eagle eye on the young misses." Casting an appraising eye around the crowded ballroom, he added, "Looks to be a bumper crop this year."

"Colin," cautioned his blushing wife. "How can you speak so of the young ladies? You will put Grace quite out of face."

"Not at all," he said, making sure they were situated near the punch bowl, where every gentleman must eventually pass. "Didn't mean the girls, but the men. Look at 'em, Grace," he said, sweeping the room with a flourishing hand. "They're ripe for the plucking. Mind, you pick a good 'un."

Once more, Amity gasped in shock, but Grace could not restrain delighted laughter.

Colin spoke the truth; the ballroom was crowded with all manner of men—from Friday-faced clergymen and bankers, to haughty members of the country gentry who lacked an introduction to higher society, to their younger brothers or sons who were aping the manner and dress of their social betters. These last garnered flirtatious glances from the youngest ladies in attendance and disapproving ones from their elders. Flirtation won over respectability. The dandies seemed no more willing to change their ways to suit middle-class standards than was the Corinthian set willing to tone down its rowdiness to suit the high sticklers of their own class.

All in all, it was the usual set of attendees. Grace experienced an involuntary disappointment that *he* was not among the crowd. Realizing the futility of such hopes given the fact that this was a bourgeois ball, she lowered her gaze to her clasped fingers.

"What is this?" Amity whispered conspiratorially.

"One would think you did not find a 'certain gentleman' in attendance."

Grace lifted an ironic smile toward her sister. "I cannot help it, I confess I was looking for someone . . . different."

"What? Have your tastes run to Belcher neckerchiefs then?" Amity laughed. Grace allowed herself to smile more broadly until her sister snapped open her fan and hissed, "Do not look, sister, but even as we speak, a 'different' sort of gentleman is making his way toward you."

Of course, Grace turned her eyes in the forbidden direction. The gentleman striding forward made her eyebrows lift in wonder. Attired in a wasp-waisted gray dress coat, embroidered brocade waistcoat of the purest white, gray pantaloons into which he appeared to have been poured, he walked with an air of consequence that Grace did not find in the least appealing.

When introduced, Mr. Blake requested the favor of a dance. She was so startled by his condescension that she did not know how to refuse. Thus Grace found herself taking a place opposite him in the set.

As the music began, she became entranced almost against her will by her partner's stiff execution of the steps. She wondered if the sharp-edged collar would eventually separate his head from shoulders too obviously enhanced with buckram padding. As they joined hands with another couple prior to circling to the left, she wondered what did one do if one's partner lost his head in the middle of a dance.

The gruesome, ludicrous thought occupied her mind until she decided that if his extreme fashion actually did cause him injury, his wide linen neckcloth would serve as both tourniquet and bandage. An amused smile lightened her countenance.

When her partner claimed her hand to pass down the length of the set, he spoke in a voice as starchy as his cravat. "Pray, Miss Penworth, accept my compliments."

She had no idea what he was complimenting. Whatever it was, she desired to know, so as not to repeat the error. But all she said was a noncommittal, "Thank you, Mr. Blake."

"I am persuaded we make an admirable couple," he said. "And judging from your enchanting smile, you are of the same opinion."

They completed a graceful turn, and suddenly Grace feared that her rigid partner was reading too much into her unrepressed amusement. "I beg your pardon, sir," she stammered. "How came you to that decision?"

But her curiosity was of necessity unfulfilled until their next turn down the set. By this time, her partner seemed so much more puffed with his own consequence that she was not surprised to hear, "I must say you are sufficiently fair to draw the eyes of most of the company. Naturally I share their admiration."

"How kind of you to say so," she said demurely, feeling more and more vexed by his presumptuous manner.

"The choice of one's first dancing partner is so important," he went on. "Having chosen you, I feel certain the evening will prove successful beyond measure."

Good manners required her to acknowledge his tribute. However, she seemed for a moment to have lost her voice. When she regained her power of speech, she could only say, "How nice for you, sir."

Fortunately the dance was concluded, and she made haste to return to her sister's side. Mr. Blake did not seem at all put out by her breach of manners, but followed at her elbow and complimented Amity for bringing such a pretty partner to the ball. "To be sure, Mr. Blake," Amity said as she fluttered her fan and cast triumphant glances toward her sister. "Such a lovely couple you made, pray do not hesitate to call at home." Upon hearing her sister's gracious invitation, Grace's mouth snapped open in dismay.

Mr. Blake surprised her by clicking his heels together and executing a crisp bow. "T'would be my pleasure," he said, adding his wish that Miss Penworth perform the supper dance with him.

Grace was opening her mouth to decline, but Amity said, "She would be happy to," with a stern stare that silenced Grace's own protest. Mr. Blake seemed so delighted by the lady's acquiescence that he nearly tripped over the toes of his dancing slippers as he took himself off to favor another lady with his company.

Smiling, so as not to frighten away other prospective partners, Grace demanded, "Why did you condemn me to sup with that puffed-up coxcomb?"

"My dear, he is everything that is nice; how can you fault him?" Amity said in a chiding tone. "He called you a pretty partner, after all."

"I cannot thank him for the compliment," Grace said behind her furiously fluttering fan.

"Whyever not?" Amity demanded.

"He chose me only to enhance his own appearance. Said he was 'sure the evening would be successful beyond measure.' "

Amity's critical moue crinkled into disbelieving laughter. "No! Did he truly say so?"

Grace realized her sister was accusing her of telling tales out of school, and she defended herself. "For once, Amie, I am not concocting a banbury tale."

"But this is beyond anything wonderful," Amity said on a note of laughter. Then, seeing that Grace misunderstood her, she added, "Dear one, do not take offense. Your stories are always so amusing, one never knows whether they are true or merely figments of your imagination. But I daresay if Mr. Blake can command a fair number of pretty partners after looking well with you, you ought to look forward to a full dance card yourself."

True to her sister's prediction, Grace did not lack for partners. Several old friends, after dancing with her, introduced her to newcomers to their social set, every one of whom claimed a dance.

She introduced Amity to her publisher, Mr. DuBarry, a handsome, muscular man who unfortunately wore spectacles that magnified his brown eyes so that he appeared to be suffering from gout. But he seemed congenial, and Amity felt no compunction about sending Grace onto the dance floor with him.

However, as he led her away, he veered from the dancing area, setting their course toward the refreshment tables. Most of the guests were merely sampling the array of hors d'oeuvres, but to Grace's humiliation, Mr. DuBarry ate his way down the long table, all the while remarking on the selfishness of the feast in light of the many poor who had gone to bed without supper.

Grace, who usually concurred with his charitable opinions, could only respond pettishly, "It is too bad your actions do not match your sentiments, Mr. DuBarry."

"One must know how the privileged live to appreciate the plight of the Great Unwashed," he countered, unselfconsciously stuffing snails into his mouth, then washing them down with great gulps of champagne. "You ought to eat more; it will sharpen your pen."

Realizing there was nothing to be said, Grace heaved a great sigh and propelled herself toward her sister, who was still sitting among the other chaperons. Though she hoped her publisher would forget about her in favor of the tartlets and pastries at the far end of the refreshment table, he followed in her wake, carrying a plateful of delicacies which he offered to her.

"You must try one," he urged, shoving the plate forward until Grace rolled her eyes and accepted a candied raspberry. He then said in a sarcastic tone, "You see, ma'am, even my Miss Penworth is not immune to the lure of pleasure."

Dropping the untouched treat on the overloaded plate, Grace glared at him. "Please, Mr. DuBarry. I am not 'your' Miss Penworth, except as a writer."

"Of course," he mumbled around a lemon pastry. "That is what I meant. Speaking of writing, we must stir up the ink a little; sales of your book are rather sluggish." Wiping his fingers on a napkin he had tucked into his waistcoat, he suggested, "Could you not do something shocking, but ladylike, of course, to call attention to our publication?"

"Do not listen to him," Amity warned, bestowing a look of dark disapproval on him. "It is bad enough you have written such an unflattering picture of the Regent—where came you by the scandalous information about his 'various wives,' Grace? I'm sure Mama and Papa never mentioned such indelicate gossip within your hearing. And shame on you, Mr. DuBarry, for leading my sister down such a dangerous path. She was reared to be a lady, not your cat's paw." Fanning herself furiously, she wished him a firm good night and turned toward Grace until he had taken himself off to plague another lady.

"Where is the romance in talk such as his?" Amity asked.

"Don't tell me you were thinking of matching me with him?" Grace gasped. "And how did you come to read my book? I specifically meant to keep it from you."

"Mr. DuBarry sent a copy to me," Amity replied. "I told him not to send one to Mama." She gave Grace a reassuring hug. "Don't worry, Gracie. If sales are too slow, he will soon lose interest. Better look elsewhere for romance, my dear."

But if Mr. DuBarry chose to talk of business; other gentlemen could not fail to please. A Mr. Hanover, who had been gazing at her with undeniable longing all evening, finally worked up courage to ask Grace to dance. Shy and self-effacing, he was exactly the sort of person, Amity decided, who would please their parents without repulsing Grace.

Newly returned from India with untold wealth, he was her silent partner for the Scottish reel and, when caught counting steps, apologized for his lack of refinement.

Grace laughed as she turned on his arm and said,

"Then we are a good match, Mr. Hanover; for I cannot carry a tune in a bucket or beat time on the piano."

He seemed momentarily taken aback by her confession, and she wondered if she had given him a disgust of her, but then his gauche exclamation, "Oh, Miss Penworth, I am so tone deaf, your voice is music to my ears," so endeared him to her that she was inclined to forgive his ineptitude until he trod upon her foot.

Stifling a cry of pain, she hobbled off the floor on his arm.

"I beg your pardon," he stammered, his complexion turning even more ruddy than the Indian sun had baked it.

Limping, Grace excused him. "Please, Mr. Hanover, do not think it is all your fault."

Amity, hastening to her rescue, added, "No, of course you are not responsible. My sister recently suffered a horrid bee sting."

Mr. Hanover and Amity lowered Grace gently onto a chair. Without thinking, he sat in the chair Amity had just vacated and began to treat Grace to a recitation of the agonies he underwent whenever he was unlucky enough to encounter an enraged bee. "And to think you are determined to dance," he said in an awestruck tone, "despite the pain you must surely suffer." After a moment's consideration, he enquired in a worried tone, "Do you think it wise?"

"Indeed, my foot is much better," Grace assured him, wishing they could turn the subject away from her ridiculous ailment. "Amity, please tell Mr. Hanover I am quite recovered."

"She will have it so," Amity said in an arch tone that

suggested he was not to take her sister at her word. "Perhaps some lemonade will ease your concern."

He was off immediately to carry out the request. After they had sipped the lukewarm and tasteless beverage, Amity sent him off to step on another young lady's toes while she accompanied Grace to the retiring room where they might recover from his exhaustive attentions. "Where do they come from?" Amity demanded as she repaired the damage the heat had inflicted upon her cosmetics.

Grace leaned over to inspect the damage to her slipper. A frown marred her countenance when she saw the dark smudge and dent in the toe. "Mr. Hanover came from India," she said.

"Doubtless that is where he learned to dance as if he was stamping snakes," Amity said with a giggle.

"Perhaps we can return him there," Grace said.

While Amity was concluding her facial ministrations before the mirror, Grace smoothed the wrinkles from her skirt. Amity ceased touching rouge paper to her cheek. "Poor Grace," she said on a disappointed sigh. "Does no one make your heart skip beats?"

Grace thought of the one gentleman who possessed that power. Alas, he was not here. And if he were, her perverse sense of humor reminded her, he might be more inclined to strangle her than compliment her. Shaking off the depression that threatened, she bestowed a teasing smile upon her sister and said, "No, but I have heard bee stings have this effect on some people."

Amity's lips pursed severely. "Do be serious, Grace. At this rate I'll never get you married."

Glad that she would not be forced to accept that unhappy hand, Grace patted her sister's shoulder. "Never fear, Amity. Perhaps I shall pull a rabbit out of the hat."

Amity pulled a puzzled face. "What do you mean?"

"Ah-ah," Grace replied, wagging a finger. "You know a magician never betrays the trick."

"Do you mean your book?" Amity persisted. "Why even Miss Austen is forced to live an austere life in her mother's home."

"They say her family calls her the 'best of aunts,' " Grace said in a distracted tone.

"Yes, well," Amity chided. "You ought to be more concerned about your own nursery than mine."

After masking the pain her sister's reminder caused her, Grace risked a glance at Amity's frowning countenance. Unable to make a jest of it, she said, "Be glad of it, Amity. If ever I hold a babe of my own in my arms, it will be nothing short of a miracle."

To her surprise, Amity winked at her. Grace could not help but smile as her sister said, "Let us find you a husband then, dear. He is all the miracle you need."

"Oh Amity," she sighed. Shaking with laughter, she added, "Have you been praying, too?"

Before Amity could respond, three young ladies burst into the room exclaiming, "The supper dance!"

Immediately the retiring room erupted into anxious uproar as ladies hastened to complete repairs on hems or hairstyles. No one wanted to risk losing an impatient partner to a more alert miss.

Giving herself one last glance in the pier glass, Grace tucked a curl more securely into its hairpin before she and her sister joined the crush of ladies who were returning to the ballroom.

As she accepted Mr. Blake's arm for the dance, she thought she saw out of the corner of her eye the Unknown Gentleman for whom she had been looking without hope all evening. She risked a longer glance at the elegantly attired brown-haired gentleman, who stood among a group of young bucks who seemed to be deriving a great deal of amusement from the bad *ton* of the dancers milling about the floor.

She hoped she was wrong, for his Mysterious Lordship was making no attempt to stem the cynical remarks being bandied about by his companions. Leaning a shoulder against a cold marble pillar, he was scanning the ballroom with an arrogant eye and giving every appearance of wishing to be elsewhere.

At that moment, so did she.

Her eyes engaged his before her partner led her into a country waltz. For an instant, surprise replaced the look of ennui that gave the lord such a disdainful aspect.

Despite herself, Grace could not suppress a welcoming smile. Rewarded with a grin that seemed to dim the light from the hundreds of candles suspended from three chandeliers, Grace stumbled as her oblivious partner swept her too abruptly into the dance. Before she regained her balance, he trod upon her uninjured foot. Trying valiantly not to cry out, Grace dragged her gaze from the person she was beginning to think of as the bane of her existence and forced herself to concentrate on the whirling steps of the dance.

They had completed one half of a turn around the room before she allowed herself to risk another glance toward Him. Her boldness this time was not rewarded with a pleasing display of esteem. His laughing visage had hardened into a set frown that made her feel quite the mushroom. The hard gaze traveled around the room before it once again established itself upon her.

He seemed to stare daggers at her. Then he turned to speak to one of his laughing cronies. Grace could not help but witness the sneer that tinged his scornful reply. The blush of mortification that colored her cheeks made her ears feel as if they were on fire.

Six

From the moment of his arrival at Peter Ramsey's elegant home on Cavendish Square, the Duke of Standen regretted crossing the threshold. His current companions found the bourgeois ball a great joke and the duke's association with a member of trade vastly amusing.

Standen was not of the same opinion, having been best friends with Ram since their first days at Eton. Their association, born of blood and tears during a Long Chamber scrap, soon had them dubbed Jonathon and David for their inevitable defense of one another against larger foes. Tonight as his acquaintances Lord Phillip Brabberton, Sir Freddie Gates, and the Honorable Andrew Blake needled Ram and his party, Standen was struck by the uncomfortable conviction that he had joined the Opposition.

After passing through the reception line and enduring the painful thrusts of the three musketeers' dull wit, he wondered how soon he could suggest they take themselves off to an entertainment more suited to their tastes, such as a gaming hell.

As they paused on the landing of the first story, Sir Freddie enquired on the tail of an unconcealed and noisy yawn, "I say, Standen, what gave you the cork-brained idea to come to this deuced dull affair? Nobody is here."

Standen stared his friend into silence. *"I* am here," he said in a manner which implied he did not attend balls populated with "nobodies."

"Demme, don't cut me up," Sir Freddie said. "Thought you'd take my meaning. Ain't like the place was elbow to elbow with the diamond squad."

"Forgot," chuckled Mr. Blake, nudging Sir Freddie's ribs with an elbow. "We're the diamond squad."

"Don't put on airs, Peep," Standen said quellingly. "I daresay Ram's family has a longer pedigree than your own."

A frown darkened Mr. Blake's pale features, but he refused to honor with a comment the duke's reference to his grandfather's doubtful birth. Instead he cast a critical gaze about the ballroom and sniffed. "Girls're tolerable, I'll give you that much," he allowed, separating himself from his cronies by a tentative step. "Think I'll take a turn about the room."

Sir Freddie turned to Lord Phillip and said, "Lay you odds he'll have a girl on his arm before he gets halfway round the floor."

Lord Phillip puffed himself up like a pouter pigeon and said, "Never bet against a sure thing, Freddie. Peep always was a success with the ladies. Look there." He gestured with a languid wrist in the general direction of the punch bowl. "Daresay he's set to cast a lure."

Against his better judgment, Standen turned his gaze in the direction his companion indicated. Blake was moving toward an unsuspecting female much like a spider moved upon its prey, in a sweeping fashion that would leave her no time to escape his clutches. Poor girl, he thought as he searched the crowd for Peep's most likely quarry; perhaps he ought to warn her. He began to move toward his purpose.

And then he saw her. The violet lady from the inn.

When he realized that Peep's prey was the same one who had made him feel like the king of fools at the Swan and Bell and along every mile of the road toward London, all good intentions were swept aside on a wave of fury that was more fierce than the duke had felt on any battlefield. His steps froze on the threshold of the ballroom.

Then without explanation, he ground about on his heel and began striding away from the dancers.

"I say, Duke," Sir Freddie began. "Can't leave just yet. Want to dance with that girl Peep's discovered."

"I won't stop you," he said, though he could not stem the irrational urge to drive his fist first into Peep's face, then Freddie's.

He tried to tell himself that he had no prior claim upon the girl, but logic failed to ease the unaccountable rage he felt when he imagined her dancing in the arms of another man, especially the rackety friends he'd brought along.

Digging his hand into his waistcoat pocket, he drew out his talisman of coins and clenched them in his fist. He strode downstairs against a tide of new arrivals and flung himself into a chair in Ram's well-stocked library. There he contrived to drink enough brandy to convince himself that he cared nothing for the girl.

As long as she was out of his sight, she was out his mind.

The trouble with that logic became apparent as soon as he returned to the ballroom prior to the supper dance. She looked deucedly uncomfortable as Peep claimed her hand. Standen forced himself to lean nonchalantly against a marble pillar to keep from playing knight errant to her seeming distress.

Lord Phillip strolled to his side. "Haven't seen you for awhile," he ventured. As if oblivious to the black look his friend had turned upon him, he began to expound on the pleasures of the evening. "Girls're pleasant enough; not a one so high in the instep she ain't grateful to take a turn about the floor with the second son of a marquess." He said it as if that were an experience that increased his consequence. "Punch isn't as watered down as at *ton* parties. Gaming's tame though. Only whist. Oh look." He pointed toward Peep and his partner. "He's done it again. Charmed 'er right out from under us all."

"Really?" Standen said, affecting disinterest. "And who might she be?"

"Name's Penworth; her father's a parson," Lord Phillip chuckled as if he had just told a good joke. "Can you beat that? Peep caught in the parson's mousetrap."

Miss Penworth. The duke turned the disastrous lady's name over in his mind. Miss Penworth. A parson's daughter. Definitely not anyone's light o' love. The certainty lightened his mood. Miss Penworth.

As if she had heard him speak her name aloud, she turned huge, dark-rimmed eyes upon him. He thought he had steeled his heart against her frailty, but she looked like a frightened doe cornered by a slavering dog.

He was tempted to compel Peep to give her over into his hands. Indeed, he gave up supporting the column and made as if to move toward the couple.

At the same time, her face seemed to light from within as a smile of recognition overspread her features.

It was the duke's custom to let his head rule his emotions. Custom, however, played very little part in his uncharacteristic response to this unusual woman, so little in fact, he was completely unprepared for the impact her sudden smile had upon him.

He felt he had ridden hell-for-leather from Brighton to London in less than four hours. He felt he could move mountains with his bare hands. Indeed, he thought, whatever she asked of him, he would do his best to accomplish.

Oblivious to Standen's intentions, Peep drew Miss Penworth into his arms and led her into a country waltz. She seemed to stumble into the set. Peep made no attempt to disguise the pleasure her unexpected tumble gave him, nor did he immediately place her at a more respectable arms' length.

Standen was reminded of his own instinctive reaction to her fall into his arms at the Swan and Bell. He wondered perversely whether she orchestrated such a maneuver with each gentleman to whom she was attracted. A black rage overspread his features.

Blind to the duke's inner turmoil, Lord Phillip muttered, "Uncommonly clumsy for such a pretty gel, ain't she? Don't see the charm in 'er m'self."

Standen grabbed a fistful of the Babbler's crisp linen cravat and dragged him behind the pillar and several palms before they caused a riot. Once safely out of the public eye, he released the choking lord and growled, "Could it be that Miss Penworth did not recognize your charm?"

Lord Phillip ineffectively smoothed his rumpled starcher as he attempted to regain his interrupted breathing. "Not that," he gasped. His shoulders heaved up and down, as if they might force more air into his deprived lungs. "Only, she's deuced pale. Looks like a ghost." Standen's face must have registered the increasing rage he felt, for the Babbler cried out, "Demme, Alan, has she bewitched you as well?"

"Certainly not," Standen replied in a voice that sounded as if he were aghast at the suggestion that a mere parson's daughter could have engaged his affections. "I owe something to the consequence of my name," he added lamely.

"Well, that sounds more like the Duke of Standen *I* know," said the Babbler on an encouraging note. "Why not escape this dreadful affair and find entertainment more to our taste?"

Standen risked a glance through the palm fronds. Miss Penworth was still whirling uncomfortably in Peep's arms as the orchestra pounded out a tuneless accompaniment. Realizing that he was moments from freedom from his odious companions, he said, "You go on, Babbler. Take Freddie with you, and Peep. You've quite increased Mr. Ramsey's consequence among his acquaintance tonight."

"But what about you?" Lord Phillip said. "You can't stay. Haven't played the pretty all evening. Doubt anyone'll dance with you."

Arching a dubious eyebrow that conveyed his opinion

that no one would turn down a dance with such an exalted personage as himself, Standen said, "I shall plead
an old war injury and sit out the rest of the evening
with the prettiest of the ladies at my side."

Though he hoped they would depart immediately, his
strategic removal of his three acquaintances was delayed
until after supper. Peep would not relinquish his hold
on Miss Penworth, and Freddie and the Babbler were
prevailed upon to escort two of Mrs. Ramsey's more
prominent female guests through the buffet.

Realizing what was owed to the duke's consequence
and kindness, that lady asked him to partner her through
supper. The petite Mrs. Ramsey ate a mountain of lob-
ster salad and drank an ocean of lemonade, all the while
carrying on a one-sided conversation that could have
been spoken in Chinese for all the sense Standen made
of it.

It was fortunate that she did not require an active
listener, for he was free to cast about the room for a
glimpse of the maddening Miss Penworth.

To his disappointment, the heedless miss was nowhere
to be seen. It took all his hard-earned self-control not
to excuse himself to go off in search of the girl.

At the very moment in which he was contemplating
submitting to the temptation, Mrs. Ramsey recaptured
his attention. "Our Miss Penworth is creating quite a
stir with your Mr. Blake," she was saying. "It is true,
did you not know, that he invited her to go down to
supper with him immediately after the first dance." She
washed down the morsel with another liberal draft of
lemonade, then refreshed, gave a nervous laugh. "Her

parents would be amazed to learn of her conquest. She has never taken before."

Standen's eyes narrowed as he considered Ram's rattling wife. "I'm quite sure they would be appalled," he said firmly. "Blake is completely ineligible as a prospective son-in-law to a . . ." He had started to say "parson," but quickly amended the scornful term to a more respectful "vicar."

Mrs. Ramsey's kindly but dull wit made a wrong turn. "Then you know the Reverend Mr. Penworth?"

Standen did not attempt to rein in his partner's mistake. Instead he said, "I have a passing acquaintance with the family."

Immediately Mrs. Ramsey swept to her feet. "Then you must meet his daughter." She allowed him no opportunity to refuse, but took his arm in a firm grip and drew him outside to a tent which blazed with the light of hundreds of branches of candles and buzzed with the sound of what seemed hundreds of voices. She moved through the crowd with all the grace and tact of his grandmother, interrupting Mr. Blake in mid-monologue. "My dear," Mrs. Ramsey said to Miss Penworth after making apology to the gape-mouthed gentleman, "why did you not tell me you were acquainted with Lord Standen?" completely forgetting in her excitement that her husband's childhood friend had been elevated in status to "His Grace."

Standen did not call attention to her faux pas, but smiled encouragement. He did not want her stumbling over an apology, nor did he desire Miss Penworth to turn shy or giddy. For a few minutes, he could be easy and enjoy a friendly conversation without the encumbrance of his rank.

Grace looked past Mrs. Ramsey toward the gentleman she had in tow. It was He. She felt she could not breathe, but was able to conceal the weakness behind a seemingly unconcerned, "I did not think it worth mentioning, Evelyn."

"Not worth mentioning!" Mrs. Ramsey gasped as if she had suddenly fully comprehended the depth of the social gaffe they had both just committed.

Was she determined, Standen wondered, to set him down every moment of their acquaintance? He laughed amiably, though he felt more like growling. "So like our Miss Penworth," he said when at last he was in control of his voice. "Never one to drop names. That is a great part of her charm." Somehow he managed to oust Peep from his place and impose himself at her side.

Grace could hardly draw air as he enquired with the demeanor of a long and cordial acquaintance, "How is your father? And your good neighbor, Mr. Davies?"

"I left them quite well," she replied in strangled tones.

Standen glanced at his friend. Peep seemed to wish him to Perdition, but that wish he must for the present deny him. Mrs. Ramsey still appeared as one amazed that Miss Penworth was on such easy terms with her most consequential guest. "Pray do not mind us," Standen said, determined not to let them know on what shaky ground their acquaintance was founded. "Old friends must not stand on ceremony."

Mrs. Ramsey collected herself and Mr. Blake at once.

"Of course, they must have so much to catch up with. Mr. Blake?"

Peep looked as if he would dearly love to ignore the inviting arm Mrs. Ramsey placed upon his sleeve, and tell Standen to return whence he came. But good manners overcame his hot temper, and he turned a bland smile on his hostess. "Would you care for some dessert, ma'am?" he enquired, leading her toward the buffet table.

As the unwanted pair began winding its way past the tables strewn about the tent, Grace turned hesitant eyes upon her companion. Now that they were alone, his regard seemed anything but kind. He looked as angry as when John Coachman had ruined his curricle.

"Why did you let Evelyn think we were acquainted?" she enquired.

"So she would do just what she did," he replied. "She is gone, and so is Peep, and now we can enjoy a comfortable coze talking old times. How is the bee sting?"

A smile still rested on his lips, but Grace noticed it did not warm his gaze. She suppressed an unconscious desire to shiver, saying, "I am quite recovered, thank you." After an uncomfortable silence, it occurred to her that she ought to reciprocate. "How is your curricle?"

"Not at all well," he said in a regretful tone, as if he were discussing an invalid relative. "Still stove in at Newbury."

"That is too bad," she concurred for lack of anything more original to say.

"Yes," he agreed, clenching his fingers around her shillings. Perversely he said, "I ought to be receiving the bill at any time."

"Yes, well, I hope you will allow me to repay you in installments," she said haltingly.

"I was willing to allow you to discharge your debt in *one* installment," he replied fiercely. Then, skewering her with a pointed look that made her eyes widen, he said, "All I wanted was a ride into Town."

Grace's conscience stung more painfully than had the bee, but she pushed aside the prickings. She tried to tell herself she had done nothing about which to feel guilty.

If anyone ought to feel the sting of conscience, it was Lord Standen. After all, he had deliberately decided not to make himself known to her during their accidental meeting.

A chiding voice within told her it was her Christian Duty to have taken him into the coach. She countered with his own argument that a lady did not ride in a closed carriage with an Unknown Gentleman, adding her own monitory "no matter how pleasing his outward appearance or manner."

Heaven knows she had proven too susceptible to his superficial qualities to be an impartial judge of his inner character. But she did regret having caused him additional discomfort and vexation by forcing him to make his own way into Town, for she was convinced she had not lived up to her Christian upbringing. Penitently she said, "I beg your pardon, my lord, for abandoning you on the high road. It was poor-spirited of me."

Surprised by her apology, Standen laughed. "Not at all," he said, abandoning his earlier intention of snubbing her. His resentment seemed to vanish like mist in the sun. "It showed remarkably good sense."

Grace repeated her apology, this time on a note of disbelief. "I beg your pardon?"

"I cannot deny I thought rather unkindly of you while slogging to Town, but now I understand I overstepped myself in our short acquaintance. Had the circumstances been reversed, I would have flown from a man who failed to introduce himself."

Grace could not stem the rush of warm color that tinged her cheeks.

He smiled as if her blush confirmed his assessment of her innocence. "I hope you will not hold it against me," he said. "You see, it isn't every day I meet a lady who doesn't know who I am and falls over herself trying to—"

Grace's eyes widened in awe of his admission of consequence. He laughed good-naturedly. "Well," he allowed. "Perhaps I overstate my importance."

Lowering her gaze, Grace said, "I am sure you completely understand it, my lord. Only I hope you do not think I threw myself at you because of your exalted position in society."

"No," he assured her. "The step broke."

"Yes," she said, "And even if I did know who you were, I assure you I would treat you no differently than a *Mr.* Standen." She directed a level gaze at his amused one and said, "I was reared to show courtesy to one and all."

"And I shall treat *you* no differently than I should a duchess," he replied. "Common courtesy," he added when she laughed at the absurdity of someone calling her "Grace Your Grace."

Extending two fingers toward him, she inclined her

head to its most haughty level and intoned in teasing
tones, "Mr. Standen, is it?"

Arising from the delicate chair, he swept a courtly
bow, saying, "Your Grace," when he accepted her fingers and kissed the air over them.

Although he did not actually touch his lips to her
hand, Grace felt the air crackle between them as if it
were charged with electricity. She wished he would release her fingers, for they seemed to be afire, with the
rest of her form smoldering dangerously. She was not
certain the feeling was healthy.

The orchestra was playing the first tentative notes after its intermission, and other couples were making their
way toward the ballroom. Grace attempted not to mark
their progress with her eyes, and she lowered them after
casting a fleeting glance toward Lord Standen. Immediately he said, "I hope you will not hold my odious
conduct against me, but will perform this dance with
me. I . . . would be honored."

Without hesitation, she smiled up at him. She could
not quell another blush from tingeing her cheeks a becoming rose color. "Indeed, my lord," she said as she
allowed him to lead her toward the more crowded ballroom, "I am honored."

The dance was a Scottish reel. At first she was disappointed it was not a waltz, but when it was their turn
to pass down the set, she became grateful that he must
of necessity remove his hand from her person. Every
time he possessed himself of her hand or brushed past
her during a figure, she received a jolt, almost galvanic
in nature, that made her pulse and breathing accelerate.

It took all her concentration just to remember the steps of the dance.

Glad to have her to himself again as the set ended, the duke led her from the floor and seated her in the shelter of an oasis of palms near a cluster of respectable and sharp-eyed duennas. "Shall I fetch your chaperon?" he enquired, hoping she would decline.

"That is unnecessary, my lord," Grace replied as she began to breathe in a more regular rhythm. Since he had removed his hand from her arm, blood was returning to her head and with it her customary sense. "My sister is not at all sympathetic to such missish airs. Indeed, I am not usually so weak-kneed." She bestowed a shy smile upon him and said with a return of her impish humor, "Although you might suppose dancing is another lack in my list of accomplishments."

He placed himself in the chair at her side and directed a steady gaze toward her as he said, "I will not say so, however much you protest it."

Grace felt the warmth of Lord Standen's gaze almost as if it were the sun's light. For the first time in her life, she was taken speechless, although her thoughts were far from empty. They tumbled over one another without regard to sense or logic, and none were such as she could comfortably confess.

She tried to rein in her imagination, but to no avail. No matter how sternly she chided herself, she could not keep from speculating as to whether Lord Standen might possibly be as deeply affected by the dance as she. It had so unnerved her as to compel her to admit a foolish desire that he would fix his affections upon her.

If she must be married as everyone insisted, she could find nothing objectionable in being married to him.

His considering gaze turned of a sudden enquiring. "A pansy for your thoughts," he said.

Appalled by the direction her thoughts had taken, Grace said nervously, "I hope you will have a care to whom you offer pansies, my lord. They are for lovers' thoughts."

As soon as she uttered the words, she regretted them. Lord Standen's blue eyes hardened and his indulgent smile froze as if she had sunk in his opinion. Nor could she beg his pardon, for at that moment their tête-à-tête was interrupted.

"There you are, Standen," Sir Freddie whined. "I have been waiting an age. Are we going or not?"

"I told you to go without me," replied the duke in a distinctly uncordial tone.

"Can't." Freddie popped himself uninvited into the empty chair on Grace's right hand.

"Would you mind telling me why you cannot?"

"Came in your carriage, that's why." Sir Freddie sniffed. "Tea rose. Nice."

Grace turned in her chair and nearly bumped her head against the knight's. An oily smile overspread his lumpish features as if he had been peeping down her dress. She was hard-pressed not to shudder.

"Do you wish to leave?" the duke demanded.

"Not particularly at this moment," replied Sir Freddie unctuously. The orchestra was beginning another set. He came to his feet. "Rather dance. Miss Penworth?"

Although Grace preferred a bee sting to dancing with

another of Lord Standen's friends, she could not very well voice such impolite thoughts.

Neither could she excuse herself by saying that she had promised this dance to another gentleman. No gentleman of her acquaintance would dare contest a titled gentleman's invitation.

Nor could she expect Lord Standen to stand up with her two dances in succession. That would be construed as tantamount to a declaration. And he had made clear by his icy look his opinion of lovers' thoughts. So she resigned herself to spending twenty minutes keeping her toes out from under Sir Freddie's.

Thanking Lord Standen for the preceding dance, she placed her fingers in the knight's cold ones and allowed him to find a place among the dancers.

Fortunately they passed the duration of the set without incident. At least, Grace did not think anything of note occurred. She was rather distracted, recalling the way Lord Standen's hand felt under hers and how nice he smelled.

When the dance concluded, Sir Freddie returned her to her sister, bowed perfunctorily over her hand, then collected his friends, including Lord Standen, and the four gentlemen took their leave.

Amity shot open her fan and fluttered it furiously. "Well, I never!" she exclaimed.

"Never what?" Grace enquired in a disappointed tone. She was watching Lord Standen's broad back descend the staircase, remembering he had not asked to call on her.

"Never saw a gentleman so full of his own consequence."

"Do you mean Mr. Blake?" Grace asked, finishing her query on a disappointed sigh. Lord Standen had not even said goodbye.

"Certainly not," Amity snapped. The breeze she was creating with her fan flared out tendrils of her blond hair so that she looked as if she were in full sail. "I meant His Grace, the Duke of Standen." Of a sudden she ceased fanning herself and used it as a screen. "I ought not to complain, my dear, since he favored you with a dance. But he did not ask my permission. And he danced *only* with you."

"Do not come to any mistaken conclusions, Amity," Grace said. She was still preoccupied with her own disturbing thoughts, most especially that Lord Standen—that is, the *Duke* of Standen—had once again chosen to conceal himself from her. She wondered why and preferred to go home herself to ponder in peace. But she could not very well plead a headache, and offered an excuse instead: "We were already acquainted."

Amity's face took on a thoughtful expression, as if calculating the consequences of her sister's prior acquaintance with a duke. But she said nothing on that head, only reminded Grace to have a care when dealing with the nobility, before sending her to dance with their host.

Grace passed the rest of the ball as one in a dream. If one had asked her with whom she had danced since the first set after supper, she would not have been able to name one partner. After she returned to her sister's home, she recalled Amity's revelation that Lord Standen—that was, the *Duke* of Standen—had danced only with her.

Common sense intruded to tell her that he danced with her only because they were acquainted, but his lack of consideration for other ladies dimmed her delight in his company. That height of manner served in no small way to rein in her pleasing thoughts.

Still, however foolish they were, she could not help but remember the children's simple, heartfelt prayer and her father's homily based upon the Scripture lesson, "The fervent prayer of a righteous man availeth much."

Just before Grace fell into an exhausted slumber, a lowering thought occurred to her. How righteous was it for a country parson's daughter to desire to engage the affections of a duke?

The gentleman was quite above her touch.

The next day, Grace received callers and accepted small tokens of esteem from her partners of the evening before. Several bouquets arrived for her, one of them anonymously. Amity almost made her send it back, but Grace took it to her room. She liked the combination of violets and miniature roses more than any other posy she had received.

Mr. Hanover sat in her sister's apricot- and cream-colored salon for a quarter of an hour. Sir Freddie delivered a spray of flowers in person. Mr. DuBarry laughed as she told a story to the children, but told her she was only wasting her time "making up fairy tales." This lowered him beneath contempt in her opinion.

Even Mr. Blake made an appearance and did not protest sharing the comfits he had purchased for Miss Penworth with her niece and nephews. He was so cordial, she quite forgot herself and accepted his offer to drive her in the park the next day.

Everyone did the pretty, except for the Duke of Standen. His regard was conspicuous by his absence.

Grace tried not to let her disappointment show.

Amity was not so forbearing. "I do not know why you keep looking out the window," she said. "His Grace is not coming today, or ever." Stabbing a needle into the fabric she was embroidering, she added, "You cannot expect an exalted member of the *ton* to darken the doorway of a house on Harley Street."

Mortified, Grace let the lace curtain fall closed over the window. "I did not think you disliked your address," she said, taking up the handkerchief she was hemming.

She had not spoken truthfully when she had told Lord Standen—she did not like to think of him as a *duke*—she could not sew. She could cut cloth and stitch a straight seam every bit as well as a seamstress, and the dress she wore gave tribute to her skill with a needle. Only, ladies did not make their own clothing. It smacked too much of gainful employment.

Amity lowered her tambour. "You know I do not despise the station in which the Lord has placed me. But depend on it, the duke's friends will mock our address to him. And he will think less of us for it."

Grace could not suppress the lowering vision of Sir Freddie and Mr. Blake regaling the duke with her middle-class lodgings. It in turn was succeeded by the gloomy conviction that *he* simply would not stoop to coming to Harley Street.

She told herself she did not care.

Seven

It is a perverse fact of life that the more one tells herself she does not care that a gentleman has snubbed her, the more one actually *does* care. In the days that followed, Grace could not restrain herself from flying to the window every time a carriage rolled to a halt outside. That the occupants came on her account as often as they called upon Amity did nothing to raise her spirits. None of the visitors was the Duke of Standen.

When more than a week had passed, she called herself a fool for having allowed her hopes to fly away with her. She was possessed of an infatuation for a person who held such an inflated opinion of his worth that he could not even leave his card at a house on Harley Street. Telling herself that such a stiff-necked individual did not merit a second thought, she proposed an outing to the children for the next day.

It seemed doomed from the outset. A rainy morning delayed their start until after luncheon. Kate wept so over the poor animals incarcerated in the menagerie at the Strand that Teddy vowed he would open the cages and free the prisoners. Only Grace's fiercely offered threat that they would not stop for pineapple ice at Gunter's on their way home and Hugh's forceful restraint kept the little boy from putting his plan into action.

As the footman lifted the children into their coach, Grace could not suppress an affectionate but rueful smile as Teddy said, "Well, I *would* have liked to let the tigers loose, because they did not look at all happy in their cage, but I should have had to wait until after feeding time at six. Mustn't set hungry tigers on the City. Anyway, I would hate to disappoint you, Aunt Grace. I know how much you like pineapple ice."

It seemed everyone in the little party liked pineapple ice. Teddy claimed two helpings as he had been such a good boy all day. Kate was happy with one dish of ice, but cast prayerful looks in the direction of the candy display, saying their governess deserved some token from their outing. Laughing, Grace allowed her to make an additional purchase "since it is for Miss Cornthewaite."

After taking their refreshment, Hugh declared, "We promised you a stroll in Hyde Park. Now is as good a time as any."

"But it is so crowded," Grace protested, her eyes opening wide upon the crush of traffic attempting to go through the gate at the corner of Park Lane and The Carriage Road.

"Of course," said Hugh with all the sang-froid of a man about town. "It is five o'clock—the perfect time to be seen." He rapped on the trapdoor of his mother's carriage and elicited their driver's promise to collect them in half an hour's time, before throwing open the door and leaping to the pavement.

Grace believed a promenade in such a crowd was not a good thing. However, before she could voice her objections, Teddy had followed his brother out the door and was calling, "Hurry, hurry, Aunt Grace!" as he folded down the step.

"Oh, very well," she said, descending from her sister's coach and offering a hand to Kate. The little girl climbed out in a manner every bit as ladylike as her aunt's descent, but once on the ground, she clapped her hands together and bounced up and down gleefully. "What an adventure!" she crowed. "Mama must never find out."

If Grace had been possessed of misgivings before, that statement served to solidify her opposition. "I do not think . . ." she began, but her objection failed to dissuade her excited charges. Teddy and Kate each grasped a hand and tugged on her arms until she was compelled to accompany them. Hugh followed on their heels as did a vigilant footman. They plunged into the flow of pedestrians who had come to the Park to see the Fashionable World strut its stuff.

On the flood tide, they were propelled through the gate and moved on apace until Teddy began to complain, "I can't see!"

Remembering her own childhood, Grace knew the poor child's view must be limited to waistcoats and walking sticks, and bosoms and elbows, one of which rudely connected with his ear. "Ow!" he cried, and came to an abrupt halt in the middle of the crowded footpath.

The stream of humanity rushed past them, parting, then closing, as if they were an insignificant island in the middle of a spawning stream.

With the footman offering what protection he could from the noisy onslaught, Grace dropped to her knees

to console the little boy who was making a valiant effort
not to cry. "There, there, my dear," she crooned, soothing the hair above his reddened ear. "Shall we find a
fountain in which to dampen my handkerchief? It will
take some of the heat from your bump."

"No," Teddy sniffed. Another individual jostled them.
Teddy caught his cap before it fell under the stampede.
His little chin quavered. Then, taking a deep breath, he
controlled the unmanly tears and said, "I'm all right,
Aunt. We had better move on."

Glancing around, Grace shot to her feet. A couple of
persons each the size of a second-rate ship of the line
were bearing down on them. "Merciful heavens!" she
cried as she tried to get the children out of the way.

The couple sailed past. Teddy was swept out of his
aunt's hands in the turbulent wake of their passage. The
crowd swirled around them, leaving him adrift in a colorful sea of humanity.

"Oh help!" he cried as he was dragged along. Looking about in confusion at the surge of black- and gold-
striped waistcoats and high-waisted muslins, he called,
"Aunt Grace, where are you?" He looked upward, hoping to glimpse her rose-colored parasol among the array
of bonnets and yardage of sunshades towering above his
head. "Hugh? Kate?" His voice began to quiver as he
gave over to fears that he was lost.

Every nightmare his old nurse had used to compel
him to be good occurred to him at once. A wicked
chimney master would steal him and force him to climb
dirty, hot chimneys, or he would be taken up by a tribe
of Gypsies and taught to steal handkerchiefs for which

Jack Ketch would hang him. His blue eyes swam with frightened tears as he cast about for a sympathetic face.

Everyone was glaring at him with hard eyes, except for two pretty ladies advancing upon him, their eyes twinkling just like Aunt Grace when she was about to share one of her stories. He moved into their path and, holding out a beseeching hand to one of them, said, "If you please, miss, I am lost . . ."

Hugging her reticule to her bosom as if she expected him to steal it, one young lady puckered her pink lips in an ugly moue and snapped, "Get away, brat!"

"Did you ever?" queried the other lady on an indignant note as she linked arms with her companion. Pushing past him, she trod upon his toes. "Come, Amabelle, let us leave the nursery."

Behind the girls came such a crush of people that Teddy was compelled to scramble aboard a statue of a mounted hero to escape being trampled. Without regard to dignity, he dug his fists into his eyes and sobbed.

Catching sight of a rather unusual addition to the Park's statuary, Standen excused himself from his charming companions and urged his high-blooded steed against the oncoming tide. Reining in before the stone-faced hero, he lifted enquiring eyebrows at the forlorn waif clinging to the stone and said kindly, "Hello, Zaccheus."

"Never heard of Zacch . . . whoever. Name's Teddy." He ran a braided sleeve across his snub nose and smeared his tears dry.

"Hello, then, Teddy." A concerned smile softened Standen's usual haughty expression. "Are you lost?"

"Not if you're a Gypsy or the chimney master," Teddy replied bravely. His eyes swept the passing throng as if he had merely climbed aboard for a better view of traffic. "I'm watching the promenade."

The duke could not restrain a good-natured laugh. It was the first time in two weeks that he had felt so untroubled. "Did your nurse frighten you, too, with Gypsies and sweeps?"

"Do you know Miss Cornthewaite?" Teddy gasped.

"No," Standen offered. "But my old nurse, Miss Bliss, must have gone to the same school. I was forever on the lookout for those bogeymen." He reached forth a hand. "Name's . . . Perry," he said, his natural wariness intruding and causing him to use his former title.

Recognizing a kindred soul among strangers, Teddy allowed his new friend to take his hand. "Pleased to meet you, sir."

"Pray do not stand on ceremony, Teddy," Perry said. "We are fellow veterans of nursery wars."

"Yes, I suppose we are." The little boy's tear-clouded eyes cleared.

For some reason, the pale gaze struck Standen as one with which he was achingly familiar. "Your mount must be devilish hard," he said. "Care to join me?"

Teddy seemed to hesitate as if warring against warnings not to trust strangers and his own need to rely on someone. His gaze darted once more around the area, then returned trustingly to Perry. "I'd be obliged, Perry, if you could help me find my Aunt Grace."

"Come aboard, Ted, and I shall return you to the bosom of your family." Sidling his mount nearer to the statue, Standen enabled the boy to mount behind him. "How shall I recognize 'Aunt Grace'?"

"Oh," Teddy said, clinging to his hero's pockets as he guided them into the flow of traffic. How did one describe a grownup? "Well, she is old."

"Half the population is London is 'old,' " Standen said around an irrepressible grin. "What other identifying characteristics has your aunt?"

"What do you mean?"

Standen glanced over his shoulder. Teddy was peering around his waist, puzzlement screwing up his tear-stained face. "Does this ancient relative of yours have warts or walk with the aid of a cane?"

Teddy giggled. "Oh no, she is not *that* old, Perry. She is only a little old . . . like you."

"I like that," the duke interjected, laughing. "I shall have you know, whelp, that I am in my prime!"

"Is that why those horrid girls were casting out their lures to you?" Teddy enquired. "They called me a brat and ran away."

"Did they?" Standen altered his opinion of Miss Amabelle Mock and her sister Clara. "Then I am just as well shot of 'em." He noticed that Teddy was craning his neck from side to side. "See anyone you know?"

"Not yet," Teddy replied, sighing as if to rid himself of a heavy burden.

"Just a matter of time," Standen assured him. "What is your aunt wearing?"

"Oh," ruminated the boy. "You know, one of those dresses . . ." He tried with his hands to indicate a short waist and high neck.

"Of what color?" Standen persisted.

This time the boy did not hesitate. "Like a boiled prawn."

"Red?"

"Pinkish," Teddy corrected.

Standen's gaze swept over the crowd. Fully one-third of the ladies were clad in some sort of pink frock. He realized he had his work cut out for him unless Teddy could be brought to reveal some outstanding feature. "Is your aunt brunette?" he asked, indicating with his riding crop a horsey-faced young woman who was directing anxious looks around the park as if searching for a lost child.

"Ugh!" Teddy recoiled. "No, my aunt ain't ugly." Standen felt him shudder behind him. "And she don't have black hair. Her hair is pale, like mine."

"At last, something to go on," Standen said, noting the white-gold sheen of the child's locks. "Your Aunt Grace is blond and pretty." He chuckled as he added, "But old."

"Well," Teddy giggled. "She would not like me to say so, of course. But she's been to Town so many times already, Mama says she's hopeless."

"Does she?" Standen shifted his searching gaze from a very pretty blonde in a frothy pink confection to a more sober-looking lady in a dusky rose pelisse.

"Hugh and Kate and I are determined she will not die an old maid," Teddy was saying as if he had known Perry all his life. He uttered a sigh. "She is so much fun, I wish she was my mother."

Under the shadow of an arching beech, Standen reined in and swiveled in his saddle to regard the little boy. Teddy was searching the forest of colorful bonnets and sunshades for one he recognized. Suppressing a sudden longing to meet a lady who could inspire such affection in a little boy and recalling the aloofness, nay, iciness, of his own mother, Standen said, "Unfortunately, Teddy, one does not choose his mother."

"No, worse luck." Teddy leaned his cheek against his hero's back.

Standen sensed the loneliness in the dependent posture and reached round to pat the boy's chubby arm as he said, "Not as bad as that, surely?"

"Well, Mama does not like dogs—at least she will not have one in Town—and we hardly ever visit Somerset where Grandfather keeps his hounds."

"That is no reason to dislike your mother," Standen said quite severely. "I think you must be very spoiled."

"So Mama says," Teddy said, not at all offended. "I shall try to do better. Because if I am horrid, Mama will not let Aunt Grace tell us any of her famous stories."

"Your mama rules with an iron hand?"

"No," Teddy replied thoughtfully. "She sighs and raises her eyes just so." He gave a remarkable impression of the early Christian Martyr that elicited an understanding nod from his rescuer. "I see you know how it is."

"Yes, and I suppose Aunt Grace does not affect such missish airs?"

"Oh no," Teddy assured him. "She is . . . 'a woman of . . . rare good sense,' " he said, hesitating over the compliment his father had once paid her. As if to cap this praise, he added, "Aunt Grace likes dogs."

At this the duke laughed aloud. "Come, boy, let us

find this paragon of womanhood before another fool recognizes her virtues and snaps her out of our hands."

Teddy tapped his jaw for a few moments as he thought. Of a sudden, it occurred to him that Perry might be the answer to their prayer for Aunt Grace. He was every bit as handsome as a fairy-tale prince, and he was kind, at least to frightened little boys. And judging by the fashionable cut of his coat and the blooded animal he rode, Perry must be rich.

Yes, Teddy decided, he might do very well. But it wouldn't do to appear too eager. "Well," he said at last, as if he were concluding a business deal, "I like you, Perry, and so I will take you to my aunt."

"I hope you remember what she looks like," Standen said, amusement tingeing his declaration with laughter.

"Of course," Teddy replied, his clipped tone indicating how foolish he thought grownups sometimes were. "She looks just like . . ." Glancing from left to right, he exclaimed, "Oh, look, Perry! Look, there she is!" He began to wave furiously enough to startle Standen's war-horse into a skittish dance. "Aunt Grace!" he shouted. "Here! I am here!"

Standen caught the reins in an iron grip before the charger reared and spun about. He heard a woman cry out, "Oh, Teddy, I was so frightened!" in a voice that had haunted his dreams for two weeks. Aunt Grace was "our Miss Penworth."

Reining in his uncharacteristic start of delight, he reminded himself sternly how she had insulted him in Newbury and how she had made over Andrew Blake at Ramsey's ball, then smilingly accepted Freddie Gates's invitation to dance just as they were enjoying a com-

fortable conversation. Then she had not even acknowledged the posy he'd sent after that accursed ball. Reluctantly urging his mount toward the treacherous female and her excited charges, he decided he would do
the civil by her for Teddy's sake, but when that was
done, whether or not she liked dogs or little boys, he
would go on his way, unencumbered and glad of it.

"Oh, Teddy, you gave us such a fright," she was saying as she placed a hand on the boy's foot. "How can
I thank you for . . ." Of a sudden, she glanced toward
her nephew's champion. Despite the rosy lining of her
bonnet, Standen saw her face go white, and she seemed
to stagger.

Handing Teddy into the care of his brother, Standen
swung himself from the saddle just as a footman appeared to take his animal's head. Without regard to his
firm resolution not to become entangled in this lady's
coils, he offered his arm to her.

"I . . . did not expect to see *you* again," she stammered as he led her toward a bench away from the press
of the crowd.

"I was . . . busy," he said as he placed her on a
bench in the shade.

"Yes," Grace said, trying to calm her racing pulse. "I
knew you must be."

"Oh, are you acquainted?" Teddy queried, excitement
making him jump about like a grasshopper. "This is
wonderful, Perry!"

"Quiet down, brat," said the duke. Concern for "Aunt
Grace" sharpened his otherwise indulgent tone. "Your
aunt is taken ill."

"Oh, not at all," she protested breathlessly. "Only, I

am relieved, and so glad to see you again!" At her intemperate confession her color began to rise, lending truth to her nervous utterance even as she embraced Teddy and stammered, "I mean to see Teddy again."

"Well, *do* you know Perry?" the child demanded, squirming against her hug.

Eight

Both adults stared at the little boy, Standen with a look of stern reproof and Grace affecting a silent plea to mind his own business. Finally releasing him, she said, "We are acquainted, Teddy." An embarrassed smile flitted across her face as she said, "It seems we must always meet by accident, Your Grace."

"Perry," he said on an impulse.

"I think we must endure the formality," she said regretfully, rolling the sound of his name in her mind. "Society will not allow 'Grace' to fall from your lips, nor condone such cordiality on mine."

"As you wish," he said. "Only Teddy and I will not stand on ceremony."

"No, of course not," she allowed breathlessly. "You are old friends."

"I should say so!" Teddy said in firm accents.

"Well, and so are your aunt and I," Standen said. "Only when Teddy praised his 'Aunt Grace,' I did not think it could be you."

"No, I can see that you did not," she replied in mortification, wondering if he *had* known, would he have left Teddy adrift in the crowd? Such cruelty could not be borne, and she thrust the ungracious thought aside by saying, "Children cannot be held accountable for their relatives."

"How true," he responded, in what Grace thought was a bored tone. Why, she wondered in frustration, couldn't she rattle him the way he unnerved her?

The tension in the air between the adults made the children exchange speaking glances as if saying, "So that is how it is."

Grace felt more embarrassed than ever as the children began to enumerate her various charms to the amused peer. She was thrifty, she paid attention when the elderly sisters down the street rambled on about their salad days, and . . . whatever their mother said, she was *far* from being at her last prayers.

At this final tribute, Standen could not restrain a whoop of laughter that sent Grace's spirits plummeting. Kate smoothed her frilly muslin frock and defended, "Well, *you* might laugh, Your Grace. For I have never heard it said that a gentleman was at his last prayers, but you are much older than Aunt Grace . . ."

"That is quite enough, Katharine," Grace commanded in the sternest voice she could muster. "The Duke of Standen has better things to do than play nursemaid to a pack of disorderly children. I am certain he is wishing that I take you home. And your mama must be beside herself with worry."

As children who have been told their expedition is over are wont to do, the three set up a loud complaint. Hugh growled, "Mama always spoils our fun."

Kate wailed.

Only Teddy seemed to possess enough presence of mind to blurt out, "Well, we will go home then, but we must take Perry with us, so he can persuade Mama that we are all safe. P'rhaps she'll invite you to stay to tea! Our teas are wonderful, Perry," he added with all sincerity. "We always have shortbread biscuits."

"Shortbread?" Standen interjected.

Grace was at once in a panic. If the duke had not cared enough to call or leave his card after the ball, he could hardly be expected to tolerate nursery tea. Hoping to save Teddy's feelings, she offered, "I am certain your friend must have another engagement for which he is late."

"You are mistaken, Miss Penworth," Standen said, lifting Teddy and Kate into the saddle. "My time is my own. Besides, I would be remiss if I did not see you safely home."

Motioning for the footman to lead the way, Standen offered his arm to Grace. When she blushingly reposed her hand upon his sleeve, they set off toward Hyde Park Corner.

Hugh, walking beside the footman, kept casting longing looks toward the animal. As they reached the carriage, he reached forth a hand and offered the horse a piece of sugar. To his delight, the huge steed took it delicately, then rubbed his muzzle adoringly against the boy's cheek.

Depositing the other children within the carriage, Standen turned to Hugh and enquired, "Do you like to ride?"

"Oh yes, sir . . . Your Grace . . . Perry," Hugh stammered, taking his hand from the animal's arched neck. "But Mama says it's a wasteful expense to keep a stable in Town, and she does not like me to ride the livery hacks, so I do not often get the chance."

As she was lifted into the carriage, Grace felt herself cringing at her nephew's unthinking confession. What must the duke think but that the middle-class residents of Harley Street were possessed of hopelessly pinch-penny ways? But he surprised her by saying, "Well, your mother is right, Hugh; it is a wasteful expense if the animals get no exercise. How would you like to ride one of my mounts?"

"Now?" Hugh blurted into the steed's ear. The startled horse blew into his hand.

"Not now," Standen said, remembering with tolerance his own boyish impatience. "Would tomorrow morning be too long to wait?"

"Oh, I say, that would be famous!" Hugh said, offering his hand manfully to seal the bargain before he leaped into the coach.

Grace saw the look of dismay which crossed the duke's face as he regarded the moisture on his palm. However, he said nothing as he swung into his saddle except, "Drive on, Coachman."

As the driver eased his team into the stream of traffic, Standen entertained Hugh and Teddy with stories of his service with Wellington, while Grace sat subdued in the corner of the coach. Though she did not like to admit such feelings, she was waiting for his engaging chatter to become less cordial as they traveled beyond fashionable Mayfair. But the only comment he made which made her heart pound anxiously was a stern remark directed toward Teddy, who was hanging out the window.

"Take yourself inside the coach, young man, or your mama truly will be overset by your adventure."

Grace was about to assure him that their mother was normally quite inattentive to her offspring, but Teddy said, rather wickedly, "She might take to her bed or throw a fit or—"

"Stow it, Teddy. Your stories aren't nearly as entertaining as Aunt Grace's," Hugh chided. He was lounging against the window, envying the nobleman's ease in handling his mount in heavy traffic.

But Standen seemed to have heard neither Teddy's dire prediction nor Hugh's set-down. He was considering their direction with a lowering aspect every bit as threatening in Grace's anxious eye as a thundercloud. As they pulled to a halt before their destination on Harley Street, she thought she perceived a sneering set to his mouth. She felt her heart sink. Amity had been right. He did think them beneath contempt.

Desiring above all things to avert what she feared most—that he would offer a heartless snub to the children, who could not help their parents' unfortunate choice of residence, she said, "Well, we are home," as she made to step to the pavement. "Thank—"

Of a sudden words failed her as the duke's hands spanned her waist to swing her from the carriage. When her feet were firmly on the ground, he did not immediately remove his grasp from her person. She felt dizzily as if she might float away when finally he turned to assist the children to the flagway.

She strove to regain her customary sense of balance as he responded to Teddy's incessant, "Perry . . . Perry . . . Perry," by ruffling the little boy's blond hair and laughing, "That's my name, Teddy-o; do you mean to wear it out?"

To her dismay, the duke seemed completely unaffected by the gallant gesture that had left her bereft of speech and almost incapable of standing, but he teased the two boys and their sister as if he had known them all their lives. And the children for once were the bane of her existence. They were jumping on and off the mounting block and curbstones, and singing and dancing up the doorstep like crickets. Everyone seemed oblivious to her sudden silence.

The footman managing at last to herd the children inside, Grace was left alone with the duke, who, tying his mount to the ring at the mounting block, seemed suddenly every bit as shy as she.

"Thank you for bringing us home," she ventured. Clasping her hands before herself anxiously, she could not refrain from saying, "I'm sure no one would expect you to . . ." She felt a hot blush stain her cheeks, and she dropped her gaze to the pavement. "That is, if you do not wish to come inside, I understand . . ."

"Miss Penworth," Standen said severely, sweeping to his full height after what seemed like an eternity spent securing his steed to the block. Compelled by his chiding tone to look at him, Grace stumbled backward at the intensity of his blue-eyed gaze. Of a sudden his visage alighted in a mischievous smile as if he had intended merely to gain her undivided attention, and he enquired, "Are you ashamed to introduce me to your family?"

Despite the gloved fingers which flew to her mouth, Grace could not suppress the happy giggle which arose to her lips. "No, Your Grace. Only I confess, after our disastrous introduction, I feared you might not like to make *their* acquaintance."

He gave his head a rueful shake and, as he offered his arm, confessed, "I fear an apology is in order."

Linking her arm with his, she gazed at him in a direct manner that intrigued him more than if she had peered flirtatiously at him through fluttering lashes. "You have it, Your Grace. I am not usually so waspish. Only, when you did not call or leave your card after Mrs. Ramsey's ball, I own my pride was pricked." She released a pent-up breath before she added, " 'Twas foolish of me. You have no obligation to do the pretty."

"But I do," he insisted. Hastening her through the wide door to deny the public a clear view of their affairs, he said, "I mean, you were right in your expectations." Eliminating the support of his arm from beneath her fingers so she might remove her bonnet and pelisse, he clenched his hands as if their conversation offered him considerable pain. "I ought to have called. But I sent a bouquet—violets and miniature roses."

"Oh, did you?" she enquired, startled into turning to look full in his face. "Several posies came for me the next day. I assume your card was lost." Blushing, she said, "Your flowers were the prettiest—all tied up in white ribbon. You must have wondered why I did not acknowledge them," as she led the way toward her sister's salon.

"It is of no consequence," he said, smiling from ear to ear now that he knew she liked his flowers the best.

"I only hope you are not confirmed in your original

opinion by this visit," Grace said. "We often take tea with our children."

"If I cannot tolerate children for a few minutes in the afternoon, you may throw me out the door," he vowed in, what sounded to her, completely serious tones.

Grace was obliged to bestow an anxious, questioning look upon him as they passed through the door into Amity's salon. His gaze meeting hers, he bestowed a reassuring wink in her direction. She could not restrain an impish smile from curving her full lips, as she returned, "I hope that may not be necessary, Your Grace. Harley Street would never recover from the shock."

"And the children shall lead them," Amity called out in a dry tone. "Where have you been, Grace? Teddy exploded into the salon nearly five minutes ago, boasting of his new friend." She raised her shoulders in a graceful but confused shrug. "He will not tell me who it is. I do hope it isn't another sweep. I cannot take on any more improving projects just now."

Drawing the duke into the salon, Grace said, "No, my dear. We have not brought a sweep to dirty your carpet today."

She could not fail to notice the color drain from her sister's countenance or the tight-lipped smile which turned her face into a polite mask as she recognized the caller. Hoping to relieve the unpleasant moment, Grace said, "I can't tell you how glad I am to have run into the duke this afternoon, Amity. He found Teddy after he had gotten lost in the park. He . . . His Grace, that is, wanted to make sure we returned home safely."

It was plain by Amity's reserved manner that she was

struggling against her former prejudice against the duke. However, years of training enabled her to overcome the pain his earlier snub had caused her. She came forward extending a welcoming hand and said, "We seem to be forever in your debt, Your Grace. Will you stay to tea?"

"I had rather hoped you would invite me, ma'am," he said as Teddy whooped in celebration. "Teddy said you might have shortbread biscuits." He directed a fond look upon the cavorting child. "I haven't had shortbread since my nursery days."

Amity gave him a look which seemed to enquire why a blooded nobleman should care whether he partook of shortbread when there were so many other more delectable treats to be had as an adult. To distract him from her sister's inquisitive stare, Grace directed him to a chair.

Waiting until she had placed herself in the chair beside his, he seated himself, then volunteered, "I like shortbread."

That a duke should be defending the privilege of eating shortbread in a salon on Harley Street appealed to Grace's sense of humor. Amity hastening to assure him that they must have shortbread in the house, as if the lack would never allow her to appear in society again, raised the exchange to a level of absurdity Grace could not resist. She began to giggle.

Leaning against Grace's knee, Kate enquired, "Did somebody tell a joke?"

"No, my dear," Grace replied between giggles. "I beg your pardon, Amity. Only . . ."

"Your imagination has gotten the better of you again," her sister helpfully supplied.

"A story! Aunt Grace is going to tell a story," Teddy announced. "Oh, Perry, wait till you hear." He flung himself full-length on the floor in front of his aunt, propping his chin upon chubby fists. "What's it about?"

"A story?" Standen enquired. "Does Miss Penworth spin yarns?"

"Yes," Hugh said in serious tones. He placed himself in a chair at the duke's elbow. "She is a famous story-teller. Aunt Grace, tell us the one about the wicked bee queen."

"Tea!" cried out Amity as if announcing a reprieve from the hangman's rope as a maid wheeled in a tray laden with the service and cakes and sweets and short-bread. After dispensing refreshments all around, she nodded at her sister. "Let us have a story, Grace. But *not* the one about the bee."

"Very well, Amity," Grace said. Holding her teacup in front of her and peering into it as if she were divining the leaves, she began quietly, "Once there was a lost little boy."

"Me!" Teddy shouted.

"Not you," Hugh insisted. To the duke, he said, "He always wants to be in Aunt Grace's stories."

"Not at all like Teddy," Grace said firmly. *"This* little boy had no one to love him."

"Is that why he was lost?" Kate said breathlessly.

"Don't interrupt," Amity shushed, leaning forward on her chair.

"He was lost," Grace said, still peering into her tea cup, "because he had taken the wrong turn on the road to Brighton. He was lost in the New Forest . . ." Her voice softened mysteriously, and she looked around her audience in a tantalizing manner that made the children squirm. "And it was getting dark."

Kate clung tightly to her knee. "I don't like the dark."

"Neither did Alan," Grace said, looking up from her tea leaves in surprise when the duke coughed on the tea he had taken.

"Was that his name?" he gasped. "Alan?"

"Yes, Alan Lightfinger," Grace replied, wondering why he was gazing at her in that speculative manner. "He . . . was a pickpocket."

"Oh," Amity said, shuddering. "I don't like him. Tell another story, Grace."

"I want to hear *this* one," said the duke, settling back in his chair and crossing his legs, one ankle over the opposite knee. The delicate chair joints creaked as if protesting the pressure. Then leaning forward on his propped-up knee, so as to relieve the strain on the fragile wood, he said eagerly, "Go on, Miss Penworth."

At his urging, Grace told the story of a little lost pickpocket who, in retrieving a diamond necklace from a highwayman and returning it to its rightful owner, found not only a home, but a loving family. All the time she knew with breathless satisfaction that the duke was hanging onto every word she uttered with as much fascination as the children.

When she had done, he said, "You ought to write them down."

"She does," Amity said in an offhand manner. "She writes books."

"For children?" he enquired.

"No," Grace said. "These stories are for Hugh and Kate and Teddy." Normally reticent about her gift, she found it more difficult to say exactly what sort of stories she did write down. Of a sudden they seemed sordid and bitter aspersions on the character of the man sitting only an arm's length away.

"She writes critical essays," Amity said without hesitation. Laughing, she added, "I have tried to get her to write romance, but she will not. I suppose it is because she has never fallen in love."

The duke's mouth tensed; Grace feared it was in disgust with her occupation. To her surprise, he said, "On the contrary, ma'am." She was forced to look away from his warm, approving look. "I have never met anyone as much in love as your sister."

Grace gasped that a gentleman she scarcely knew should think her in love. What if he ascribed that emotions as owing to himself? It was beyond any conceit she had yet witnessed in anyone of noble birth.

Amity sniffed. "I am not aware of it, Your Grace. If my sister were in love as you claim, she would share her good news with me." Slyly she enquired, "Or are you hinting at your own feelings?"

"Amity," Grace cried, "what will our guest think?" When everyone looked at her, she hid behind her cup as befitted a poor relation who had overstepped herself.

"If my emotions are engaged, I shall not hint," Standen replied haughtily. "No, and neither will our Miss Penworth. That is why I know she is head over heels in love with life."

Grace nearly drowned in her tea. Coughing, trying to catch her breath, she could only be grateful that the duke had not claimed she was wearing her heart on her sleeve for him. "I wish you will tell me how *you* know so much," she said in a miffed tone, resolving to guard her responses more carefully from now on, lest someone mistake her zest for life for affection.

"I cannot explain myself," he said, accepting another shortbread biscuit from Teddy. "Except to say that I have never seen your enthusiasm among Society's daughters. They pale in comparison."

Grace heard Amity's gasp of surprise and pressed her lips together in a frown to quell the flutter in her own breast. It would not do to let hope fly away with her again. She and the Duke of Standen lived in different worlds. His would never accept her, and he would soon hold her in as much contempt as his peers. But her pulse would not settle down into a more regular rhythm.

Hoping to quiet the unusual sensations within her breast, she said, "Flattery becomes you ill, Your Grace. How can a vicar's daughter compete with daughters of earls and marquesses?"

He laughed. "If I thought you truly wished to enter that race, I could tell you nothing more except to be yourself."

"If that is the extent of your advice," Grace said severely, trying without success to suppress the thrill his laughing compliment had incited, "it is just as well I do not care to join the competition."

"No?" he said, raising a dubious eyebrow. "Then why are you in Town?"

Knowing it would not serve any useful purpose to dissemble, she replied, "To do my duty toward my family."

"Aha," Standen said. He sounded very much as if he were prosecuting a case against her. "And do you not wish to secure the most flattering offer?"

Struggling against outraged embarrassment, Grace said, "You are well-aware that is the expressed desire of every female in the realm. Some of us, however, are able to make our own way unassisted or unhindered by the bonds of marriage."

"Really?" Clasping his hands loosely together, he leaned forward on his chair. "I have never met such an independent lady. How do you keep body and soul together?"

"With my pen," Grace replied.

"Beg pardon?"

"I told you," Amity said. "She writes critical essays." Arising from her chair, she glided toward a low bookcase, selected a slim volume, and placed it in the duke's hands. "Mama and Papa think she is here to snare a husband; in truth, she is here to keep her publisher honest," Amity laughed.

"Cock and Bull Stories," Standen read aloud. Perusing a passage, he pursed his lips together as if he found her unusual opinions distasteful. Then, gazing at Grace in such a manner as to raise a blush to her pale cheeks, he added, "Definitely *not* children's literature."

"No, Your Grace," she concurred, feeling her cheeks flame hotter as he opened the book and began to read other passages. To her mortification, he began to chuckle.

Lifting his gaze once more to hers, he raised his eyebrows as if surprised and said, "Very enlightening. Would you mind telling me how *you* know so much?"

She did not lower her eyes, but looked at him in a straightforward manner and replied, "I have seen much suffering in my father's parish and know it to be widespread in the realm."

"I do not doubt it," he said, closing the book to her great relief. "My grandmother would like to meet you."

"I hope you do not mean to use my meager talent to shock her," Grace said.

"No, the old girl is shockproof." To prove his point he said, "She is one of the few ladies who still receives Caroline Lamb."

"Really, Your Grace," Amity chided as she shooed Teddy and Katherine upstairs. "I hope you will not introduce our Grace to that fast set."

Ignoring Amity's admonition, Standen asked, "Would you like to meet her?"

"Lady Caroline?" Grace enquired. "I cannot think she would care to meet *me.*"

"No, goose," Standen responded. "My grandmother. The Dowager Duchess of Standen." As if they might not have heard of her, he added somewhat lamely, "Lady Perry, the poetess."

"Oh," Grace said in awe. The duchess was a living legend. "I would be honored to meet her."

"But only if Caroline Lamb is not—" Amity said.

"Nonsense," Grace interjected. "She needs every friend she can muster."

Standen chuckled. "Your sister is right, Miss Penworth. My grandmother might admit a rackety sort into her home on occasion, but she is mindful of convention as it concerns young ladies. Your reputation will be safe with her."

As if mindful that he had extended his visit beyond polite limits, he arose. "I am driving to her estate in Kent on the weekend. Perhaps you'd accompany me . . . ?"

"Kent?" Amity cried out. "Out of the question; you

cannot travel that far unchaperoned, Grace. Mama would forbid it." As if to take the sting off her prohibition, she added, "Perhaps if the duchess comes to Town . . ."

"She never comes to Town," the duke replied. "My grandmother is an invalid." He looked out the window as if searching for a way to induce Amity to relent, then said in regretful tones, "It is too bad, she needs cheering up."

"Nevertheless, I cannot be comfortable—"

"Do not be foolish, Amity," Grace said. "Papa would think nothing of my going to comfort an invalid. I think he would rather chide me for not relieving her loneliness."

"I do not know," Amity wavered. "Perhaps if you took one of the children . . ."

"Hugh," Standen said emphatically. "He will not get homesick and spoil my . . . my grandmother's peace."

Amity seemed to be considering the duke's offer. Grace found herself hoping that her sister would agree to let her eldest child chaperon her on the outing.

"We are committed to the Opera tomorrow," Amity said, thoughtfully. "And a musicale on Saturday. Not to mention Church."

"Then we shall depart Monday," Standen said. "Hugh, if your mother agrees, I will come for you tomorrow morning for our ride."

"Capital!" said Hugh, leaping to his feet in a burst of boyish enthusiasm. Then, recalling his manners, he quelled his start and said, "I mean, may I, Mother?"

"Only if you remember to say . . ." Amity said.

Hugh needed no further prompting. "Thank you, Your Grace," he said fervently.

"Don't mention it, boy; I told you my horses need exercise. And we needs must discuss your visit to Bon Chance." Turning to Grace, he asked, "Will ten o'clock be too early?"

"I am used to get up much earlier in the country," she said with all the enthusiasm of a child anticipating an unexpected treat. "We will be ready, Your Grace. And thank you."

Nine

After watching Hugh ride off with the duke on Friday morning, enduring screeching sopranos and tenors whose voices cracked painfully on Saturday, and a long-winded sermon depressing the pretensions of those who attempt to rise above their stations in life—which Grace felt was aimed at her—on Sunday, she fell asleep Sunday night dreaming that Monday would never come or that she would sleep through it.

Having awakened herself every hour or two during the long night to make sure she had not missed her outing, she presented, the next morning, an even paler aspect than was her custom. Amity started when she bustled into her bedchamber, and exclaimed, "La, Gracie, have you fallen ill?"

Grace turned her dark-circled eyes from the unkind mirror to face her sister. Chuckling wistfully, she confessed, "No, my dear, I am quite well. Only tired."

At once her sister hurried toward her and embraced her. "Oh, how unkind of me; you must not regard it. You look quite pretty in your blue muslin." Picking nervously at a little puff sleeve, she added, "Quite . . . delicate, in fact."

"Shall I cough for you?" Grace laughed, letting Amity pull her long, white-gold locks into a loose mass that tumbled over her shoulders.

"No, you know what I mean. But looking as fragile as porcelain the way you do, the duke will be driven to protect you against every evil."

"Goodness," Grace said, coming to her feet in an unexpected burst of energy, "I hope you don't mean to wrap me in cotton wool. I am sturdy enough to survive a trip to the country."

"I know that, Gracie," Amity said, fussing with her own hairstyle. "And you know that. But I saw the way he looked at you at tea Thursday, and . . ."

"And what?" Grace challenged. "The duke and I are friends, Amity."

"Friends," Amity mocked. "I *saw* how he looked at you."

"Pray, do not tell me his heart was visible in his gaze, for I shall laugh at you," Grace retorted. "We met quite by accident, and to his harm, for Mr. Davies's coach ruined his curricle on the road to Town." Picking up her gloves, Grace plucked at the fingers, saying, "He is merely concerned about his grandmother."

"Were that so, my dear," Amity laughed, "he would keep her out of your way. Your unusual sentiments concerning the nobility must offend even one as liberal-minded as the poetess Lady Perry."

Before Grace could enquire as to her sister's meaning, Hugh burst into her room. "He's come, Grace!" Running to the window which faced the street, he exclaimed, "Oh, what a rig. I knew when he took me riding Friday that all his cattle would be sweet goers. And oh, Mama, goodbye, I can't wait!" Throwing his arms around his mother's neck, Hugh bestowed a sloppy kiss on her cheek before racing down the stairs to throw open the door to his hero.

Grace stared after her nephew, suddenly fearing the trip. At her side, Amity gripped her hands and urged, "Courage, dear. Hugh likes him, and so do Teddy and Kate. If he has their approval, he can't be bad at all." Then placing a kiss on her cheek, she said, "Besides, it's all grist for the mill, isn't it?"

Distracted by anxiety, Grace turned a puzzled look upon her sister. "What?"

"Your essays," Amity said, drawing her toward the stairs. "I know you have one you've been working on in the bottom of your trunk. Is *he* in it?"

Grace could not help blushing crimson. "I did not know who he was at the time I drew the character. But he is nothing like . . ."

Laughing, Amity gave her a little shove. "Only because you have grown to like him, in spite of his down-the-nose manner. Grace, you are as transparent as glass."

"That, dear sister," Grace answered in a smiling tone as she glided downstairs toward the masculine voices in the foyer, "is a cliché which shall never dull my pen. But I do not mind if he knows I like him. We are living in an enlightened age when men and women can be friends without inviting gossip."

"Only if they are married, my dear, only if they are married," Amity responded in a voice meant only for her sister's ears. In a more general tone that covered Grace's gasp of dismay, she said, "Here, she is, Your Grace; ready on time."

Grace stopped on the bottom step and grasped the banister so that she wouldn't flee upstairs. She was suddenly possessed by the fear that the duke would think she had accepted his invitation merely to snare a husband. The look he was giving her did nothing to ease her apprehension. He had turned from Hugh and was regarding her as if dumbstruck. Hoping to turn his appalled silence into a joke, she quipped, "Ought I to have kept you waiting twenty minutes, Your Grace?"

In stricken tones he confessed, "No, only I did not expect . . . Hugh did not tell me . . . how pretty you look." He tore his eyes away as if the sight of her gave him extreme pain, and laughed at something Hugh mumbled before saying, "Yes, Hugh, your Aunt Grace *is* different from any lady I ever met."

Grace felt Amity's gaze bore into her back as she moved toward him. His tribute elicited a smile she tried to quell, especially in the wake of his subsequent comment. However, the usually stifled romantic in her soul assured her it was quite all right to be different as long as the Duke of Standen thought she was . . . pretty.

And as long as she remembered they were merely friends.

Offering his arm to her, he said to her sister, "You have nothing to worry about, ma'am. I will bring her—*them*—back safe and sound."

"You may have them as long as you like," Amity said, waving them through the door. "I'm sure Her Grace will not wish to part too soon with my sister. And you and Hugh will have all of Kent in which to ride."

By the time they reached Bon Chance later that evening, Standen was wishing Hugh anywhere but on the road to Kent. The boy had ridden between him and the traveling coach in which he had installed Miss Penworth, and had kept up such a steady chatter that the duke had not been able to hear himself think.

Not that the duke needed to be hit between the eyes with a board to recall his thoughts. They had been full of Miss Penworth, as they had been for weeks—had it only been *three* weeks ago that she had wrecked his curricle and wounded his heart?

It seemed as if he had been trying forever to dispel visions of her from his mind, and now, when he had her in his sights, he couldn't see her for this gabbling impediment with which he had saddled himself. Why, he wondered, as they turned finally onto the shaded drive toward his favorite estate, had he not placed her on the front seat, so he could gaze at her without craning his neck and converse with her without raising his voice.

The first sight of Bon Chance never failed to move him, and tonight he anticipated it with even more expectancy. As they rounded a wooded bend which opened onto the vista of the huge main house, which had originally been built as a fortress, then expanded and turned into a palatial country home, the setting sun illuminated its brick facade with a golden pink glow that elicited a whoop from Hugh and a quieter, but more gratifying, "Oh my," from her.

He wanted to see her face as she saw his home for the first time. And so, when the footman let down the step to hand her down, he brusquely told the man to help Hugh dismount instead and offered his own hand to his quiet traveling companion.

She hovered in the coach door, turning wide open eyes from one side of his home to the other as if counting the steps it must take to get to the farthermost wings. Suddenly she gazed at him, visibly unsettled by the grandeur which presented itself. He wondered if she feared she had entered the enemy camp.

Embarrassed by the ostentatious display, which usually filled him with pride in his heritage and his hard work, he could not help but raise his eyebrows as he grinned boyishly and said, "Big, isn't it?"

"How do you find your grandmother in there?" she said, grasping his hand at last and descending to the stone drive. To his satisfaction, she did not release his fingers at once, as if she were frightened she might lose him.

Taking advantage of her reliance, he tucked her hand around his arm as he laughingly said, "Fortunately, Grandmother likes the garden. If she's not in her salon, I usually find her tending roses." Drawing her up the broad limestone steps and into the pedimented front door, he called out a nonchalant, "Coming, Hugh?" that compelled Miss Penworth's nephew to follow hastily or risk being left behind in the expansive marble-tiled foyer.

Grace did not know whether the fluttering pulse which assailed her was due to shock over the lavishness of the duke's country home or to the fact that he had possessed himself of her hand and showed no inclination of releasing her. He was pulling her so quickly past closed carved doors, telling her in proud boyish tones

which room they guarded, that she could no more remember which was the gold salon and which was Cu-
pid's salon than she could catch her breath.

"Please, Your Grace," she gasped, as he paused at a
junction of two wings as if considering the right path,
"you've quite taken my breath away." She collapsed in
the middle of a red- and gold-striped bench. Hugh followed her example, panting like a winded puppy.

"Shall I request a litter to carry you the rest of the
way?" Standen teased.

Immediately she shot to her feet, saying, "Absolutely
not!" Then smiling in embarrassment, she said, "I am
used to walking miles at home, but never inside."

Laughing himself, Standen said, "It is marvelous exercise, and one can do it in the rain."

"Without an umbrella," Hugh piped excitedly. Then,
more wistfully, "But no puddles to splash in."

"As I recall, the roof in the nursery wing leaks.
Plenty of puddles there."

"But I've outgrown the nursery," Hugh said.

"So you have," Standen allowed, raising Grace to her
feet. "Come, we're late, and Grandmother hates to be
kept waiting."

"I think we ought to run then," Grace said, staring
down the endless hallway which was ornamented along
one long wall with carvings of trees and flowers that
made it look more like a garden than an interior, especially as tall windows on the west wall let in the last
golden rays of the sun.

"Do you?" Standen enquired with raised eyebrows.
Grace was beginning to regret her impulsive statement
when he laughed and threw open a door. "There is noth-

ing I should like more than to indulge you, Miss Penworth, but a race will have to await another day. Here is my grandmother's suite." Leading her within an enormous room decorated in shades of green and yellow and rose, he leaned over her ear and said, "And here is my grandmother."

From a pile of pillows on a couch came the mellow sound of a woman in love. "Alan, you naughty boy; I've been waiting all day to meet your friends. Couldn't you have driven faster?"

Hearing the sound, Grace focused on the pile of pillows and discovered in their midst a diminutive lady dressed in what seemed like a rose garden. Her gown was richly embroidered with the fragrant flowers, and even her cheeks seemed to be painted with rose petals.

Leaning over the frail-looking woman and bestowing a kiss on her dry cheek, the duke said, "I didn't drive, my dear. Elwood did, and he sets a pace that will impress people with your consequence, not mine."

She seemed to pout as she patted his cheek. "I shall discharge the old fool if he cannot move my cattle faster." Looking over his shoulder, she directed a stern eye at Grace and her nephew. "Well, come here where I can see you better." As they did, she drew in a breath and exclaimed, "You did not say she had a child."

"Nephew, Your Grace," Grace said, curtseying as the dowager frowned forbiddingly.

"Grandmother, do not stare Miss Penworth out of countenance," Standen said as he took Grace's free hand and squeezed it reassuringly.

"What else am I to do," she snapped, "when I've kept dinner waiting hours for you."

"Poetic license," he said, grinning down at Grace. "Grandmother eats at six o'clock."

"And it's now half-past seven," the dowager announced. "So let's get introductions out of the way, without standing on ceremony." Reaching forth a soft, wrinkled hand, she clasped Grace's fingers and said, "Elsie Faulkner, and you're . . . ?"

"G-Grace Penworth, Your Grace; and my nephew, Hugh Spencer."

"Come to chaperon, has he?" the dowager chortled. Grace was of the opinion the old lady would have elbowed her in the ribs had she been standing. As it was, she tugged her onto the cushions with her. "Tell me how it is between you and my grandson, Miss Penworth."

Grace could not hide the furious blush that colored her cheeks as she said, "We're friends, ma'am."

"Friends," the lady parroted dubiously. She did not let go of Grace's hand.

"Yes," Grace asserted, caught between the duke and his suspicious *grandmere*. "He thought we—that is you and I—might enjoy one another's company, as we both write."

"You write?" The dowager duchess patted her hand as if she would like nothing more than a comfortable coze with another sister of the pen. "What is it you write? Romance?"

"No, ma'am," Grace said, gazing steadily at the older woman's face. "I write critical essays."

The facade seemed to slip a notch as the dowager sniffed. "Critical of whom?"

"Social conditions," Grace responded.

TO GET YOUR 3 FREE BOOKS
'ILL OUT AND MAIL THE COUPON BELOW

Mail to: Zebra Regency Home Subscription Service
120 Brighton Road
P.O. Box 5214
Clifton, New Jersey 07015-5214

YES! Start my Regency Romance Home Subscription and send me my 3 FREE BOOKS as my introductory gift. Then each month, I'll receive the 3 newest Zebra Regency Romances to preview FREE for ten days. I understand that if I'm not satisfied, I may return them and owe nothing. Otherwise, I'll pay the low members' price of just $9.90 for all 3 books and save over $2.00 off the publisher's price (a $11.97 value). There are no shipping, handling or other hidden charges. I may cancel my subscription at any time and there is no minimum number to buy. In any case, the 3 FREE books are mine to keep regardless of what I decide.

NAME

ADDRESS _____ APT NO.

CITY _____ STATE ____ ZIP

( )
TELEPHONE

SIGNATURE _____ (if under 18 parent or guardian must sign)

RG0594

Terms and prices subject to change. Orders subject to acceptance by Zebra Home Subscription Service, Inc.

ZEBRA HOME SUBSCRIPTION SERVICE, INC.
120 BRIGHTON ROAD
P.O. BOX 5214
CLIFTON, NEW JERSEY 07015-5214

AFFIX
STAMP
HERE

"Eh?" the elder woman demanded.

"Parish relief," the duke interjected before Grace could edify the duchess as to her poor opinion of the aristocracy.

"Oh." The duchess's dark eyebrows knit together. Grace began to yearn for the exalted person's approbation when she saw the dowager's gaze slide toward the duke. The noblewoman demanded, "How came you to meet?"

"We met by accident," he said hastily. "Now it seems as if fate put me in her path."

The dowager's eyebrows shot up at his avowal. Giving him a dubious appraisal, she muttered, "And you say you're friends."

"I'm afraid that's all we can be, ma'am," Grace explained. "You see, I'm not of the nobility. My father is a clergyman in Cherhill."

"Quite ineligible," the duchess said bluntly. "But Alan, really. Friends?"

"I'm comfortable with that," Standen said, grinning. Before his grandmother could take issue with that, he ushered Grace and Hugh toward the door. "Why don't we get you installed in your rooms where you can change for dinner," he said, forestalling the protest that seemed to be forming on Grace's lips.

Keeping a carefully friendly smile on his mouth, he continued, "And I'll fetch you in half an hour to escort you to the dining hall." At the door he gave them into the hands of a silent footman who took them down the hallway toward a sweeping staircase which led to the South Wing.

Before they were completely lost to him, he heard Grace call out, "How will you find us?"

"Throw out bread crumbs," he answered, shutting the door on her delighted laughter.

"Friends, my good eye," the duchess said, patting the cushion at her side. When he placed himself beside her, she scolded, "I wish you will stop bringing your *friends* to entertain me. I want great-grandchildren."

"And so you shall have them, Gram. As soon as I convince Miss Penworth to give up her foolish prejudice that she is quite ineligible and accept a proposal of marriage."

Shaking her head, she said, *"You're* the ineligible one, Alan. Her father is a clergyman. Won't approve of you or me *or* our free-thinking friends."

"Well, she did say that her parents wouldn't like the way we met," he confessed. "But they're more likely to force a marriage than to forbid one."

"And is that what you want? A bride forced to marry you?"

"No, how can you think it?" he defended. "Only she does not know the way the wind blows, which works to my advantage."

"How so?"

"Despite her serious occupation, she is the sort who reads romance into everything," he said, recalling the charming story she told at nursery tea. "As long as we are 'friends,' she will be comfortable in my company."

"Until you divulge what your heart is full of," Elsie cackled, "then she will bolt like a spooked filly." She slapped his hand with her fan. "Foolish boy. Sweep her off her feet; don't give her time to 'be comfortable in your company.' "

"But I want her to trust me," he said, "not fear me."

Giving him a look that spoke volumes of her contempt of his self-restraint, the dowager duchess pushed to her feet. Leaning on a silver-handled walking stick that was every bit as long as the ones footmen carried in Town, she snapped, "Then remain silent, Alan, and she'll accept another offer before you can bend the knee. And you'll spend the rest of your life loving another man's bride."

Ten

Alan stared at his grandmother, unable to believe she expected him to fall victim to the family curse involving firstborn sons. Everyone of them, beginning with the first Duke of Standen's heir, excepting Alan's grandfather, had lost his true love. And Alan admitted his grandfather might have lost Elsie to another nobleman had she not taken matters into her own hands and taken him to Scotland.

But with their firstborn son, the curse had reasserted itself. His Uncle Roderick had named Alan his heir after the woman he had chosen for his bride married a mere marquess. His uncle having remained unmarried to his death, Alan was the final hope of the Standen house. If he failed to marry, the line would end.

"What are you Faulkners about?" the dowager demanded. "Never cautious in war, but in love, ready to throw in the towel before the first salvo is fired."

"I'd hardly call us cowards," Alan said in defense.

"No one said you were cowardly," she snapped, pounding her walking stick on the parquet floor. "Only too cautious. Don't understand it. You were all of you very popular with the ladies. Even Kendrick." She sighed as if remembering her husband. "He enjoyed the muslin company, but treated me as if I were china that might break." Pressing her dry lips together, she said in a voice that was not to be denied, "Don't make that mistake with your Miss Penworth. She looks delicate, but she's made of sterner stuff than most ladies. And I heard her laugh outside before you presented her. Delightful."

"So you do like her?"

"What does it matter whether I like the girl, Alan? The question is, do *you* like her?"

In his mind, he conjured up Grace Penworth, appearing in her stalled coach, flinging off an attacking bee, clinging to him, fleeing from him, dancing in his arms, welcoming a lost little boy into her arms. How he wished she would welcome him . . .

Warning himself that such hopes were premature, he directed a stricken look at his elderly relative, confessing as he moved toward the door to dress for dinner, "She drives me mad, Gram."

"Then do something about it," commanded his grandparent, "or you will fall prey to the same curse that's afflicted seven generations of Faulkners."

He bestowed a long-suffering look on her. "You are forgetting two things, Gram."

"Which are?" she asked in a voice that suggested she would not be easily convinced.

"I am not the heir to the title and not a green cub with no experience with the world."

She smacked her walking stick on the floor. "Neither of which signifies. You are our only hope."

"Then trust me to do the right thing," he urged. "I will not kidnap her to Gretna. *That* must surely prove her bias against our class."

"What bias?" demanded the unhappy duchess.

"That we are all self-centered, arrogant snobs, possessing no conscience whatsoever." The duke tempered his unflattering comments with an indulgent smile. "I expect I affirmed the worst of her convictions on first and second meeting."

Giving him the eagle eye, the dowager said, "You have known each other long?"

"Less than a month," Standen said wonderingly. How could it be that in such a short time, a simple country girl should turn his world upside down? Standen decided it must be madness. But if it were, he would be the happiest man in Bedlam.

The little gilt clock chimed eight times. "Pray, excuse me, Grandmother," Standen said, startled out of his confusing but satisfying reverie. "I must fetch Grace from the labyrinth, or her expectations will once more harden against me." Without awaiting her leave, he strode toward the door and made for the stairs.

"Grace, is it?" Elsie mused when he had gone. Perhaps there was hope after all.

The object of his insanity would have flung herself at the door when he knocked, had not a maid been possessed of a lock of her hair. "No need to hurry, miss," said the maid confidentially as she coiled the lock and secured it to the elegant topknot of curls she had designed. "A gentleman likes to be kept waiting if the results are worth waiting for." Cupping the finished hairstyle in her capable hands, she directed a considering gaze at Grace's reflection.

Grace could not help but catch her lower lip anxiously between her teeth as she watched the maid tilt her head from side to side as if passing judgment on her handiwork. "Well?" she said at last when she could no longer abide the suspense.

"I'd prefer to lace a ribbon in the curls," said the maid, taking away her hands. "But that'd be gilding the lily, so to speak. And knowing His Grace, he'd not notice anyway."

Fear that he wouldn't notice her new hairstyle made Grace propel herself toward the door. "Why did you bother then?" she demanded. "If he takes no notice of such things."

"I did not say he won't notice you," said the maid as she tidied up the vanity. "How could he not? Only, he wouldn't pay any attention to ribbons. Men don't, you know."

But Grace did not know what men noticed. She only knew that the duke had praised her for not keeping him waiting in Town. And she repaid him by making him cool his heels outside her door the very first time he came to fetch her for dinner. Drawing open the door, she apologized for being so slow in dressing.

Hand raised as if to deliver another blow to the door, he seemed dumbstruck when she appeared and offered an apology. "I'm not used to having maids pull my hair," she explained nervously, putting a hand to the side of her head. The style was so heavy and seemed so precariously piled, she feared it might tumble down at the slightest breeze. And he looked anything but approving, staring at her with glazed eyes that glided over her frame from head to toe and back. "If you do not like it," she said, lowering her hand and smoothing her gold-striped silk skirt, "I could ask her to put it back the way it was."

"No, don't," he said, taking hold of her arm when she made as if to return to her chamber. "It's pretty. Different." Bestowing a wry grin on her, he indicated the wispy curls that framed her face. "I like the way they sort of curl around your cheeks."

Pleased with his compliment, she coiled one lock around a finger. "Thank you, Your Grace."

Offering his arm, he led her down the hall. As she walked beside him, trying to still the nervous flutter of her pulse, he kept looking at her in much the same way Colin had gazed at her sister before the Ramseys' ball. His heated stare made her feel increasingly self-conscious, and all too conscious of his virility. A heated blush colored her cheeks as she considered the incongruity of their association.

But he seemed determined to set her at ease, for he said, "Grandmother likes you. I think she wishes to adopt you."

Assured by his statement that he had no evil designs on her person, Grace smiled up at him. No gentleman, even if he were a rake possessing the worst of the noble traits with which she was familiar, would introduce his grandmother to the woman he'd decided to give a slip on the shoulder. And the Duke of Standen was by no means the worst nobleman of her acquaintance.

That dubious honor must go to his friends, Lord Phillip Brabberton, Sir Frederick Gates, and that insufferable coxcomb, the Honorable Mr. Blake; all of whom had drooled over her as if she were one of Gunter's famous confections. The duke, for all the privilege of his exalted station in life, seemed remarkably unspoiled and mindful of her genteel upbringing.

But she could not like having him think of her as a relative, and so teased him. "It is all very well for Hugh and Teddy and Kate to call me 'Aunt Grace,' Your Grace; only, I will not brook having *you* address me in such aging terms."

Standen smiled down at her in such a warm manner that Grace's laughter died in her throat. "I believe my grandmother wishes to address you as 'granddaughter,' " he said in a light tone that gave Grace to understand that he did not entirely take his elder relative seriously.

Breathing a sigh of relief, she decided she would humor them both and said, "I have never had a big brother, Your Grace. It might be rather fun."

"Would you not rather think of me as your friend?" he enquired, his tone still carefully light. "A brother, after all, can be a devilish marplot." Halting their progress at the double doors leading to the great dining hall, he regarded her with a look that was definitely not brotherly.

Beset by an unfamiliar yet compelling hunger, Grace lowered her gaze from his appraisal. It was all too attractive a magnet to resist, however. Risking a glance upward, she was rewarded with a teasing grin that incited her pulse to run riot. Of a sudden, she realized why brothers so often played spoilsport—to protect gullible girls from their tendency to trust handsome men. Smiling, she said, "I don't have a brother, Your Grace, but it is my understanding they act in one's best interest."

Standen winked as he replied in a conspiratorial tone,

"I should hate to spoil your fun, Miss Penworth." This left Grace wondering whether she ought not to trust him after all.

"Wait! I say, Aunt Grace." Hugh skidded to a halt on the slippery parquet floor beside the couple, breaking the spell. "I thought I should never catch up with you. Did you not hear me calling for you to wait for me?"

"No, Hugh," Grace replied, turning from the heart-pounding sight of the duke's teasing smile to regard her nephew. "How rude His Grace will think you to shout so in his home." Straightening the collar of the boy's rumpled dinner jacket, she placed a kiss on his flushed cheek. "My," she said in surprised concern. "You are rather warm."

Standen brushed an absent hand over the boy's fore-head. "Comes from running in the halls," he said, indulgently ruffling Hugh's damp combed hair. "Go inside, young sir, and announce us. Mind you take your time. Your aunt has something to say to me, I think."

The footman led Hugh into the cavernous chamber, and Standen possessed himself of both of Grace's hands, so that her cheeks were infused with a becoming pink tint. Averting her gaze so as to calm her lurching pulse, she said, "You are mistaken, Your Grace. I have nothing to say to you."

"Said in the expressive tones of a lady who has every intention of dressing one down," he laughed. "I see how it would be if you *were* my sister."

She heaved an embarrassed sigh.

"Eloquent silence and speaking sighs meant to depress my consequence," he went on. Giving her hands a firm shake that raised her eyes to meet his still-teasing gaze, he said, "I can tell you now, my friend, it would not suit." He grinned maddeningly at her. "You would harass me unmercifully until I should have you married off within the month, just to impress you with my power."

Grace had heard tales of the Marriage Mart, in which young ladies were married off with not the slightest attention paid to their heart's preferences if an alliance benefited the family. She did not wish to think he would be so cruel as to carry out his threat, but what did she really know of the Duke of Standen? One of the most powerful men in the realm, he could no doubt do whatever he wished. Her slumbering imagination awakened, she tugged on her hands, protesting, "Surely you would not."

He winked at her. "Since you are fortunately *not* my sister, you will never know for certain. Aren't you glad you are my friend?"

"Yes," she replied in breathless accents. She was glad they were friends, even if they could be no more than friends. She had never enjoyed a comfortable relationship with any man save her father and brother-in-law, for everyone else seemed determined to consider her a potential bride. That Standen did not caused her a moment's pain. Intellectually attributing her discomfort to Injured Pride, she quelled an unbecoming tendency to pout.

Immediately she heard the strident tones of her nephew's voice calling out, "His Grace, the Duke of Standen, Marquess of Faulkland, Earl of Faulkner, Viscount Perry . . ." Hugh heaved an audible sigh as if catching his breath, adding in equally stentorian tones,

"And my Aunt Grace Penworth, of Cherhill, Wiltshire."

"Our cue, Miss Penworth," Standen said, laughing as he released one hand and led her into the long, high-ceilinged hall. "Your nephew must have been prompted by Latham, my protocol minister . . . and underfootman." He chuckled, seemingly unaware of Grace's sudden self-consciousness. "He never misses an opportunity to puff himself off by reciting my various ranks and titles."

In awe of the duke's consequence, Grace could not at first reply. What was *she,* the young daughter of a country vicar, doing in such lofty company as the Duke of Standen?

A cynical inner voice that sounded very like Mr. DuBarry hinted the duke found her an amusing counterpoint to the sophisticated ladies and innocent debutantes with whom he had hitherto been acquainted. He probably did not count among his extensive acquaintance many ladies capable of entertaining a thought more serious than which modiste to patronize. A female essayist must strike him as being as unusual as a talking monkey.

The unflattering inner suggestion made Grace burn with the desire to ask him whether he thought her a freak of nature.

"Strange," mused the duke, startling her out of her self-conscious preoccupation long enough to wonder whether he had the ability to read her mind.

She could not refrain from asking, "Who, me?"

He gave her a searching look, then smiled as if deciding he liked what he saw in her. The approving glance made her glow. "Definitely not you," he said at last. "No, Miss Penworth, you are the most normal of my acquaintance."

His tribute failed to please. An essayist she might be, with ideas and thoughts beyond the pale, but she was still a young lady who longed to hear a handsome gentleman dedicate pretty compliments to her. "Normal" sounded strangely flat to her ears.

Laughing, he conceded that he had not meant to offend. "Indeed, I was reflecting on Latham's curious penchant for reciting all my titles, yet omitting my favorite rank."

Didn't he have enough honors? Grace wondered as he seated her. Aloud she enquired, "What is that, Your Grace?"

"Colonel," he said, sliding into the chair next to hers.

With a start, she realized he was sitting at the head of a very long table; one that looked as if it might comfortably seat two hundred wearing court dress.

Against her will she thought of the poor unfortunate souls she had abandoned in her father's parish to present herself to any eligible offer of marriage she might attract this spring. To her shame, she had even dropped the necessary obligations of balls and soirees to go chasing after the most ineligible bachelor of her acquaintance.

She clasped her hands tightly in her lap to keep from decrying her foolishness and the unfairness of life that so few should enjoy such abundance. That was what she ought to do, but the duke and his grandmother had shown her such kindness, she could not in courtesy offend them.

How like a traitor she felt. She was no better than those bubbleheaded socialites who cared nothing for the plight of their poorer countrymen and women. In point of fact, her conscience told her she was worse, for she *knew* how bad conditions were for the poor in the country.

The Reformer in her wished Mr. DuBarry could see this lavish waste of material comforts.

Giving herself a mental shake, she decided she did not want him to intrude on her visit with the duke. Mr. DuBarry would only find fault in every little thing, just as he had done at the Ramsey ball. Why, she wondered, drawing her golden eyebrows together critically, did he not understand that everyone, rich and poor alike, needed some joy in their lives?

Lost in her contemplation, she did not realize the first course had been laid. All she could think of was the way Mr. DuBarry's eyes would bulge out in self-righteous rage. It was a most unattractive prospect. Grace could not suppress a delicate shudder.

The dowager duchess leaned across the table. "Is something not to your liking, my dear?"

Grace gave another start as she pulled herself back to the moment. "Were you addressing me, Your Grace?"

"Do you not like salmon?"

Grace looked at her untouched plate on which reposed a portion of poached salmon, asparagus, potatoes, and young carrots. "Oh," she said, knowing she must speak now if she was to hold her head up among her charges back home. "No, everything is delightful. I . . . I was just thinking of the parable of the banquet which was opened to the poor and infirm. How many of those unfortunates could sit at your table." She did not fail to see the speaking glance that passed between the duke and his grandmother, and she tensed herself for the reproach which she felt their bruised consciences would heap upon her.

"So pretty," said the dowager, surprising Grace with a benevolent smile. "And kind-hearted, too, Alan."

"Yes," agreed the duke in the tones of one who has discovered a pearl beyond price. "I have also heard it touted that she likes dogs." He bestowed another of his heartwarming smiles on her.

Grace felt strangely light-headed. Did he know how his smiles affected her? She could scarcely breathe, and her heart was pounding the way it did whenever she climbed White Horse Hill.

Heavens! she thought, making an attempt to rein in her pulse. She was merely his friend, after all, and ought to be immune to flirtatious glances.

Still, that he thought her kindhearted brought a pleased smile to her lips as she voiced a somewhat embarrassed, "I don't see how I could be less concerned with my poor brothers and sisters than with our four-footed friends."

"Comes from living in a religious home," said the duchess.

"I beg your pardon," said Grace, ducking her head as she belatedly remembered her manners. How she wished she could hide behind her napkin until the guilty color subsided from her cheeks. "I have no right to ring a peal over your heads." Addressing at last her neglected platter, she confessed, "Oh, this is very good," then reverted to her apology. "You see I could not help following my father about the parish. My sister showed little aptitude for parish work."

"No doubt her interests lay elsewhere," prompted the elderly woman in an attempt to make her guest more comfortable.

Hugh was quick to agree. "Mama prefers organizing bazaars and balls to visiting the poor. Says she can help more of 'em her way than Grace can."

Startled by her nephew's revelation, Grace choked. The duke alternated between patting her back and offering her a glass of water, which ministrations only increased her discomfiture even though they eased her fit. A warmth having nothing to do with embarrassment suffused her veins when he suddenly ceased striving and rested his hand on her back. Pressing her own hand to her bosom to quell the rush of heat ushering from the region of her heart, Grace directed a hesitant, sidelong glance at Standen that caused him to withdraw his hand in a manner that suggested he had been burned.

Secretly pleased by Grace's ardent, yet modest reaction to her grandson, the dowager directed a scowl toward Hugh. "Have you been listening at keyholes, boy?" she demanded.

"No," he stammered. "Mama just says things."

"And you repeat them, even if they must hurt someone's feelings," persisted the duchess.

"Pray, do not regard it," Grace whispered, still in a flutter of confusion. "*I* do not, most of the time. And I do owe you an apology for thinking unkind thoughts while enjoying your hospitality."

The duchess waved an imperious hand in the air, saying, "So you are normal, after all, Miss Penworth. Alan was painting your portrait as a saint. But now, since I know you entertain occasionally catty thoughts, I can be comfortable with you."

The dowager's confession surprised Grace and momentarily nonplussed her. However, catching Hugh's eye, she saw a brightness within his gaze that was most unlike him. "Are you feeling all right?" she enquired, coming out of her chair and moving around the end of the table to feel his brow. It was devilish hot. "You are not well!" she exclaimed. "How long?"

"Not long," Hugh said in a pained voice. "This morning."

"Why did you not tell us *then?*" Grace demanded in a gentle tone. "You would have been tucked in your bed and cosseted all day."

Hugh pressed his lips together as if, now his secret was out, he was tempted to revert to the actions of a little boy. Manfully he contended with tears, saying after a moment, "Mama would not have let you come if *I* could not."

Grace wrung her napkin anxiously. "And she will never forgive me should your fever carry you off." Clenching her hands in impotent rage against Hugh's senseless sacrifice, she cried, "I should have known you were not yourself." Addressing the duke, who had risen to stand behind her, she said, "He is never such a chatterbox unless he is coming down ill or is frightened."

Standen placed a soothing hand on each of her arms, an action which proved anything but calming. "In which case he takes after his Aunt Grace," he said, drawing her gently back to her abandoned chair. "He will not expire before the physician sees him, Miss Penworth.

And if he is indeed sick, and not merely overexcited from the journey, you will need whatever sustenance you can take now."

The duke's hands were still firmly pressing her down in spite of her determination to go to Hugh's aid. "But I must get Hugh to bed, Your Grace."

"Latham will see your nephew to his room," Standen said, directing an inarguable glance toward the under-footman. "And our housekeeper will see he is tucked in and fed a light broth."

"Oh, this is too much," Grace said, throwing down her napkin and coming to her feet, despite the pressure to keep her seated. "If you think I shall abandon my nephew to strangers, you cannot—"

Hugh coughed in his napkin. "Please, Aunt Grace," he choked. "I don't wish to spoil your fun. The rest will do me good . . . but if you have the chance, could you p'rhaps tell me a story before you turn in?"

Before she could respond, Standen said in an inarguable tone, "Your aunt will look in on you after dessert. If you are not asleep, you may have your story. Now say good night, my man; I will send the physician to you directly."

Scraping back his chair, Hugh found his feet and made a childish bow. "Thank you, Your Grace," he coughed. "Beg pardon, ma'am," he said to the dowager. Hugging his aunt, he said, "Good night, Aunt Grace, I am glad you got your special trip." Letting her go, he followed the stiff-backed footman to the doors.

When he had gone, Grace glared at the duke. "You are mistaken if you believe I will allow that boy to go to bed without his story."

To her fury, he began to laugh. Chuckling, he held up a staying hand. "Hugh needs a story like he needs spots. No, my dear Miss Penworth, don't cut me up. The best you can do for him is let him rest. Especially after Dr. Toombes finishes with him."

Though she was still warmed by the duke's proximity, Grace suddenly felt as if all the color had drained from her face. Frightened, she demanded, "He will not . . . bleed Hugh, will he?"

"Who knows?" Standen said, as if it did not matter to him what treatment the physician ordered.

Immediately Grace flew toward the door, saying, "I ought to have known you would not care." At the doors, her flight was halted as the duke imposed himself before her. Standing toe to toe with him, she demanded, "Kindly remove yourself from my path, Your Grace. Hugh needs me."

Scowling, Standen gave every appearance of prohibiting her from leaving. But Grace was too concerned about Hugh to know that no one in recent experience had dared to question the duke's will without receiving a well-deserved rebuke. Still, she could not fail to hear his grandmother's shocked inhalation, and recalled herself to who she was and where she was. Indeed, she expected at any moment to hear the icily voiced query, "Who do you think you are?" which never failed to set Nobodies in their place.

Instead, the duke stepped aside. "You are right," he said gently. "We would think less of each other if we continued dining as if nothing had occurred." He cleared his throat as if the concession was costing him his dignity. "Go, assure yourself of your nephew's comfort. We shall have a tray sent to you." But his eye gleamed menacingly as he added, "And I expect you to eat every bite, or I shall assume you are courting illness and send you to bed as well."

His threat was no idle boast, Grace knew. Recalling the way he had swept her up in his arms and carried her into the Swan and Bell kitchen elicited a frisson of fear and delight along her nerve endings. Grace compelled herself to quell the fluttery sense of anticipation. It was not at all pleasant to be so short of breath and lightheaded. Such missish airs affected her ability to concentrate on anything save the duke's handsome visage, virile form, and manly character.

Of course, she could not allow him to see how he affected her. Drawing herself to her full height, she stared daggers at him, saying in a voice that trembled more than she would have liked, "That won't be necessary, Your Grace. I'd rather go to bed alone." Blushing furiously in the face of her indelicate slip of the tongue, she fled the dining hall without taking proper leave of her hostess, who seemed on last glance to be suffering an apoplectic fit.

Choking back laughter, the dowager looked down her nose at her grandson. "That was very naughty of you, Alan."

"Yes, it was, Gram," he allowed, laughing himself.

"I shall not allow you to plague your little friend," she persisted.

Standen reclaimed his seat at the head of the table. "I don't mean to plague her." Taking up his fork, he downed a portion of cold salmon. "Ugh," he complained, throwing down the utensil. "Take this away.

And tell Cook not to send it to Miss Penworth. I want her to eat something that will distract her from her sick nephew." When the silent footman had removed the unsavory first course, he fixed a glittering stare upon his grandmother. "I only want some time with her."

The devilish duchess chuckled over a glass of wine. "You're not the first one to refer to it as 'time,' my dear, but I wish you will recall to whom you are confessing such an impolite declaration."

"Confound it," Standen growled. "I don't wish to ruin her reputation. I want to learn where Grace Penworth came by her outrageous, no, *dangerous,* ideas, and whether or not she can think kindly of any aristocrat."

Further conversation on the subject was necessarily delayed until the second course was laid and the duchess had directed a light dinner be laid in the sick room for Miss Penworth. As soon as they were left alone, she bestowed a measuring look upon her grandson. "Do you mean to convert her?"

"Please," he protested, "don't make it sound so religious."

"My dear, any deeply held philosophy is religiously defended when it comes under attack." The furrows in her white brow deepened. "Your Miss Penworth sounds like a dangerous lady to befriend. Perhaps I ought to read her shocking little book."

"Not so shocking," the duke said, thoughtfully addressing a portion of vol-au-vent of chicken. "Merely imprudent and naive, because she bares her heart to the world."

Elsie regarded the duke thoughtfully as she digested his words. Then lowering her perceptive gaze, she said,

"Indeed, that is dangerous. She would be safer if she wore her heart on her sleeve for some*one* rather than an ideal."

Nodding, Standen said, "I certainly think so."

When they had finished with dinner, the duchess lay a commanding hand upon his sleeve and asked, "Will you tell her, or shall I ask a few pointed questions?"

Standen tucked her hand within the crook of his arm and began to draw her down the hall. "You cannot fool me. You want the nursery filled again. But I will not allow you to pressure Miss Penworth into revealing her feelings."

"Why, Alan," chuckled the grande dame as she patted his sleeve, "don't you wish to know whether your suit will prosper?"

Smiling down at his grandmother, Standen said, "It is enough that the lady is here, Gram. And although she is concerned with her nephew's fever, I will not allow her to become obsessed with it." Delivering her into the keeping of her abigail, he kissed the papery cheek and said, "Now if you'll excuse me, she promised Hugh a story. Maybe she'll let me listen in."

Eleven

After consulting with the physician and sending him home, Standen strolled into Hugh's room as much at ease as if he were entering his club. But as soon as he saw Miss Penworth drowsing in a chair at her nephew's bedside, he felt as unsure of himself as if he were in the throes of calf love.

Sheets of paper covered with delicate handwriting lay in her lap, her ink-spattered fingers curled protectively over them as if she was deep in thought. Standen wondered if the writings were inflammatory prose or a letter to Hugh's mother informing her that her eldest son had developed a fever and cough.

A crease knitting Grace's elegant brows together and the stiffness in her posture told him the depth of her concern. Unable to help himself, he strode forward and gently rubbed the tension from her shoulders.

Grace started awake at his touch. Fearing Hugh had taken a turn for the worse, she burst from the chair, neglecting to remove her writings, which scattered to the floor. Leaning over her nephew and brushing his hair off his hot, dry forehead, she assured herself that he was still asleep.

While Grace saw to her nephew's comfort, Standen

knelt to retrieve her fallen papers. He managed to read a few lines and was relieved to discover they reflected an aunt's anxieties for her nephew's health. Smoothing the paper together, the duke wished he had the right to ease her concerns.

Satisfied with Hugh's quiet repose, Grace turned to face her host. He was stacking pages together, seemingly uninterested in the content of her letter. Clasping her hands together to keep from holding them out to receive her writings, she said, "I have been waiting to tell him his story, but he is sleeping," her explanation dwindling into breathless accents as the duke took her hand and drew her from the sickbed.

"No chance of that now," he said, directing their steps toward her chamber. "Dr. Toombs said he gave Hugh a sleeping draft. Best thing you can do for the boy is get some rest yourself." When she made as if to protest the selfishness of such indulgence, he frowned in his best Lord-of-the-Manor fashion, saying, "I have recruited Latham to act as Hugh's nurse tonight. He was too impressed with his own importance."

Knowing her conscience could not let her rest while Hugh tossed feverishly on his bed, Grace also knew further argument with her host was useless. Turning at her door to face him, she smiled wearily as he handed her the letter. Despite his kindness, she gently accused, "You are heartless, Your Grace."

"It is a consequence of my rank," Standen said with an odd catch in his voice. Self-consciously he cleared his throat and clenched his hands behind his back to keep from embracing his preoccupied guest.

Grace giggled. Standen seemed so boyish and vulnerable—not at all heartless—that she was compelled to testify in his behalf. "You so rarely attempt to impress one with your title, I should think you despised it."

"I don't think about it much," he said, rubbing his chin thoughtfully. Then, grinning a challenge, he leaned a hand against the doorframe over her shoulder and enquired, "Is that why you like me so well?"

Tucking her papers like a shield against her bosom, she blushed involuntarily, then stammered, "Y-you are too sure of yourself." She dropped her gaze self-consciously. How could he suppose she liked him only because he was a duke?

Lowering his hand from the wall to cup her chin, Standen raised her face and smiled down at her. She fairly glowed in the half light of the hallway, and he found it difficult to speak. His mouth felt dry of a sudden, as it had done when he was called to recite sums he had forgotten. Running the tip of his tongue across his lips, he said, "I have never had reason to doubt myself before."

Mesmerized by the sensual motion of his tongue over his lips, Grace lay a hand upon his lapel, saying, "You are a rare man."

"Yes, I am," he said proudly, yet lightly. "Would you like to know me better?"

His voice drew her toward him, and she shivered in his tender grasp, wanting him with a shameless longing that betrayed her upbringing. With their disparate backgrounds, she knew better than to throw herself at him. Still, she could not help but confess what they both wanted to hear: "I wish it above all things."

He hovered above her like a hummingbird over a

flower, and she wondered giddily whether he was going to kiss her. As soon as the warming thought kindled in her mind, she drenched it with the reminder that he wouldn't risk blackening their comfortable friendship with fires of passion.

Goodness! she chided. *How like a romantic I sound. And how foolish.* She judged by the bemused expression on his handsome face that he must be looking at ink smears on her cheek while reminding himself that she harbored sentiments that placed her beyond the pale of Parliamentary Society.

She felt herself foundering on the lee shore of loneliness. No matter how lofty were her stated purposes to comfort the poor and infirm, to raise up women and protect children, Purpose was not Love. For the first time in her life, Grace felt the lack of love as if she was drowning.

But of course she could not confess her deepest desires to a man she scarcely knew. Dropping her gaze from his to conceal her submerged hopes, she stammered, "I have heard the best way to discern a man's heart is to watch him at play."

"I have never heard such foolishness," Standen grumbled.

"My father is often accused of spouting nonsense," Grace allowed. "But he is also a rare man who tells the truth."

"Very well, Miss Penworth," Standen said, lowering his hand from the soft silky curve of her chin. "Why don't we play a game of Pharaoh?"

"No, Your Grace," she replied. Her heart hammered painfully as she realized again how much the circumstances of their lives distanced them. Her experience did not include the high-stakes game of chance in which he probably thought nothing of gambling a fortune a night. "I regret I don't know how to play Pharaoh."

A teasing smile creased Standen's cheek as he said, "No, I didn't think you would. What then do you suggest we play? Fox and Geese?"

"Fox and Geese is for children," she chided, setting her papers on a desk within her chamber. Returning to the duke's side, she said teasingly, "Although I usually let Teddy and Kate win, I should not be so lenient with you."

"Chess then," he suggested with a grin he was careful to keep "friendly."

"I happen to play chess very well," she boasted. "Only tonight I am rather distracted."

"Meaning you do not like to lose?" he persisted. He offered his arm in a peremptory manner that did not allow her to refuse.

"No one likes to lose," she replied, hesitantly placing her hand on his arm. "I should think you'd rather play a worthy opponent and earn an honest win."

"Touché." He directed their steps down the staircase and through a long gallery. Casting a sidelong glance toward her, he enquired, "Ever play billiards?"

"Never," she said. "It is not ladylike, according to my mother."

"She's right," he laughed. Moving forward happily, he propelled her down another long hallway and thrust her into a cavernous game room whose main piece of furniture was a large baize-covered table. "But since you claim at least one *other* skill that is not ladylike, I'll teach you."

His enthusiastic, teasing promise raised gooseflesh and compelled Grace to gaze upon her host as he racked up the balls. He did it in an innocent manner that assured her they were nothing more than friends.

Not knowing why such a comfortable relationship made her feel increasingly dissatisfied and restless, Grace took a turn about the room, examining hunting scenes. In one she was surprised to find in the center of the fray a likeness of the duke astride a magnificent black steed. Turning in his saddle, he seemed to be looking directly at her. It was so well-done as to take her breath away. "Did you commission this?" she enquired in awed tones.

"I did not do it for my own glory," he said in an arch manner, taking a cue down from the wall, "but to support an artist whose family had turned him out because he chose to go to the Royal Academy instead of Oxford."

Grace blushed. "Pardon me, Your Grace, I did not mean to criticize. I was only surprised to see you gazing back at me from the canvas."

He laughed and said some nonsense about her being the first to notice, before drawing her toward the table. "Take hold of the cue," he said. When she grasped the stick as she would hold a broom, he positioned them correctly. "Like this." Then, instead of taking his hands away, he leaned over her, drew the cue back, and snapped the tip against the ball. He poised over the table, Grace fitting against him like a hand in a glove, then stood up to observe the shot.

Breathlessly pinned between him and the stick, Grace watched the ball smack the opposite rack of balls, sending them flying into various corners. "Oh, look!" she laughed. "One fell into a hole."

"I meant for it to," Standen answered.

"That particular ball?" she asked, turning her face to gaze wonderingly upon his profile.

"That one in particular," he replied. He lowered the cue so that she turned completely to face him.

"Why that ball?" she asked, glancing upon the table.

"Because I should have lost my turn," he said.

She nodded, perfectly satisfied with his reasoning. It was not considered ladylike to admit such competitive feelings, but she could understand his point. It was rather like waging war. One did not give the advantage to his opponent if he hoped to survive. "Do you always hit your mark?"

He grinned, saying with a measure of honesty that surprised her again, "Often enough, and *always* when it counts."

She smiled up at him. "We are evenly matched, Your Grace. I don't like to give up a point either."

To her surprise he frowned, as if not entirely pleased with her declaration. Raising the cue, he directed her attention once more to the table. "Then I must see to it that we are always on the same side." Moving around the side with her hand in his, he again directed another well-aimed shot at the cue ball. Another ball dropped from sight. On each of the next several shots, he managed to pocket one ball, and he took pains to assure her that it was the very one he had aimed at, even when the ball had been struck a glancing blow by a second ball.

Grace could not concentrate on the game. All she could think of was the duke's warm bulk supporting her, directing her steps, his arms encircling her, his thighs and hips pressing against hers as they leaned over the table to execute a lightning-fast shot, and his warm, fragrant breath tickling her ear and inciting gooseflesh on her arms as they waited for the target to fall. Despite sternly telling herself to attend the rules, she could not help wondering what game they were playing.

His enthusiastically voiced "Yes!" when the last targeted ball dropped into its pocket assured her that he, at least, was playing billiards. That she did not affect his concentration as deeply as he influenced hers did nothing for her feminine pride until he hugged her impulsively and said, "I say, we do make a good team."

Breathless from the shock of being enclosed in such an exhilarating embrace, Grace made an attempt to rein in her racing pulse, but was only capable of saying, "I . . . think so, too."

He bestowed such a long, approving look upon her that Grace was of a sudden compelled to lower her gratified gaze to his broad shoulders. As she looked away, he did not release her, though he did gentle the grip around her waist.

Caught in inescapable, but oh-so-welcome bonds, Grace felt unaccountably shy and ashamed of herself. In her impulsive statement, she had virtually asked him to declare himself. How could she have been so stupid and self-serving? Hoping to redeem herself in his estimation, she said, "You play very well in spite of the handicap I present you."

"Look at me, Grace," he said in a husky voice that compelled obedience. As she hesitantly raised her eyes to his, he said, "I've never known anyone like you."

"I daresay you haven't," she giggled nervously. "Amity said God broke the mold when He made me."

"I think He outdid Himself," he said, brushing a gentle finger across her cheek.

Grace felt his touch as if it was a trail of sparks, but his next words threw water on rekindling hopes. "For the first time in my life," he said, "I know what it means to be a friend."

Her heart plummeted into the pit of her stomach as he went on, seemingly oblivious to her shock. "I know people, Miss Penworth, who can advance your career, people who can accomplish your . . . charitable concepts, people who count."

"Like yourself," she said in dull, disappointed tones.

Startled, he said, "Well, yes. Contrary to your unflattering portrait of the nobility, there are many who care about social justice. I could not hold up my head if I did not take care of my people."

Stricken by his blunt rebuke, she turned to stare at the billiard table. Rolling the cue ball beneath her fingers, she said, "I am sorry, Your Grace. I did not come to spy on you."

"No," he said with a self-deprecating chuckle. "You came at my invitation, and now I am treating you to a lecture in manners." A clock chimed midnight in a hallway, and he seemed to recall himself to his duty as a host. He led her toward the doorway. "Would you like to meet the people on whose shoulders falls most heavily the burden of Bon Chance?"

"Of course, Your Grace," she said in stiff, formal tones. Then, smiling, she added, "If I can be of help to anyone while I am here, I hope you will call on me."

Clasping her hand in a firm grip as he drew her up the stairs, the duke bestowed a fervent gaze upon her as he said, "I know at least one person who needs you. You may depend on it."

Thinking the duke meant her nephew, Grace was up at first light. Assured by his drowsy nurse that Hugh had spent a relatively undisturbed night, she settled onto the chair at the side of his bed but was immediately on her feet. In the candlelight spilling over his sleeping face, she could see an unmistakable rash. "Dear heaven," she whispered, brushing back the boy's forelock and raising the branch of candles overhead.

Her first fear was of smallpox, but upon recalling that Colin had insisted upon having his family inoculated, Grace breathed a sigh of relief. It was short-lived.

Hugh had not had the measles.

Her heart began a slow, tortured, fearful pounding.

He stirred in his sleep. Immediately Grace snuffed the candles and made certain the heavy draperies were drawn against the light. At all costs she must keep him quiet and in the dark.

Standen found her sitting in Hugh's darkened room. When he made to open a drapery, she stayed his hand. "No, Your Grace, don't," she said. "I fear he has the measles."

He took her hand in a gentle, reassuring grasp. "Measles?" he demanded, thinking back to the childhood diseases he had endured. Measles was not among them. Knowing that, he should have withdrawn from the sickroom at once. But the woman at his side kept him from ignominious retreat. He must be strong for her, to let her know she could depend on him the way others seemed to depend on her.

Grace nodded, drawing strength from him, but was completely unprepared when he slid an arm around her shoulders and drew her into a quiet embrace. "You will need all the help I can give you," he said.

Grace could make no reply but could only lean against his solid form, willing her heart to cease its joyous leapings. She told herself he was only offering the comfort of friendship, nothing more; but her heart persisted in its tumultuous, bounding rhythm, even when he withdrew for his morning ride around his grounds, saying his tenants liked to see him about. Dropping a brotherly (she told herself) kiss on her forehead, he promised to return shortly. "I, too, would like to hear Hugh's story."

When Hugh awakened and demanded in querulous tones a drink of water and complained that the darkness gave him a headache, Grace was still filled with an inexplicable joy. She bore his complaints with good humor and promised to tell a story as soon as the duke returned from his morning ride.

"I want a story now," Hugh croaked.

"Impatient wretch," growled Standen as he strode into the sickroom and threw off his gloves. "Will you not even allow me to rid myself of my dirt?"

"You smell like outdoors," Hugh said. "I wish we could open a window."

"I don't think one open window will harm him," Standen said, easing open a pane on the southern exposure to allow a warm breeze to drift into the stuffy room. Then smiling upon the boy's lovely nurse, he sat on the edge of the bed and declared, "Now, I am comfortable. You may tell us the story, Aunt Grace."

"The one about the bee," Hugh prodded obstinately. "I feel as if I'm being pricked to death by their stings."

Handing him a cup of mild tea, Grace placed herself in a rocking chair and closed her eyes. She felt two pairs of eyes boring a hole in her forehead while she collected her thoughts. Then quietly she began.

"The hive in the gum tree hummed with the satisfied activity of a thousand worker bees. It had been a good summer, and the combs were full of enough good, sweet honey to see them through the long cold spell of winter.

"But one among the hive was not happy," she continued. A frown marred the white perfection of her brow. "In all the hive, the one bee who ought to regard this wealth and harmony with pride and satisfaction was pacing up and down the royal comb in agitation."

"Who was it?" Hugh demanded.

"The queen," Grace replied.

"She ought to have praised her workers," Hugh remarked. "Without them, she'd go hungry."

"Hush," Standen urged, taking the boy's cup so Hugh could roll onto his stomach the better to enjoy his story.

"She was very vain," Grace explained. "I suppose it is because she had been pampered and petted all summer while she laid her eggs, so much that she had grown to depend on the hive's adoration."

"Girls are like that," Hugh said disgustedly.

"Only because they are given very little else to occupy their minds," Grace replied patiently. "But since her Season had come and gone, the hive was occupied with the more pressing details of survival, and she was very hard to live with.

"Until a worker bee flew into the hive with a fragment of mirror clutched between its legs. He thought the queen might like to admire herself. And she did as long as the autumn light lasted." As she spoke, Grace unconsciously affected the posture of a pretty girl appreciating the image of herself in a glass. Standen leaned back against the pillow next to an itching Hugh, thoroughly enjoying Grace's unconscious display.

"But the days grew shorter," she said darkly, "and the queen had less time to preen before the mirror. With the single-mindedness of Monarchy, she decreed that one of her workers must fly to the nearest house and take a candle. And another worker must contrive to bring back a coal with which to light the wick."

"Is there no army in this story?" Hugh complained, rubbing an irritated spot on his back. "And how is a bee supposed to carry a live coal?"

"Stop interrupting, young man," Standen commanded, leaning forward eagerly. "Go on, Grace."

Grace chose not to call attention to the duke's inadvertent slip of the tongue and returned to her story. "As impossible as it might seem," she said, "the hive *did* manage to bring a candle and a light into the queen's chamber. Candlelight made the combs glow golden, and the queen was enchanted with the effect and with the blessed warmth. She ordered the candle to remain lit all winter.

"Unfortunately the heat began to melt the wax. Honey began to ooze down the walls of the queen's chamber. Workers rushed to the rescue, beating their wings furiously to cool the melting combs, only making the candle burn more brightly, which melted the combs even faster.

" 'My queen, we must put out the candle,' " said one brave bee, 'or the hive will surely perish.'

" 'Never!' cried the queen. Then, reason seemed to return to her. All her babies would die if she remained stubborn. In a foolish and misguided act of courage, she clutched the mirror, commanding her workers to carry her and the candle outside where she might admire herself."

"But that was stupid," Hugh said. "She must have frozen to death."

"Of course she did," Grace replied in matter-of-fact tones that implied the story was done. Coming to her feet, she twitched a blanket over Hugh's feet.

"What happened to the Happily Ever After?" Hugh demanded. "Your stories always end happily."

Grace sighed. "Real life is not always so kind, Hugh. But you must remember, the foolish queen saved the hive. And that, in beedom, is the only thing that matters. So in a sense, there was a happy ending." Then, turning toward the duke, who was scribbling on a piece of parchment, she tilted her head and laughed. "What are you doing, Your Grace?"

"Acting as your secretary," he crowed, producing the story, minus interruptions, and including an illustration at the bottom of a bee admiring herself in a mirror.

The drawing was very well-done for having been executed so quickly, and looked remarkably like Grace herself, with wings. "You have a hidden talent as well," Grace said in awe. "But I told you these stories are for Teddy, Hugh, and Kate."

"You will be glad of them someday for your own children," he persisted, taking the story back. "And don't you think others might like to hear one of Aunt Grace's bedtime stories?"

"I don't mind sharing your stories," Hugh said, running a hand over his itching face. "And anyway, Teddy and Kate would like to hear what they missed."

"That settles it," said Standen. "As long as you're here, I'll write down the stories you tell Hugh. Now come with me, Miss Penworth. Hugh needs a soothing bath, and you need some fresh air."

Her protests that she was not dressed he waved away, saying, "On the contrary, Miss Penworth, you look well enough to charm my tenants and all the bees in my apiary." He did, however, let her go to her room to comb her hair and remove her apron.

Twelve

When she was satisfied that she would not embarrass him by her appearance in a round dress of peach-colored twilled silk topped with a spencer of white-striped lutestring, she met him in the great foyer. She was glad for the broad-brimmed leghorn bonnet that concealed her blush when he raised an eyebrow and teased her for the vanity of changing ensembles to engage in good works. "I did not think bluestockings cared about their looks," he said, laughing in tones that betrayed approval.

Taking the arm he offered so gallantly, Grace slid a flirtatious, sidelong look toward him. Smiling, she said, "Oh, yes, Your Grace, it helps to distract the opposition if we present a pleasing aspect in debating issues of reform."

Leading her outside, where his carriage awaited to carry them round his vast farm, he allowed, "I hope you will take pity on a poor, distractable male, Miss Penworth."

Smiling beneath her bonnet brim, Grace allowed herself to be handed into a curricle on which was inscribed the Duke of Standen's crest. Recalling his concentration while playing billiards, she said, "I doubt anyone could distract you from your purpose, Your Grace," while disposing her full skirts about herself.

Standen moved to the far side of the vehicle. Taking a firm grasp on the railing, he climbed onto the seat. After considering her for several moments, he said quietly, "Do you think I am ruthless in the dispatch of my designs?"

"I do not like to endorse your opposition," she said, removing her gaze from the duke in confusion. She took from a silent footman a basket which the duchess had seen fit to fill with various jellies and healing preparations, and promised the elder lady when she appeared through a sunny door on the ground floor to wish them Godspeed that she would dispense them to their tenants.

"Don't forget to make it known to the steward if any of our people are in want," the Duchess of Standen said with a twinkling grin that did much to alleviate Grace's pangs of conscience regarding her valiant tongue the night before. "From your experience in doing parish work, you will know what they need, and I trust you to make sure they're not cold or hungry."

"Thank you for your confidence, Your Grace," Grace said, blushing when the frail woman clasped her hand in an affectionate manner. "I won't fail you or your people."

"Then, if Alan is agreeable," said the duchess, glancing toward her grandson as he climbed into the driver's seat, "we'll have a comfortable coze during tea, my dear."

Taking the reins in his hands, Standen winked at his grandmother and said in teasingly, "Of course, that is why I brought Miss Penworth, Gram, to visit with you."

"Go on then, you naughty boy," laughed the elder lady, releasing Grace's warm hand to wave goodbye. "Don't, I pray you, let him tease you anymore, dear girl," she said indulgently. "I shouldn't want you to brand all aristocrats heartless fools on the example of one."

"Now Gram," said Standen in loving, but warning tones, "I have already promised to be on my best behavior. Don't listen to her, G—Miss Penworth," he concluded in an aside that turned the tips of his ears red.

Delighted to be a part of the affectionate family exchange, Grace giggled. "No, Your Grace," she said, waving to the dowager a moment before Standen urged his pair into motion, "I confess the duke is already amending my unfortunate prejudice."

"Well, thank God for that," cried the duchess. "I have no worries for you then, children; our tenants will chaperon your outing admirably, *and,*" she added in confidential tones for no ears but her own as she accepted the arm of an omnipresent footman for the return to her suite, "give me their good wishes for your happiness."

As soon as they swept down the smooth-packed drive, Grace was uncomfortably aware of the duke's proximity. His thigh pressed intimately against the length of hers on the narrow seat, and his shoulder and left arm rubbed along her own in such a manner as compelled her to turn into the corner of the curricle so that she might breathe again. Hiding behind the brim of her bonnet to allow her crimson cheeks to cool, she inwardly confessed that she was glad not to have shared that closed carriage with him on the road to London a little more than three weeks ago.

"What?" he demanded, turning down a well-cared-for side road. "Am I crowding you?"

"No, Your Grace," she replied, clinging to the basket of medicants and the railing as they rounded a corner that slid her into her former place. "I merely was giving you room to drive."

"To atone for John Coachman's sins?" he enquired, turning a teasing, sidelong look upon her.

Grace could not quell another rush of hot color from staining her cheeks. "I knew you were no gentleman," she giggled, grasping the railing once more as they rattled over a plank bridge. "And I am beginning to think John was not completely to blame for our accidental rendezvous."

"Indeed?" Standen asked, urging her to explain.

"Truly," she replied breathlessly, releasing the railing to hold onto her bonnet with a shaking hand. "I have never driven so fast, Your Grace. Are you sure we shall be safe?"

Throwing his head, Standen laughed. "As long as a drunken coachman does not swing a wide turn onto the lane before us, we are perfectly safe. But," he added, moderating the pace somewhat, "I shouldn't want my tenants to think you are a wild-eyed radical today."

"No need to fear; I shall mind my manners, Your Grace," Grace said penitently, wishing the duke thought as well of her as she did of him.

"No, don't come up prim now," he chuckled, turning into the square that was surrounded by a cluster of neatly kept cottages and shops which were proclaimed a village by a mile marker with the word *Standen* on it. "Pray, don't tease me for naming the village after myself," he added, noting the direction her gaze took. *"That* vanity belonged to my great-uncle who, having failed to set up a nursery at Bon Chance, insured his immortality through a country village."

Gazing around the bustling square, Grace absently nodded, understanding by the duke's roundabout explanation that his forebear had left no legitimate heir. Wondering whether the former duke had populated the village with illegitimate offspring, she felt her old intolerance rising like an angry bulldog. She beat it back down, saying, "It is a pretty village, Your Grace. How many people reside here?"

"At last count, eighty souls," he said, tying off the reins when a boy took his leader's head, and stepping to the stone-paved road. "But I've no doubt we'll soon be welcoming a few new inhabitants." He moved around the curricle and offered a hand to Grace. "Grandmother has most likely included a few packages for our expectant families. Shall we visit them first?"

With the duke's help, Grace alighted from the carriage and allowed him to carry the basket. "Ah, yes," he said, stopping at a cottage ringed with a spring garden of pinks, forget-me-nots, bluets, and coral bells. "Gram has always delighted in babies," he said, knocking politely on the freshly scrubbed door. "And this family, the Crocketts, satisfy her expectations every year." Then, in a voice that scarcely carried to Grace's ear, he added in what sounded like mortification, "Please excuse me, Miss Penworth. I assure you I am not in the habit of speaking so freely with every young lady of my acquaintance."

Grace was prohibited from replying as an obviously expectant woman opened the door of the cottage and exclaimed in soft-voiced accents, "Your Grace! Come in, but you've caught me unawares."

"Morning, Sally," Standen said, drawing Grace within the spotless home. "I've brought Miss Penworth, who is visiting my grandmother. Grace," he added, looking down at her, "this is Sally Crockett."

Grace offered her hand. This flustered her hostess, who dipped a respectful curtsey, then accepted the gloved fingers hesitantly, saying, "Pleased to meet you, Lady Penworth."

Rather than call attention to Mrs. Crockett's flattering but mistaken address, Grace said, "I am very glad to meet you as well, Mrs. Crockett."

"Oh," said the housewife, blushing to her ears. She dropped Grace's hand, covering her heated cheeks and saying, "I'm nae but Sally."

Rummaging within the basket, Standen discovered a jar and packet marked *Crockett.* "Knowing how busy you are with your brood, we won't stay but long enough to drop off a few things and—"

"Take a cup of tea with me, I hope," Sally interrupted, reaching for Grace's bonnet and offering another curtsey, her movements impeded in no way by her increasing waist. "Most of the children are off at school with the vicar. And the little ones," she glanced sideways, "are napping, so I've plenty of time to chat."

Removing the headdress, Grace allowed Mrs. Crockett to place it on a peg at the door. As she performed this task, Grace took a moment to survey her surroundings, praying that she would find nothing for which to criticize the duke.

Sunlight streamed through the windows, dancing off

the furniture and a shining floor and reflecting from a shelf of glassware. Grace smiled at the blushing housewife, who whisked a nonexistent speck of dust from a cushioned settee.

"Pray, sit yourself down, my lady, Your Grace," she invited, scurrying to heat a pot for tea while her guests made themselves comfortable. When the tea was ready, she presented a pretty tray laden with teapot, cups, and a plate of scones.

"I hope all the Crocketts are well," Standen said when tea had been served and he had delivered his packages into Sally's hands.

"We can't complain, Your Grace," Sally said, beaming. "And that's the gospel, my lady," she added over the rim of her cup. "Our Standen stands by his people, no matter what. Did you know his doctor treats us?"

"I . . . yes, he is everything that is kind," Grace said, feeling a pang of conscience to be enjoying herself while Hugh lay wretched in bed with measles.

"Of course, I don't bother the good physician about havin' the babies," Sally said, patting her belly. Then, recalling to whom she was speaking, she blushed and apologized. "Beggin' your pardon, my lady. Not a fit subject for your ears."

"Nonsense," Grace cried, trying to stem a blush of her own. "I am used to helping in parish work, Mrs. Crockett; nothing shocks me."

Grinning because he had seen her modest blushes, Standen said, "So you have said before, Miss Penworth. But I pray you will not argue the point. Your cheeks rival Sally's pinks just now." Then he engaged his hostess in a discussion of estate business, eliciting from her the surprising news that several roofs in the village needed repairs.

"They would not tell you themselves, Your Grace," Sally said with a bob of her head. "Not wishing you to think they were grumblers. But I have seen the pots in the Widow Rankin's cottage and believe the reports I've heard about old Mr. Pennywhistle's hut, that you can see daylight through the thatch."

"I see," Standen said, his brow furrowing thoughtfully. Both the widow and the elderly man wished not to trouble him, he knew, but why, he wondered, did they not realize delaying repairs was more costly than giving them prompt attention? "Don't trouble your head about this, Sally," he said after a moment, when he grinned. "I shall set the boys on both their houses and have them put to rights again."

"You won't let the old people know I told you," Sally said apprehensively.

"Oh, I assure you, they'll not know who tipped me. Now," he said, setting aside his cup and coming to his feet, "we have several stops before lunch, and we'd best be on our way. Grace?" he said, offering his hand.

Sally scurried to fetch Grace's bonnet and open the door. "You mustn't worry, my lady; our duke won't harm the old folks. It's only they're proud and don't like to think they'll make trouble for anyone." Shrugging and giving a little laugh, she said, "'Course anyone of us would just fix the roof ourselves. Must be hard not to be able to do for yourself."

"Yes, I suppose it is," Grace agreed. She tied a bow beneath her ear as her father had taught her, then walked around the square with the duke, stopping obediently when he met an individual on his grandmother's list. With each visit, he learned of another cottager in need of help or a tenant in trouble with the law. But when he introduced her to those same troubled people, he did not betray by so much as a glance or word his knowledge of their difficulty, as if he knew that to do so in public would discommode them and cause them to trust him less.

When their errands were accomplished and they were riding toward an open field for a picnic lunch, Standen eyed her with a grin. "You are bursting with something to say," he said, giving his pair their heads on the straight road.

"It isn't my place, Your Grace," she said, clasping her hands together in her lap.

"I give you permission to dress me down," he laughed.

"No, I have nothing to say against you," she said, "Only I am so embarrassed to have paraded my foolish bias against you."

"Against me personally?" he enquired, steering into the early shade of an oak.

"No, you as a class," Grace stammered. "You are so kind, Your Grace; bearing with everyone's complaints like Moses."

"If I recall, Moses lost his patience more than once," Standen said.

"Well, anyone would," she allowed. "Only, you recall he mediated disputes and stood in the gap when the people were particularly odious to their God."

"I am no miracle worker, Miss Penworth," he said, helping her to the ground. He was tempted to pull her against him, but this talk of miracles and Moses recalled him to a sense of propriety. Removing his hands from her waist, he directed her to a spot overlooking his home, where a picnic had been spread out, several footmen standing at attention around the table. "Right now, I am hungry. Shall we see whether Cook has prepared manna and quail for our lunch?"

When he had wrapped his hands about her waist, Grace had felt another distressingly potent current pass between them. To her chagrin, she hoped he would kiss her, but he had set her down with alacrity. Attempting to reply to his joking query in kind, she said, "As long as it isn't salmon," immediately regretting her complaint, for it sounded pettish instead of whimsical.

Directing her toward the picnic site, Standen nodded, saying, "If he is so foolish as to repeat himself, we shall send it back."

"I don't think that will be necessary," she replied, hungrily eyeing the small damask-laid table that was laden with two roast chickens, boiled potatoes in butter sauce, cold asparagus, a salad, bread and butter, jams, and various fruits, including early strawberries. "Oh, there is so much, and it looks so good. Thank you, Your Grace."

"I shall relay your good will to my chef, Miss Penworth," Standen grinned as he seated her. "And I make no doubt he will strive to please you as long as it pleases you to remain with Grandmother."

As he lowered himself into a chair at her elbow, Grace turned a puzzled gaze upon him. His answering gaze warmed her apprehensive heart, for it was plainly written in the lingering look that he was putting the only respectable face on her visit. They had not known one another long enough to have formed a lasting attachment. Nor did Grace expect that he had done so, however much she might wish it. But that he was careful to say she was his "grandmother's guest" made it clear that he had no dishonorable designs on her, even if he did not mean to declare his intention to marry her.

Telling herself not to expect a fairy-tale ending, she allowed her considering look to turn to one of quiet amusement and said, "I shall be pleased to remain as long as it pleases Her Grace."

Grinning from ear to ear, Standen picked up a knife and fork and began slicing a chicken. Serving her the most delectable portions—the wings—and generous portions of vegetables, he said, "Good. Now eat, Miss Penworth, or Gram will think I've starved you."

They returned from their afternoon visits at three o'clock. Pleading neglected business with his steward, Standen relinquished Grace into his grandmother's keeping, saying with a contrite grin, "Wilkins will expect me to show some interest in his ledgers, I suppose." He jammed his hands into his pockets, looking for all the world like Teddy when compelled to attend to his sums. Then he brightened, adding, "But I shall return in time to hear the story you tell Hugh."

At her nephew's name, Grace felt a pang of conscience for having left him all day. She ought to dash upstairs to see how he was getting on. But Lady Standen had made the effort to come into the foyer, and Grace knew she could not scurry away from the person who was very kindly sponsoring this visit.

"Hugh said to tell you not to bother him until after teatime," said the duchess, noting the direction of

Grace's gaze as it swept toward the west wing. "I left him playing with Alan's soldiers. He told me to inform you that he was 'whipping Boney all the way back to Paris.' Come into the solarium, my dear. Tell me the news of Standen Village."

Seating themselves in the shade of a fig tree which was planted at the side of a man-made stream which gurgled happily, they took tea from an attentive maid, then the duchess waved her servant away to hear the news of her people. Satisfied that the Widow Rankin and Mr. Pennywhistle would be cared for, she assured Grace that they would not go wanting in the future simply because they did not wish to bother anyone. The dowager then engaged Grace in conversation about Cherhill society.

"There isn't much society in Cherhill," Grace confessed after accepting a second cup of tea from the duchess's hands. "Mr. Davies is widowed and doesn't often entertain, and of course it isn't proper for the vicar's family to entertain lavishly. But we do attend Spring and Fall Assemblies, which my mother calls the Country Marriage Mart." Blushing, she added, "However, neither of her daughters found a match at any of the local balls. We were compelled to go to London, where, Father says, gentleman are more forgiving."

To her consternation, the dowager did not laugh, but said, "Not in my experience. You must introduce me to your set."

"I fear you would find us quite dull," Grace responded, turning even more crimson at her inability to be quiet. "The men do not gamble, except on the Exchange, and the ladies do not spend money except as it saves them a few pennies. We're all quite common."

She did not miss the speaking look the dowager duchess passed toward her grandson, who had appeared during Grace's humiliating confession. The duchess smiled benevolently and said, "Not all, my dear. You, I find most *un*common. Don't you think so, Alan?"

"I have always said so," he maintained, seating himself at Grace's elbow. To her amusement, he stole a biscuit from her plate and munched on it while she passed a cup of tea to him. "She tells the most uncommonly good stories, Gram. Why do you not hie yourself upstairs this afternoon for a listen?"

Chuckling, the dowager said, "These old bones do not 'hie' themselves above the first story, as you well know. However, if you find yourself in need of a chaperon, I shall lend my dresser's attendance at the party." Sensing the discreet presence of a footman at the door, she directed a cursory glance upon the liveried servant. "Yes, Tidwell?"

"A visitor, ma'am," he said, glancing toward Grace. "For Miss Penworth. I put him in the book room."

"Well, where is this visitor's card?" demanded the lady, irritated that her tête-à-tête was being interrupted.

As if accustomed to his employer's gruff demands, Tidwell bowed, saying, "He did not present a card, but said his errand was urgent."

Clutching her wrap regally about her shoulders, the dowager said, "You need not see anyone who does not identify himself, my dear."

Grace's first thought that her father had hauled himself down to Bon Chance to save her from ignominy propelled her from the garden seat. "No, Your Grace, it might be Papa."

That, Grace told herself, was highly unlikely, as he rarely bestirred himself beyond Cherhill. Colin, however, could have driven down from London to make sure Hugh was in no danger. Clasping her hands together prayerfully, she added, "Or perhaps my brother-in-law came to see how his son is doing. Please, excuse me."

Following the footman into the duke's library, she heard, in an unwelcome and all-too-familiar, carping voice: "You might have let me know you were decamping." Coming to his feet from the leather chair in which he was seated, Mr. DuBarry removed his spectacles and directed a wide-eyed stare at her as he demanded, "Have you joined forces with the enemy?"

Thirteen

DuBarry's aggressive, bulldoglike stance did not produce the effect on Grace he must have intended, for she neither burst into tears nor blurted out a self-righteous defense of her presence at Bon Chance. Instead she regarded him quietly while her tumbling thoughts fell into a semblance of order. She then said with dignity, "I fail to see why you have the right to question my actions."

"Our Understanding lends me courage," he said, moving toward her. "We are of a like mind in so many things, Miss Penworth; surely you cannot have failed to notice that my interest in you exceeds professional limits."

"I am sure you are mistaken," Grace retorted, "when your every comment emphasizes sell-throughs." She compelled herself to stand firm in the face of his advance. Despite her resolve, she discovered she had placed herself immediately before a leather sofa from which there was no possibility of escape. And Mr. DuBarry's expression was not that of a publisher intent on increasing book sales. His potent regard was more like that of a disgruntled lover, dark and brooding and . . . menacing.

Against her will, Grace took a step backward and stumbled onto the cool surface of the sofa. Immediately

Mr. DuBarry seated himself at her side and was blurting out what must have been, for him, a passionate avowal of love. "Oh, perverse woman," he cried, righting her with a vehement shake. "Why do you think I care so much that people read your book?"

Placing a hand to her spinning head, Grace stammered, "I have no answer to that, sir, aside from the fact that you wish to profit from my work."

The avaricious gleam in his eye did not escape her notice, but he was quick to stifle it and say in self-righteous tones, "I cannot have been so mistaken in your character as to believe you wrote your essays for money. No, Miss Penworth—Grace—you must have written them out of your heart's longing for Justice. And I cannot help but . . . respect you for your . . . courage."

As this last was said while his bulging eye lingered on the agitated rise and fall of her bosom, Grace was persuaded he was not as respectful of her feelings as he claimed. "Let me go, Mr. DuBarry," she said, cringing when he palpated her upper arms as a baker might knead bread dough.

"How can I release you?" he cried. "Grace," he raised his eyes once more to hers and gazed at her nearsightedly, "we share the same sympathies, express the same views. Why, sometimes we speak as if we share the same mind. We belong together, you and I."

Grace knew that if they had spoken with the same mind, it was only because Mr. DuBarry had taken over a thought and completed it when she began to express one that opposed his. Once again he had reached a conclusion with which she could not agree, and this time, she would not remain silent. "Please, Mr. DuBarry," she said, wriggling out of his forcible grip and leaping from the couch, "I wish you would say no more."

He came haltingly to his feet, but did not pursue her when she sidled away. "Indeed, I must have surprised you," he confessed in tones that revealed his own discomfiture. He ran a finger between his constricting collar and his reddening neck. "To be truthful, I surprised myself. But now that I have come, I must speak my mind, for I am certain you will agree with my decision."

Closing her eyes in fury and frustration, she admitted to herself that there was no help for it but to listen to him. "I do not share your optimism, sir," she said warily. "But since you have come so far on my account, go on."

"I was mortified when your sister informed me that you had come here with the duke," he said. "You can have no notion of how it appears."

"I am sure you will tell me," she said, crossing her arms before her.

"Standen comes from a long line of well-known rakes and libertines," DuBarry said in hushed tones of revulsion. "Surely you know he is only playing with your affections."

"I believe you are mistaken," Grace said. "His Grace has been all that is kind and respectful."

"Nevertheless, he will only ruin you."

Raising a dubious eyebrow, she enquired, "And what can that possibly mean to you?"

"Why, of course, it will further depress the sales of your book," DuBarry said automatically when she sniffed in disdain. "But beyond that, I cannot stand the thought of you as the *on-dit* of the Season."

Understanding dawning, she asked, "Because it will reflect poorly on you?"

"Precisely," he said. "Grace, I want you to marry me. You have a marvelous mind, but it needs guidance . . ."

"And you are willing to mold my ideas to suit your own," she concluded. Really, she thought when he nodded, the man had finally exceeded the level of arrogance of which she believed him capable. Wanting to marry her to control her mind. That insensibility alone cost him whatever respect she felt she owed him. But he seemed insensible of her determination.

"You see?" he exclaimed. "Our minds do run in the same circles. One wonders what we could accomplish if we put them together for all time."

"I shudder to think," she began. Before he could continue, she raised a quelling hand and commanded, "Pray, say no more, Mr. DuBarry. I cannot marry you."

"Whyever not?" he asked.

Grace was not so naive as to enumerate the true reason for her refusal, that she was hopelessly in love with the Duke of Standen, and so said, "You deserve a wife who is willing to submerge her entire being into your life's work, sir. I am too selfish to give you that happiness."

"Oh," said Mr. DuBarry on a troubled note. "I had not considered that. Is your own career so important to you, then?"

At the moment, it was the furthermost thing from Grace's mind, but she could not very well confess that to him. Taking a breath and uttering a prayer that she might be forgiven the lie, she said fervently, "It is my only hope, Mr. DuBarry."

He heaved a great sigh as if he was attempting to

bring his disappointment under control. Settling his spectacles over his nose, he said, "I wish you joy in it, then, Miss Penworth."

"Why, thank you," she replied, somewhat surprised by his grudging acceptance.

"And while I must say I am disappointed in your decision," he said, collecting his broad-brimmed hat from the chair on which he had tossed it, "The least I can do is to promote your book in a manner that will assure its success."

"That would be very kind," she said, wondering if she had perhaps misjudged his character.

"Oh, I admit I shall reap some satisfaction and a profit in doing so," he said with a stiff grin creasing his face. "That is the nature of business. But I trust you will not hold it against me for long."

"Of course," she said, putting out her hand to show that she did not begrudge him her friendship.

After a moment, he took her fingers and shook them. Then, dropping them in an attitude of distaste, he said, "Well, I tried to get you to see reason; now you must accept the consequences for your refusal. Good day, Miss Penworth."

As Mr. DuBarry strode toward the front doors, Standen stepped into the library. "What did he want?" he asked.

Grace immediately brightened to see her good friend, even if he looked anything but happy to see her. A frown creased his handsome forehead. Grace longed to smooth it away, but knew such familiarity would not be proper. "He came to take me home," she said in a small voice.

Miraculously the furrow in his brow disappeared.

"You are still here," Standen said with a smile that intensified her confusion. "May I take that to mean you prefer my company to his?"

Raising her shoulders in a delicate shrug, she confessed, "I should *like* you to think so; however, my nephew's health must keep me here whether you want me or not."

"Miss Penworth," said the duke, narrowing his eyes upon her, "I would move heaven and earth to keep you here." His avowal left her breathless with longing, but his next words left her in no doubt as to her real worth. "You are amazingly entertaining. I can't wait to see what story you will dream up next."

"Are you not perhaps concerned that I might turn your tenants into radicals?" she enquired.

"I have never seen them more contented," he said, confidently moving toward her. "Or so glad to see a guest of mine."

As he advanced, his eyes darkened as if he had passed into a shadow, but he did not appear menacing. On the contrary, he was relaxed and very attractive.

And that frightened her.

She was a simple country parson's daughter who ought not to look on the duke with anything save awe. She ought to be glad he found her "entertaining" enough to hold his interest. But she could not help but feel disappointed in his compliment until he took her hands in his and smiled down at her.

"Poor Grace," he said, raising their hands between them so that she gazed at him over their clasped fingers. "Do I disappoint you so terribly?"

Shaken that he had read her mind, she tried to make

light of her sensibility. "Not at all, Your Grace. I own I was surprised by Mr. DuBarry. I must not have recovered from the shock he gave me."

"Shock?" Concerned by her disclosure, Standen led her to a chair and pressed her gently into it. "Surely he did nothing to harm you?"

He seemed perfectly in control of his emotions, except that he squeezed Grace's fingers too tightly as he bore her across the room. Clasping them in her lap when he released her, she stammered, "No real harm. Only he commanded me to marry him."

Of a sudden, his grandmother's warnings that had seemed last night like nothing more than superstitious nonsense revealed themselves as premonitions of disaster. "Marry him!" the duke exclaimed, clenching his teeth in an effort to stop from commanding Grace to marry himself instead. He ground out, "Am I supposed to wish you joy?"

Grace's spirits plummeted at his amazingly rigid query. She needed to explain herself to regain the duke's respect, and she felt her face heat in embarrassment as her tongue stumbled over a disjointed rationale. "No. I did not make him happy. I suppose I ought to be thankful to have received the offer. Mama will call me stubborn."

Standen felt a warm rush of happiness pulse through his veins, and he had to compel himself not to hug Grace in relief. But he could not stem the grin that turned his stern visage into a mask of boyish mischief. "Will she, Grace?"

"Yes, because I turned down the Reverend Mr. Gladstone last year, and I was supposed to accept *any* offer this Season."

Delighted to learn that his Grace had possessed the good sense to turn down two unsuitable bachelors in order to give him the opportunity to make her his own and put to rest his family curse, Standen could not resist teasing her. "Why did you not obey her then?"

Suppressing an involuntary shudder, Grace considered her clasped hands for a long moment while she battled the disturbing impression that the duke thought she should have accepted Mr. Dubarry's offer. She wanted to make him understand her reasoning was not just a girlish whim or romantic fancy, but was based on her understanding of Love as her father taught it. "I cannot like his manner, Your Grace. He kept telling me how alike we were, how similar our thoughts. But we are nothing alike. He never lets me voice an idea contrary to his."

"Never?" Standen looked as if he doubted any man's ability to stifle a lady's opinion—especially this lady's— but he did not express such shocking sentiments. If he did, Grace would only think him as opinionated as the gentleman she refused.

"He tells me I must learn from him; that it isn't proper for me to instruct him. After all, he is a Fellow at Cambridge."

Standen's hand closed into a fist. Grace wondered if she had earned his contempt by her unbridled criticism of a fellow man. She half-expected him to deliver a stern set-down of her pretension. To her surprise, he only said, "That explains his Whiggish tendencies at least." Then he further confused her by enquiring, "Am I to understand you never encouraged his suit?"

"No, never, Your Grace. I know what it would be like

if we *did* marry: he would forbid me to put pen to paper except to copy his essays."

He grinned, as if amused by her stumbling explanation. "I think you might prefer to have a secretary of your own."

Grace covered one burning cheek with her fingers. "I cannot deny my own projects weigh more heavily on my conscience. But it was selfish of me to have said so."

"Fustian," said the duke. He crossed his arms in an impatient but aristocratic motion to keep from throwing them around her. "If anything, you were unflinchingly honest."

"You are not the first to say so," Grace said in sinking tones. "The phrase has always been 'honest to a fault.'"

He did not answer at once so that she raised her eyes to his. Immediately he bestowed a teasing grin on her that she could not resist. When she was smiling again, he said, *"I* cannot fault you for it."

"Thank you," Grace said.

His approbation made her glow within. She wanted more than anything for him to like her, but that was a confession no lady could easily make, even one who was normally honest to a fault. So instead, she said, "I expect the fault lies in not knowing when to keep silent."

"Or in trusting the wrong people," Standen added in thoughtful tones that sent shivers down her spine.

She did not know whether the vibration was warning her of future danger or of the impossibility of her desires. But suddenly her hopes did not seem quite so impossible, for he was drawing her to her feet and saying, "I know I have no right to ask anything of you, but I hope you will trust me."

"As a friend?" she asked in a reminder to herself that that liaison was all that she could hope for.

Why had he ever suggested such a ludicrous arrangement as friendship with this lady? he wondered. And why did she keep throwing it in his face? Was she frightened of him?

He exhaled a long breath before nodding. "As you wish," he said at last in disappointment, suggesting she see how Hugh had fared in the care of his housekeeper, adding in commanding, but boyish tones, "But don't tell him a story until I finish one last piece of business with Wilkins." Then, after she had leapt to her feet with a gasp of alarm and hurried upstairs to tend to her forgotten duty, Standen ordered Wilkins to have a man watch DuBarry. A rejected suitor who promised "consequences" to a refusal was dangerous.

Of this concern, Standen made no mention later when he joined Grace and her nephew. Hugh was happily directing troop movements among the bedsheets with the duke's collection of painted soldiers, and Grace was scribbling at the desk. When Standen entered, she hastily sanded the paper and lay a blank sheet atop it as if she was loath to share her work with anyone.

Standen wondered again what she was writing, but forbore to tease her. Instead, he placed himself in a chair near Hugh's bed and asked, "What story will you have today, General?"

Instead of demanding his aunt's immediate attention, Hugh asked, "Were you in the Army, Your Grace?"

"Yes, I was a colonel with the Duke of Wellington,"

Standen said, drawing Grace onto the bed beside her nephew where he could gaze upon her as she wove the fabric of her story. "I'll tell you about it sometime if you like."

"Tell me now," Hugh said in the petulant tones of a child who is uncomfortable and bored.

Grace passed a perceptive eye over the duke. He seemed perfectly at ease, but an inner sense told her of his reluctance to speak of the battles in which he had fought. They were not the stuff of polite conversation, and she knew such memories often served to injure the one recounting them. But rather than expose any possible wounds the duke might have sustained in battle, she said, "Your tutor has already drilled you on the engagements of the late war, Hugh."

"But Stevens did not go," Hugh protested. "And all he talked about was dates and places." With a hand holding his head as if it ached, he whined, "How shall I keep them straight in my head if I don't know what they were really like?"

"I think all you need to know is that they were nothing like the battle you have spread out before you," Standen said, his voice quietly restrained but still commanding. "Tin soldiers leave behind no wives or children to mourn them when they fall."

"I know," Hugh replied, absently scratching his skin as he regarded the rows of tin men lying on their sides on the hills and valleys he had made of his counterpane. "Papa read me the reports. Well, if you won't tell me about your experiences, why don't you show me the tactics."

Cocking an eyebrow toward Grace, Standen came to

his feet and swept the soldiers into a box. Crouching low to the floor, he set them up on the floor beside the bed to form the battle of Hougoumont at Waterloo. Then, while Hugh looked on from above, he maintained a running commentary to explain what occurred, as Jérôme Bonaparte led a desperate assault against a fortified chateau which was defended and held by superior British forces.

"Were you there?" Hugh asked at last, his eyes bulging at the enormity of the losses on both sides.

"Yes," Standen said, snatching up an officer and handing it to the boy. "Here I am."

"Safe and sound," Grace murmured gratefully. "Thank God."

"Yes, my dear," Standen said almost absently, but with a smile of appreciation for her expression of relief. Pinning her with a meaningful stare, he said, "However, I lost many good men, and I am determined to keep those I am responsible for as well as I can from now on." Then, turning an imperious eye on Hugh, he said, "You have your own war to fight, my boy. Better to rest now than hear another tale of derring-do."

"But I'm bored," Hugh complained, pushing Grace away when she moved to fluff his pillows.

"No," Standen amended in stern, almost parental tones. "You are sick and seem to be losing this battle."

Curling into a resentful ball, Hugh grumbled, "It isn't fair."

"All's fair in love and war," the duke said, arising from his crouch as Grace smoothed the covers over her nephew. Then, drawing her toward the door, he said,

"Like any war, Hugh, yours will be won by obeying orders, timely advance, and tenacious digging in."

Closing the door on further protest, Standen regarded Grace for a long silent moment. She could not tell what he was thinking, for his back was to the light and his face was in shadow. But his stiff posture revealed an annoyance that she felt somehow responsible for.

"I do apologize," she said, dropping her gaze to the rich patterns of the Persian carpet that covered the hall floor.

"Why?" Standen asked. "Are you sorry you turned down DuBarry's offer?"

"No, Your Grace," she replied. "I shall lose no sleep over that decision. Only, I can't help but think your life would be . . . simpler if you had never been troubled with me."

"Simpler, Grace?" he asked, then responded with a chuckle before she could censure herself again. "I think life would have been deadly dull without you complicating things. No, don't apologize again," he said when she offered a contrite upward glance as she moistened her lips.

The unconscious flick of her tongue drew his complete attention and focused his desire in one act. He wanted to kiss her as he had never wanted to kiss another woman. But she was in no mood for romance just yet. A sudden assault on her person might damage his suit beyond repair. Mustering the reserves of his will, he restrained himself from taking her into his arms. But he could not completely resist touching her. "Go, write a letter to Hugh's mother," he said, smoothing the back of his hand along her cheek. "Or pen another scathing essay exposing man's unconscionable insensitivity."

As he withdrew his hand, Grace blinked several times to quell the hope fluttering in her breast that Standen wanted to kiss her. Of a sudden, she felt as if she was blinking back tears of disappointment. How foolish and vain she was to want him to kiss her. It was obviously the last thing he intended to do.

He was teasing her again, as a big brother might tax a troublesome sister. Through the fog of frustration that dimmed her perception, she knew she must make some response. Grasping at his suggestion, she said, "Perhaps I will, Your Grace. But I shall exempt you from the insensitivity so often displayed by your sex."

Standen's heart gave a leap of joy, but he gave no outward sign as he wondered if she was softening toward him. He had to know. But instead of asking outright how she felt about him, he said, "How came you to this agreeable conclusion?"

Turning an open, smiling gaze on him, she said, "Your many kindnesses to children," adding an inward, *and your unfailing kindness to me.*

Despite her calmly voiced commentary, Standen felt as if she had bestowed upon him her highest compliment. It was not that she seemed to regard him in any romantic light, though he was eager for that glow to kindle in her gaze. But he could not fail to see trust shining forth from her pale eyes, and he was buoyed by the growing hope that she returned at least a measure of his esteem. He longed to tell her that everything he did was for her, but suspected such a bold confession would only embarrass her or make her shy away from him. So he only grinned at her in a foolish sort of way and deprecated his tolerance as he said, "Thank you, Miss Penworth. I shall leave you now before I blot my copy book."

And before I say anything more foolish, he thought, striding down the hall, mentally thumping his forehead with the heel of his hand. He sounded more like a befuddled schoolboy suffering from pangs of calf love over a kindly governess than a peer of the realm who had fallen hopelessly in love with a beautiful woman who seemed to regard him with the affection due an older brother. And despite her confession that she thought he was kind to children, he wondered whether she truly believed him a pattern card of manly virtue or if she was merely attempting to be polite for her nephew's sake.

During the next week, Standen had more than one occasion to regret that Hugh had come down ill. He felt sorry for the boy, of course. His rash made him miserable, as did his cough and runny nose, and the fact that he was confined in a darkened room.

But despite his sympathy, the duke had to confess that he had more selfish reasons to rue the boy's isolation. Grace was preoccupied in caring for the cranky invalid and too busy to pay Standen any mind, except on her host's command to wait upon him and his grandmother of an evening. Even then, she appeared abstracted, and toward the latter part of the week, Standen began to feel listless and neglected.

For her own part, Grace was kept so busy easing her nephew's discomfort that she scarcely had the opportunity to notice the duke's decline. She was hard-pressed to keep Hugh quiet, and depended more and more on Standen for relief, for he rarely refused an opportunity to play a quiet war game with her nephew or show him a few magic tricks while she refreshed herself. Immediately upon her return, however, he excused himself, pleading an obligation to business, appearing again only when she sat down to spin a yarn.

And when Hugh finally recovered his strength, she knew she must tell the duke it was time they returned to London. Marching into his study while she had the courage, she caught Standen sneezing into his handkerchief. He then convulsed in a fit of coughing that raised beads of sweat on his forehead. Without waiting for an invitation, she hurried toward him, offering him a glass of water. When he controlled the spasms, he set the glass on his desk and said in a husky voice, "Have you come to lighten my dull day, dear Grace?"

She touched a gentle hand to his cheek in a gesture reminiscent of her practice with Hugh. "Oh, no" she cried out, cupping both hands along his jaw as a sudden fear pounded through her veins. "You have a fever!" Then, mastering her fear and the near-overwhelming desire to pull him into a protective embrace, she gazed narrowly at him and asked, "Do your eyes hurt?"

Standen passed his hand over them, saying in a tired voice that made her heart ache, "A little, Miss Penworth. But I have work to do."

"It will wait," she assured him. Grace wanted to shake him, but caught his hand and led him instead to a couch well away from the light that was pouring through the long windows. Sitting down beside him, she demanded, "Why did you not tell me you'd never had the measles?"

"You never asked," Standen said, feeling quite abused by her lack of interest in his past. He wondered with the wounded conceit of the sick if she cared so little for him. Certainly she had spent less than no time with him in the past week, and if what his staff had told him was true, she was planning to flee from him at her earliest opportunity. He wanted her with him. But already she was leaping to her feet, scurrying toward the mantel, and yanking on the blasted bell. "No, don't ring the bell, Grace," he commanded, waving her back, clinging to her hand when she obeyed him.

"What is it, Your Grace?" she asked, placing herself gingerly at his side. "Do you want a glass of water?"

Standen shook his head. "I want you to sit with me. *Now* what are you doing?"

She wrapped a shawl around his shoulders, saying sternly, "I am going to put you to bed."

Standen grinned mischievously and said, "Are you now? That's an idea I must say I like. How do you propose to keep me there?"

"Don't be silly, Your Grace," she said, blushing though she assured herself that his improper assumption was due to impending illness. "You're not well."

"I'm not out of my head with fever," he chuckled, holding her cool hands to keep her beside him.

She rested in his hands, smiling despite her concern for his health. He had grown too dear in the short time she had known him. Squeezing his fingers, she prayed silently, *God grant him long life.*

To her surprise, Standen laid her hand along his cheek.

Her fingers absorbed the heat that seemed to radiate in waves from his person. When she felt she was in danger of bursting into flames, he kissed her palm, then said in bemused tones, "Perhaps I am, at that. But I am not so delirious that I don't know to whom I am speaking, Grace. I don't want you to leave just now, but I can't ask you to stay here with me."

"No," she agreed, curling her fingers around his hot, dry hand. Dropping her gaze from his, she allowed, "It wouldn't be proper."

"No," he muttered, then asked, "Would you keep my grandmother company until I can return you to your family?"

"Yes, of course," Grace agreed, her spirit soaring at his request. "But look, Your Grace," she said, noticing at the door the footman who had come in answer to her summons. Holding him off with her free hand, she asked him, "Have you had the measles?" When he nodded, she came to her feet and said, "Good. Will you kindly help me get His Grace to his rooms. I fear he is not well."

Fourteen

As soon as Grace saw the duke to his chamber and relinquished him to the capable hands of his valet, she went in search of the duke's grandmother. She found her in the rose salon, feeding a Yorkshire terrier on her lap. When the duchess perceived she was not alone, she shooed the little dog to the floor and said, "Ah, how good you are to visit me, my dear. Come sit with me until my grandson can make time for us."

"He has been quite busy, Your Grace," Grace said.

"But that is no excuse for neglecting us ladies," the duchess laughed, drawing Grace down in a chair next to hers. "Eh, what's this?" she asked, noting Grace's unusual nervous preoccupation. "Surely you haven't quarreled."

"No, Your Grace, I scarcely know how to tell you . . ."

Tightening her grip on Grace's wrist, Lady Standen ordered, "Say it, my girl, or I shall be alarmed."

Grace fortified herself with a deep breath, then said, "Standen has fallen ill, Duchess; I think with measles."

"Probably," said the dowager, controlling her natural anxiety that her grandson should have contracted an ailment he was spared in his youth.

"I am sorry," Grace said. "If only I had known, I would have refused to let Standen visit."

"I doubt you could have kept Alan away," Elsie said thoughtfully.

Her forgiving confession did nothing to ease Grace's conscience. "Oh, how he must hate me for bringing this plague on him," she cried, springing from her chair to pace a circle around the rug. When she had propelled herself in a full circle, she dabbed at her eyes with a corner of her handkerchief, saying, "From the first day we met, I was nothing but trouble for him; and I promise you, I meant him no harm."

"Of course you did not." Gratified by the becoming show of concern, the duchess arose from her chair and patted Grace's white-knuckled hands. "But I fear he will not rest easily in his darkened and idle state. I hope you will tell him one of your enchanting tales."

"Yes, Your Grace," Grace said, meeting the kindly gaze of the grand lady. "I would do anything for him."

"Well, then, go on," said the dowager in gruff tones, adding in an undertone as Grace fled to obey, "I wish he would hurry up and ask."

Grace found the duke growling at his valet and demanding his draperies be opened. "I have work to do. I need the light," he shouted to Valmont's retreating back. "Come back here, you lily-livered Frog." Throwing off his covers as the valet maintained his course, he vowed, "Damn, I'll do it myself."

Directing a sympathetic look at Valmont, who was scuttling toward the duke's dressing room, Grace let herself into the chamber. She crossed her arms forbiddingly and teased, "Are you determined to be an impatient patient, Your Grace?"

"I have no time for childish ailments," groused the duke. "I have important work to do." Then, caught in a violent spasm of coughing, he did not protest when she delivered him back to his bed. However, when she covered him up, he demanded, "What are you doing in here?"

"Keeping you from terrorizing your employees," Grace said, allowing a tender smile to soften her accusation.

"Why?" he growled. "So you can write about the abominable Duke of Standen?"

"I would not do that," Grace vowed, plumping up his pillows behind him. "You have made me regret my overbearing opinions. It is wrong to condemn an entire people for the sins of the few."

"If you stay, your opinion may sink to its former depth," Standen said bitterly as he lay back against the pillows.

"If I stay?" Grace demanded, taking a tray of soothing tea from a footman. She set it on the bedside table and served the duke a dose. "I should like to see anyone force me to leave."

Coughing, Standen took a sip, then attempted to return the cup to his nurse. "I don't want it," he complained when she refused to take it back. But a gentle reproof convinced him that he would hurt her far more by spurning the medicine than himself by swallowing it. Grudgingly he drank it all, then said, "I hope you will not kill me."

"I think it will take more than this to do you in," Grace allowed, though she was far from feeling confident in her assurance. Taking the cup, she smoothed a hand over his forehead, controlling an impulse to place a kiss in its place. She may have done so for Hugh, but the duke was no mere boy who needed a motherly touch. With the Duke of Standen, she felt anything but motherly. Moving away from his side, she said, "Now I have seen you comfortable, I shall leave you to rest."

"Will you come back?" he asked, grasping her fingers before she got completely away.

"Yes," she replied, blushing. "But only if you promise to go to sleep."

"I promise," Standen grumbled. "But you must pay a forfeit."

Grace looked at him, then decided to humor his petulant whim. "As long as it isn't too outrageous . . ."

"Stop calling me 'Your Grace,' " he commanded. "My name is Alan, and I am lonely for the sound of it."

"I shall try . . . Alan," she said. He seemed satisfied, for he released her fingers and lay back on his pillows. "But only as long as you are not well; and only in private. I shouldn't wish to decrease your consequence."

"Consequence is a lonely mate," he complained, closing his eyes against the shadows. "Friends have no need of rank or consequence, Grace. But I will respect your scruples."

"Thank you," she said, leaning forward on impulse to kiss his cheek. "Good night, Alan."

Though he did not open his eyes, he smiled and murmured, "Good night, my Grace," when she slipped out the door to supervise Hugh's quiet play.

Despite her prayers to the contrary, the duke was soon

covered with a fine red rash that caused him to complain bitterly. "Blast," he cried, when Valmont let her into his room one afternoon, "Hugh was right; I feel as if a thousand bees were stinging me." He directed a pointed stare at Grace as she began to dab a soothing preparation on the spots on his face and hands. "All over."

Setting aside the bowl and sponge, Grace moved to let Valmont tend his master's needs. Standen cast a forbidding look toward his valet, who, having suffered the duke's sharp tongue for three days, sidled out of the room, muttering, "He has the bee sting, and I know when to retreat."

"Shall I summon a footman?" Grace asked, folding hands that yearned to touch him, to soothe his discomfort and her own.

"No, I should only send him away, too," Alan said. Holding out a blotchy hand, he said, "Only one person can make me feel better. Come here."

Hesitantly Grace moved forward and, taking his warm fingers in hers, sat on the edge of the duke's bed. She felt unaccountably shy as the image of a bride on her wedding night presented itself to her.

"Help me, Grace," he said, his voice a husky whisper that conveyed distress and something more, an aching need that did more than awaken Grace's compassionate heart. It kindled a desire she had long denied herself.

Startled, she raised her gaze to his and saw in his eyes an unguarded longing that matched her own.

Restraining her longings, she reminded herself that it was not the duke's intent to seduce her. Standen was a sick man. Repeating the phrase as a litany to control inappropriate desires that flickered to life, she attempted, in what she hoped was a maternal manner, to unbutton his nightshirt. But her fingers shook, she fumbled with the fastenings, and she couldn't look the duke in the eye. She knew she ought not look anywhere else. Suddenly paralyzed by conflicting feelings of desire and propriety, she removed her hands from the warm fabric, clasped her fingers together, and tried to breathe normally. It was of no use. Her fingers burned to touch him.

Standen caught her hands and held them still while he complained, "I don't want to be one of your charity cases."

"You aren't," she snapped, tugging her fingers out of his grasp. "I don't think of touching you as doing a Good Work."

She heard his sudden intake of breath and regretted her sharp tone. And when he said, "It isn't good at all," she was gripped by the fear that he did not wish her to touch him at all.

"It isn't proper," he brooded.

"No," she countered in confusion. She didn't know what was right or proper anymore. She only wanted Alan. No, that was not precisely correct. She wanted him, but not if it diminished him in any way. Grasping her courage about her like a mantle, she said, "If I threaten your peace or reputation, you may cry out; Latham will doubtless defend your honor against my encroaching ways."

The duke seemed too tired to resist. But he did mumble, "You know very well that *my* reputation isn't at stake."

Grace pursed her lips and said, "I trust you, Alan. Can you not trust me? I want to help you, not force you to . . . do the honorable thing." Then, resolving to treat him as if he were one of her father's flock of parishioners, she pushed the soft fabric off his shoulders and revealed a network of angry red welts that did look like stings. "Oh, sweet heaven," she breathed in sympathy with his pain. "I wish I had not come here."

"Don't say that, Grace," Standen commanded. "Who would take care of me if you were not here?"

"You would be very well without me," she said, near tears. Closing her eyes, she murmured, "Oh, I cannot bear to see anymore."

"Do I look that bad?" he asked, hurt.

Her eyes flew open at his query. Staring at his broad chest and its soft brown furring, she sighed. The perfection of his form was marred by the rash, but she could only confess, "No, Alan; you are magnificent." Casting a startled look into his eyes, she could not suppress the blush that overspread her features as she realized how immodest her comment sounded. Licking her lips, she hastened to explain herself, "Only you would not be ill if Hugh and I had not darkened your doorway."

Alan saw the hesitant flick of her pink tongue and was nearly consumed with a hunger to taste her sweet lips himself. But he restrained himself, thinking his appearance must repel her. Crossing his arms behind his head to keep from pulling her into his arms, he leaned back against his pillows in an attitude of relaxation he was far from enjoying. "I don't hold you responsible, Miss Penworth. Will you tell me a story?"

Taking up the sponge, Grace began to spread a soothing ointment on his shoulders and upper torso. As she
smoothed the preparation along his poor, irritated flesh,
she racked her brain for a story to tell him.

"Once there was a brave knight . . ." she began in
an almost inaudible voice. She had to compel herself
not to dwell too long on the powerful swell and curve
of his form. ". . . who was forced to rely on a troublesome young woman."

"This sounds familiar," he said, relaxing under the
spell of Grace's soothing voice and magical touch. "I
think I know the ending."

"Would you like to tell the story?" Grace asked in
strangled tones. Of a sudden, she dropped the sponge
in the bowl and turned her gaze toward the darkened
windows as she convulsively clasped her fingers together. "The knight was handsome and brave as you
must know, and he was determined to vanquish an evil
warlock who held the unfortunate lady captive."

"I wish him well then," murmured the duke.

Grace directed an indulgent look upon him. Standen
was lying against his pillows—like a sultan, she thought,
turning her eyes from his dark form. Self-consciously
she drew his nightshirt closed and buttoned it, bringing
her thoughts back to the story she had begun. "He was
riding toward the warlock's den when the lady ran into
his path."

"I have heard this tale," Standen laughed, entwining
his fingers with hers before she had the chance to draw
away. "I thought she was being held captive."

"Hush," Grace said, allowing him to draw her down
on the pillow with him. She snuggled against him like

a child, explaining, "The warlock knew the knight was susceptible to beautiful women, and used her as bait."

"I'd fall for it," Standen said, raising Grace's hand and pressing a hot kiss on her knuckles.

"She was not so weak-spirited as to allow such a handsome creature to sacrifice himself for her," Grace said, taking a calming breath as a wave of desire washed over her. Suddenly aware of the impropriety of her posture, she struggled to sit up. "She told the knight to ride away."

"Why would she do such a thing?" Standen interrupted again, controlling Grace's sudden start and attempting to soothe her down beside him once more. "Did she not like the knight?"

"I don't know," Grace stammered, tugging on her fingers. "I think she must have liked him, only . . ." She stumbled off the bed and sat very properly in a chair. "It is no use explaining everything, Your Grace."

"I thought you agreed to call me Alan," he chided.

"I think we had better return to 'Your Grace' and 'Miss Penworth,' " she said, "At least for the time being."

Standen shrugged, more to scratch a new outbreak of spots than in resignation, for he said, "I don't like it, but I will bow to your scruples—for the time being, Miss Penworth. Now, why did your lady reject her knight? Did she not like him?"

"Yes, of course she did," Grace sighed. *As much as I like you.* "Just believe the lady was very independent and did not like having everyone else order her life to their satisfaction."

"All right," Standen said, crossing his arms over his chest sullenly and glaring at her. "But I can tell you the knight is not going to ride away and leave the lady to the evil devices of that damned warlock."

"Of course not," Grace agreed. "The knight sets her on a rock out of harm's way and rides into the warlock's domain."

"Just like that?"

"How would you do it?" she snapped back, leaping to her feet and pacing alongside the bed.

"Not by riding up to the front door," Standen said wearily. But when she turned to pass down the length of the bed, he reached out and plucked her to his side once more. "Believe me," he said, turning her face so he had her complete attention, "a frontal attack would mean his certain death. And I want the knight and his lady to have a happy ending."

"So do I," Grace said, unconsciously covering his hand with hers.

"So?" Standen prompted, drawing her cheek down upon his shoulder. "How do we give them happiness?"

Of a sudden, Grace could think of nothing but the happy ending she longed for herself. For Alan, she amended. But those longings were ineligible and selfish, and not ones she could properly confess. "You tell this part," she insisted. "But remember, he doesn't win the battle right away."

"Be quiet, let me think," Standen said, squinting as he made the effort. It was deucedly difficult to think of anything but kissing Grace while he held her in his arms. Willing himself not to give her a disgust of him, he said thoughtfully, "We're agreed the knight doesn't ride into battle. He . . . walks in wearing the garb of . . ." *Something romantic,* he thought, *but what? Oh yes, the very thing.* "A minstrel."

"A minstrel?" Grace objected drowsily. "Where would he come by a lute and bells?"

"Who is telling this part?" demanded the duke. Then, squinting toward her in a hungry sort of way, he asked, "What do you think he should wear?"

"Oh, definitely a monk's robes," Grace said with a giggle.

"Blast," grumbled Standen. "He would have no weapon against the warlock's charms."

"No, but it would enable him to resist the *lady's* charms," she said, still laughing. "And it is more symbolic of the battle between good and evil."

"Very well, a monk he shall be. Go on with the story," said the duke in grudging tones.

"Thankfully the knight was educated in a monastery," Grace continued. "And he calls on the lessons learned under the direction of the good brothers during the battle of wits which immediately ensues."

"No swords?" Standen sounded disappointed.

"No, that would be too easy," she replied smugly. "The warlock initiates a series of contests in which he weaves spells which the knight—that is, the monk—has to render harmless."

"He is not going to turn me—that is, I mean the knight—into a frog, is he?" Alan complained.

"No," Grace said, smiling as she realized he understood the story was for themselves. "Frogs are not very attractive, after all. Now, let me see. I've lost the thread of the story."

"Spells," Alan said, thinking an enchantment was being cast over him at that moment. But with Grace snuggling against him, smelling of roses and violets, it was one he did not mind in the least.

"Oh, yes," she said. "All goes well for several hours, with the knight neutralizing the warlock's evil eye through faith and boldness. But when the unhappy lady appears in the doorway, the knight loses his concentration. At once the warlock realizes his adversary is the knight he has vowed to enslave, and he takes advantage of the knight's distraction to cast an evil spell which the knight cannot evade."

"Why did she come back?" Standen demanded in impatient tones that ignored the fact that the hero of the story was incapacitated. "She should have stayed safe on her rock, and—" He began coughing.

Starting out of their embrace, Grace held a glass of water to the duke's parched lips until he quieted. Setting the glass on the bedside table, she curled up beside him once more and said in a gentle whisper, "Because she knew her knight needed her."

Standen wrapped an arm about her waist and pulled her nearer to him. Laying his head beside hers on his pillows, he said drowsily, "Yes, I do, Grace." Then he turned and kissed her.

She did not expect it and met the caress with lips half-parted. His tongue slid across them in a sensuous salute that caused her pulse to thrum in a delighted rhythm which echoed the rapid thud of his strong heartbeat. But he was not well, and she knew he needed rest to recover. And so, restraining herself with reminders of what was best for him, she said, "Rest, now Alan; we have plenty of time for kisses when you're better."

Smiling, he lay back and fell asleep, keeping her securely within his embrace.

Grace felt all feminine and fluttery inside. She watched him sleep and was compelled to admit that a different heart beat within her breast—one completely at odds with her ambition of remaining single and supporting herself through the writing of critical social essays.

But this hope rising in her breast, this hope of bringing the great Duke of Standen to the marriage altar was impossible. He owed something more to his consequence than to wed a lowly parson's daughter.

True, he had been kind, but he had never given her a reason to entertain such futile hopes.

Yet, he admitted he needed her. And he had kissed her.

She clung to that unconscious admission and to his caresses as if to a lifeline. They strengthened her as she nursed him through the worst of his illness. They inspired her to spin out their story of the knight and his plaguey lady to the disgust of her nephew, who demanded to be sent home if she couldn't think up anything more rousing for their entertainment.

"So, *go* home," Standen growled in such disgruntled tones that Grace was forced to suggest that it was time they both returned to London.

"No," said the duke, dropping a pile of letters on the coverlet to clutch her hand forbiddingly. "You mustn't go. I need you to stay here, Grace," he said fervently. "With me."

"That's all very well," Hugh said with a boyish snort of disdain. "But *I* still want to go home. All you do is stare at each other like two loobies. You're no fun."

Drawing himself to an imperious height on his pillows, the duke glared at the ten-year-old and said, "You're right, Hugh, old man. But I know just the thing that will alter that state of affairs." So saying, he threw off the covers and strode toward the fireplace, yanking on the tasseled bellpull with enough force to set all the bells in the servants' hall a-chiming.

Stunned by the sight of his powerfully muscled bare legs stretching out beneath his billowing linen nightshirt, Grace hurried after the duke with his dressing gown. "Here, Alan, you'll take a chill," she said, drawing his arms into the sleeves with as much care as she would have taken with a sick child.

"Ah, my Grace," he teased, taking pleasure in her solicitous fussing while she belted his robe and smoothed its lapels. She smelled delicately like a rose garden. He longed to gather her in his arms and breathe in her intoxicating, refreshing essence. But knowing she would only suspect he was suffering a relapse and treat him like an invalid the way she had done for the past week and more, he only teased her, "Do you mean to keep me warm? Now *that* would be fun."

Meeting his enticing gaze, Grace raised a hand to the blush that heated her cheeks. "Behave yourself, Duke," she chided him, tugging decisively on his sleeve with a sidelong glance toward their audience.

"Ugh!" Hugh stumbled toward the door, making various rude sounds that eloquently conveyed his disgust at the grown ups' unconscious display of affection. "I can take a hint. You're acting just like Mama and Papa when they want to be alone."

Fifteen

Breaking the compelling gaze that connected him with Grace, Standen glared at the boy, who had just collided with Valmont as the manservant entered the chamber. "Send me my secretary, Valmont," said the duke, recalling his dignity at last and setting Grace apart from him. "And tell Latham that Hugh is to go home."

"Very good, Your Grace," said the unctuous Frenchman, holding the door for Hugh's exit. As the boy slumped into the hallway, the valet enquired, "And will Miss Penworth be accompanying her nephew?"

"Did I say she was going?" snapped the duke. "Don't look at me in that wounded manner. I shall entertain whomever I wish in my own house."

"As you wish, Your Grace," muttered Valmont, sidling out of the chamber.

Standen raised a spotted hand to his brow as if the effort expended in thinking had worn him out. Helping him to a nearby chair, Grace tucked a lap robe about his knees and leapt back when he snapped, "I am not an invalid, Grace. Leave well enough alone."

Grace lowered her gaze penitently. "Perhaps I should go, too."

"Yes, Gram said she expected you to attend her," he said as a scratch at the door heralded his secretary's arrival. "I have business to conduct now. But do not be gone long. We have a story to finish."

Grace knew she must tell him the real ending to the story but could not bear to utter the words that would only break her heart. And so she fled from him, stopped on the duchess's threshold by a footman bearing a letter on a silver salver. Noting that it was from Amity, she tore it open immediately, hoping her sister would command her to come home.

"Dearest Grace," she read. *"Mr. DuBarry is spreading the most scurrilous lies about your book. It is all anyone can talk about. People are saying the most horrible things—that you are a traitoress and ought to hang. I hardly know what to think, but Colin says you must trust the Duke of Standen."*

Grace crushed the note as she felt hot fingers of fear squeeze her heart. People were calling her a traitor. This was worse than anything poor Caro Lamb had endured. What must she do?

Her first inclination was to do just as Colin had suggested, but Alan had sent her away in order that he might conduct some business. She could not run back to him, crying for protection when he had offered none. More importantly, she could not trouble him when he was still unwell. Grace could not stand it if her trials should cause him to suffer a relapse.

And the duchess, for all her liberal sympathies, could not possibly countenance a person branded a traitoress. That was likely to cause the frail lady to suffer an apoplexy. For their sakes, she must go home.

Placing Amity's disturbing communication within her sleeve, Grace smoothed an unconcerned smile on her face. Upon entering the duchess's salon, however, she was not as successful in masking her dismay when the grand lady set aside the book she was reading and fixed a disconcerted gaze upon her. It was her own *Cock and Bull Stories.*

Judging from the dark look the dowager was directing at her, Grace fully expected to be told she was to join her nephew on his journey home which had been set for three days hence. To stave off the disappointment, she offered to take Hugh home herself.

To her surprise, Grace was not banished, but ordered to remain at Bon Chance to see whether the storm in London would blow over. Grateful as she was not to be sent away, she could not help wondering whether she was being kept under house arrest.

She did not know why she should allow such recriminations to dim her trust in her friends. The duke and his grandmother certainly never betrayed by look or remark their doubts in her innocence.

Reproaching herself for having expressed in that hateful volume the hurtful sentiments Mr. DuBarry found so praiseworthy and profitable, three days later she watched Standen's traveling coach rumble down the wide gravel drive with Hugh leaning out the window waving a happy farewell. She thought she heard him cry, "I hope you get your happy ending," just as the coach rounded the bend at the bottom of the hill, but realized it must have been her heartbeat echoing her own selfish, futile hopes.

She did not deserve a happy ending.

Returning to the house, she was sent outside with a basket thrust into her hands by none other than the duchess herself, who said, "You've been looking too pale, child. Go out and collect some roses."

"Yes, Your Grace," Grace said, dipping an unconscious curtsey before making her way through the delicate maze of furniture in the duchess's salon and into the rose garden.

Only moments later, the duke entered the salon. "I heard the coach drive off. Where is Grace?" he demanded, belting his dressing robe in convulsive movements that betrayed his fear that she had left him.

"I sent her into the garden," replied the dowager. Clutching his arm with her bony hand, she said, "Alan, I fear for her."

"There is no need for that," he said. He pressed his grandmother's fingers with his red-spotted ones. "Don't worry, Gram," he said firmly. "I shall see she comes about."

"But the charges," Elsie cried.

"Don't worry," he assured her. "If Grace must answer charges, I'll see we answer them together."

He found Grace trimming roses and laying blossoms carefully in a basket as if nothing threatened their peace. Her delicate pallor, however, told him she was not completely at ease. Striding toward her without a care to the weak sunlight that was battling the cloud cover, he enquired, "How long did you intend to keep me in the dark?"

Grace dropped the basket, spilling flowers on the crushed shell path. Kneeling to retrieve the bruised blossoms, she stammered, "You ought to be in a darkened room now, Your Grace—Alan. Your poor eyes . . ."

Standen raised a narrowed eye to the overcast sky, then drew her to her feet. "My eyes will not suffer today, my dear. And you know very well I was not speaking of sunlight, but of your circumstances. How could you think I would not find out?"

"Did Amity send you a letter as well?" she asked, drawing a piece of paper from a pocket and giving it to him.

Scanning it before handing it back, he directed a commanding look upon her and enquired, "What are you going to do?"

She could not bear having him think the worst of her. "I ought to have gone home with Hugh. You must not like harboring a traitoress under your roof."

"Hush," he commanded, giving her an urgent shake before drawing her into his arms. "We both know that's a blasted lie . . . born out of DuBarry's jealous wish to have you to himself."

"Love does that to some people," she mumbled, leaning her cheek against his lapel, inhaling his fresh, manly smell.

"Love has nothing to do with it," he protested, snugging her more protectively within his embrace. "It's greed, pure and simple."

So vehement was his declaration, all she could say was a defeated, "Oh?"

She might not like Mr. DuBarry, but she could not help feeling the pricks to her pride to learn his interest had not been fixed except in a covetous sort of way.

"If he'd cared at all about your feelings, Grace, Du-

Barry would have pulled your book from the shelves," Standen assured her. "Instead he wasted no time in promoting your 'scandalous little book.' "

Hurt by the duke's cruel assertion, Grace gasped and tried to extricate herself from his grasp. But he took her fingers in a gently inescapable grip, kissed them, and said, "Do not look so shocked, Grace; it is what *he* calls it."

Against her better judgment, she clung to the duke's hand. "I do not understand, Your Grace. I did not mean to scandalize the world. The essays were merely my observations on the necessity for the practice of Christian charity in the world." She uttered a nervous giggle. "It must be very disappointing reading to those accustomed to lurid novels."

"On the contrary," said the duke, "everyone is taking your words to heart."

"That is a surprise," she said, tilting her head in wonder. "I hadn't thought I should make such a difference in people's lives."

"You little fool," he said, dread tingeing his words with scorn. "They are calling you a traitor and demanding your head."

A frisson of fear shook her, but she straightened her shoulders and directed a brave gaze at the duke. "It would be very poor-spirited in me to hide. I ought to return to London and answer—"

"Be still, Grace."

"But if I am completely honest, Alan, I shall have nothing to fear," she protested.

"The fault, you once told me, lies in not knowing

when to be silent," Standen reminded her as he led her down the path in a box hedge maze.

"But they will find me, and . . . Oh how I wish you had not heard of my difficulty."

"Why?" he asked, stroking her soft, pale hair. "Are you so eager to languish in jail?"

"No, but if I have lost your good opinion, nothing else matters."

He passed a trembling hand over his eyes and drew her down beside him on a stone bench deep within the maze. Tucking his arm around her waist and keeping hold of her fingers with his, he half-turned toward her, saying, "I am not as fickle as that. I want an end to our story."

Wrapped in his embrace, Grace could scarcely breathe as she regarded their clasped hands in confusion. Their story had only one ending, but she could not bear to speak of it: she would go to jail for expressing unpopular sentiments which she could not recant, and he would forget all about her, except to remember that one summer she caused him so many troubles.

Resigned to the certainty of her unhappy fate, she sighed and said, "She was the cause of all the knight's troubles, and he was better off without her."

"I don't like that ending," said the duke in a voice as intractable as steel. "Let me." Drawing her nearer still, he mused, "She was the cause of all the knight's troubles, it was true," in stern tones that had Grace shaking in her slippers. But then, regarding her with a gentle look, he added in a softer voice, "But she was also the source of all his joy. Before their accidental meeting, he had suffered from Lombard fever . . ."

"And she had been too independent for her own good," Grace added.

"Quite so," Standen agreed, settling her cheek where it belonged, against his strong shoulder. "Only don't interrupt—where was I?"

"Lombard fever," she offered, turning her face up to his.

Silencing her with a finger sliding over her lips, the duke regarded her with an emotion Grace could not define. Of a sudden his dark lashes dropped down, and then her lips were captured in a compelling kiss that drove all fear from her mind.

Her arms circled his broad back as if by clinging to him, she might keep from falling into her unhappy future.

As he tenderly assaulted her mouth and she reciprocated, she admitted she had fallen head over heels with the most top-lofty noble in the realm. She was kissing him back irrepressibly, not caring who could see them, only wishing the kiss might never end. *That* would be her happily ever after.

But he drew away, abruptly, it seemed to her. And he said in a voice that sounded much weaker even than when he had been at his sickest, "But since he'd known this independent lady, the knight had never been bored."

"She was an accident waiting to happen," Grace reminded him. "And she was completely ineli—"

Too quickly for her to complete her depressing thought, the duke said, "And she needed her knight."

He was looking at her in that enigmatic way that made her feel as if she were melting into him. But though at one time the admission might have made her wary, now she welcomed the feeling. As selfish as it was, she wanted to be a part of him—to have her days begin and end in his arms, to be responsible to and for him. That would be heaven, she thought.

But she knew it was likely she'd be denied that particular bliss. Worse, if the charge against her was true, she'd doubtless be relegated to the eternal fires. The probability made her eyes burn with craven tears.

"Grace," Alan said, stroking her cheek to restore her overflowing eyes to his commanding but tender gaze. "My dear, you need me."

His avowal took her breath away and staunched her foolish tears. It was a long moment before she could regain her power of speech and say, "Don't be silly, Your Grace. I need a solicitor, not a protector."

"Is that what you think I intended to offer—my protection?"

Shrugging so as not to shame herself by confessing that it mattered very much what he intended, she confessed, "What else could you mean? Whatever you offer, it will only be temporary."

Her glib speech awakened a battle light in his eye that made her shrink from him.

"No, my dear, I am looking for a permanent arrangement," he said firmly. "If you think I should let them punish you for sedition, you are quite mistaken."

"I do not know how you can stop the proceedings," she said, hoping he would declare that that was indeed within his power.

Shaking his head, he replied to her disappointment, "I cannot stand in the way of an investigation. But I will stand with you."

"You are a true friend," she whispered, leaning on his shoulder.

"Not merely a friend," he said, turning her face upward.

Eyes filling again, she smoothed a hand over his dear features, as if to memorize them.

Kissing her fingers, he said, "There is only one way I can save you, Grace. You must marry me."

Grace sat stunned in his arms. Then slowly she said, "I am inclined to accept, Your Grace . . ."

"Alan," he said in compelling tones.

"Alan," she echoed. "Only I cannot but think you are sacrificing yourself."

"How so, my Grace?"

At his most welcome endearment, she looked a sad reproach at him. "I wish you will not, sir. You can do much better for yourself, and everybody knows it"

"Do they?" the duke enquired in awful tones. "I suppose we are the *on-dit* of the Season, the Duke of Standen and—"

"That Scribbling Woman," Grace finished. "They will say much worse if you marry a traitoress."

" 'They' would not dare," Alan said in a grim tone that made her heart sink. "Once you are my duchess, you will be beyond scandal."

Propelling herself to her feet, she clasped her hands behind her and began to pace as if it was the only way in which to keep from touching him. "Don't you see? That is precisely why you must not marry me. You need a wife whose name is above reproach, not beyond the pale."

Arising from the bench, the duke caught her arm

and compelled her to look at him. "I need *you,*
Grace," he vowed before pulling her in another breath-
taking embrace and silencing her protests with an in-
disputable kiss.

This was the man she loved, even if that love was
doomed to be short-lived. Rather, she thought, her life
was destined to be short. That dismal future contrasting
with the very pleasant present lowered her natural mod-
esty. Grace gave herself up completely to the kiss.

When she molded herself against his hard frame, Alan
broke off the kiss, leaving her bereft of reason and unable to stand on her own feet. "If I thought that kiss
did not affect you as deeply as it affected me," he said,
gazing intently at her, "I would not force your hand,
Grace. But you are too independent for your own good;
I simply cannot allow you to sacrifice yourself on your
country's altar."

"Yet you ask me to allow you to . . ."

"Love and protect you, my dear," he said as he
smoothed a tender hand along her stubborn jaw.

"Sacrifice yourself," she maintained.

He gave a long-suffering sigh and looked off into the
distance over her head for several moments, then said,
"If I offer you the protection of my name and position
in society, Grace, believe me, it will be no sacrifice on
my part."

"But I am a Nobody," she countered again. "How
can you—"

Once more a finger laid across her lips silenced her.
"You sound like one of the highest sticklers decrying a
mushroom. Trust me, Grace; I know what I am doing.
And it's your only chance."

His finger remained a bar against her lips while she considered the trouble she had caused him and would cause him should they marry.

"And don't tell me how much trouble you'll cause me," he said as she took a breath.

"I was thinking just that," she confessed.

"I knew you were," he replied, gifting her with one of his tender smiles. "Don't you know that you'd cause me far more trouble out of my life? I'd worry about you every minute."

"Would you?" The possibility that she would trouble his thoughts raised her spirits. "I wouldn't like to make you worry. But . . ."

"Then I think you owe it to both of us to accept my proposal," he said righteously.

"It is that very smugness that makes your offer so objectionable," she declared, suppressing the joyous laughter which threatened to spill forth.

"Objectionable?" he demanded. Then with a grin, he teased, "One would think you didn't want to marry a duke."

"It is the only rank I would consider," she replied, lifting a half-embarrassed smile to him. "But only because *you* are the duke."

"Since I *am* the duke, Grace," he said, kissing her, "Will you marry me?"

Flinging caution to the winds, Grace twined her arms about his neck and sighed, "Oh, yes, Alan, I will."

The duke rewarded her for her compliance with another kiss that made Grace weak-kneed and dizzy and marvelously happy. Then in an abrupt about-face, he set her on her feet and hurried her back toward the house, saying, "Now we shall return to London, and we shall face this crisis together."

Sixteen

To Grace's puzzlement the next day, her mother and father were awaiting their arrival at the duke's town house. They gave no explanation, but as soon as the Dowager Duchess of Standen had been made known to the reverend and his wife, Letitia burst into loud tears, alternating between inarticulate joy in her daughter's incomparable catch and inconsolable anxiety about her seditious writings. "Where did you learn such things?" she sobbed, adding for the duke's benefit, "Certainly not from me or her father, Your Grace. We raised her to be a good, law-abiding, Christian girl—"

"Hush, Letitia," said Andrew Penworth as he shook Standen's hand. "Grace does not have to defend herself to us."

"No, she does not," Alan agreed, extricating Grace from her mother's anxious embrace. Enfolding her under a protective, seemingly relaxed arm, he continued in a grave voice that made Grace's heart burn with fear. "But she must answer charges, and I intend to stand beside her. Will you marry us, Mr. Penworth?"

"It will take time," said the vicar. "To post the banns and do it properly."

"She does not have time for a proper wedding," said

Standen. He reached within his coat and withdrew a parchment document. "I would prefer to give her a proper defense."

"A special license?" mused the vicar. Seeing the Bishop's sanction of the hasty ceremony, he nodded as he returned the license, saying, "As you wish, Your Grace."

Unable to comprehend the speed with which her life was being rearranged, Grace looked at her betrothed and gasped, "But you were ill. When did you arrange everything?"

Bestowing a warm gaze on her, Alan said, "I must credit my secretary for his efficiency."

"Yes," interjected Mrs. Penworth. "When your happy communication reached us on the heels of the news of Grace's troubles, Mr. Penworth and I hurried to Town as you requested. Oh Grace, I scarcely know what to think, whether to laugh or to cry."

Grace exhaled an overwrought sigh as she leaned heavily on Alan's arm. "I share your confusion, Mama. Too much has occurred in too short a time to take it all in." The crushing weight of fatigue and shock having finally taken its toll on her nerves, she began to shiver uncontrollably. Casting a panicky look among the company, she said, "Please excuse me. I must beg a few minutes to compose my feelings."

"I'll take you to your room," Standen said when her parents arose to take her back to the Spencer home on Harley Street. "I understand your anxiety to have her under your roof again," he said. "However, I think Grace will rest better here."

"But, Your Grace, the proprieties," Mrs. Penworth exclaimed.

Ignoring her mother's protests, Grace went above stairs with Standen and sank limply onto a salmon-colored sofa when he ushered her into an elegant sitting room. "Grace," he said, kneeling at her side and rubbing her wrists, "you will not faint, my dear."

"No, Your Grace," she responded in distracted tones. In spite of her outward lethargy, her mind was reeling. Standen must have sent notice to her parents to prepare for their marriage at least five days ago, but he had proposed to her only yesterday. Rather than feel grateful for his concern, not only for herself, but for her parents, Grace felt an all-consuming sense of shame rob her of good sense. "I suppose I should thank you for . . . everything," she said. "But I cannot help but cringe before your arrogance."

"Arrogance, my love?" he enquired.

"I don't believe that is too strong a word for your overbearing confidence that I should accept your proposal." She retrieved her hands from his grasp, adding, "It completely sinks me to the level of a social climber whose only interest is in your rank or of a frightened goose who is unable to stand on her own two feet."

"Not you," he said, stroking a hand over her heated cheek. "I did it for your own good, Grace."

Despite the thrill his touch elicited, Grace protested, "I won't have you sacrifice yourself for my good." She shook her head so vehemently that several curls tumbled from their pins and fell over his hand. "I take it back. I won't marry you. I'd rather take whatever punishment the court metes out than subject you to a lifelong commitment you'd only live to regret."

He regarded her with the stunned look of one who has been dealt a blow to the stomach. And like one dealt such a blow, he could not at once form a reply, but only attempt to marshal his reserves of strength and control. As the silence crackled between them, Grace began to think she had convinced him of her resolve. She was possessed of a crushing despair, but compelled herself to be brave, saying inwardly that her sacrifice was the best thing she could do for him.

Finally, with a stiff inclination of his jaw, he enquired, "You are quite decided?"

"Yes, Alan," she whispered, her courage faltering. "You need a lady who will complement your consequence, not offend it."

"Grace," Standen began, lowering himself beside her on the sofa and possessing himself of her hand. Kissing it, he vowed, "I should never regret taking you to wife. I love you."

It was her turn to register shock. It had never occurred to her that he might truly return her affection. His revelation ought to fill her with joy, but it only left her numb. After a long silence, during which she attempted to form a logical argument against the alliance, all she could say was, "I love you, too. But don't you see that is why I must not drag you into this miserable predicament. I wrote myself into this corner, and somehow I must get myself out."

He sighed as if he were tired, then said, "You of all people ought to know that we cannot rely on our own strength for deliverance."

"Do you mean to read me a sermon?" she asked in chastened tones. "I have not forgotten where my help comes from."

"No?" he shot back. "How do you know I am not a part of that help you desperately need?"

"Do not tell me you are an angel sent—"

"Don't be ridiculous," he replied. "Angels don't burn the way I burn for you. But you must confess we should never have met except by divine intervention."

Bemused by his obvious attempt to encourage her, Grace could not help giggling.

He gathered her in his arms. "If you do not depend on me, Grace, your independence will be your death. And that I should regret above all things."

She sighed in confusion. "It seems that I shall cause you trouble no matter what I do."

"Yes," he grinned. "But you will cause me less trouble if you marry me, and so I shall give you no alternative. Your father has given his blessing; you cannot take back your words; and there's an end to it. We shall be wed tomorrow morning in Standen Chapel."

Then, before she could protest, he covered her mouth with his and managed with very little trouble to convince her of his single-minded devotion and unalterable determination to bend her gently to his will. And his silent arguments were so deliciously persuasive that Grace could only cling to him and murmur, "Yes, Alan," between kisses.

On the morrow with their families looking on and wearing as her bride dress a gown of white lace over a white satın slip which Amity insisted she must have and a collar of pearls which the dowager duchess clasped around her throat, Grace met her duke at the altar as he had commanded. She promised with all her heart to love, honor, and obey the man who was becoming her husband. Standen pressed her hand reassuringly and expressed his own vows without hesitation, in a clear strong voice that resounded within her soul.

And when the Reverend Mr. Penworth pronounced them man and wife and her new husband raised the veil of Brussels lace to gaze upon her, she knew without a doubt that he had not married her just to save her from trouble she had brought on herself, but because he did love her.

She knew she did not deserve his affection or his protection, but rather than decry her own unworthiness, she gratefully accepted his love. Gathered in his arms, she raised her lips to his and returned his kiss with the full measure of her own devotion.

Finally Alan broke off the kiss to look at her with an open, adoring gaze that assured her that they could stand against any opposition. Tucking her arm within his, she allowed him to lead her out of the chapel surrounded by their families, who were anxious to offer their felicitations before the wedding breakfast.

As they were making their way toward the duke's reception room to greet those guests invited to fete the happy couple, Teddy began dancing in front of his aunt singing, "Aunt Grace, Your Grace. Aunt Grace, Your Grace."

Laughing, Standen plucked the boy off Grace's satin-clad toes and playfully tweaked his nose. "What are you about, brat?" he enquired.

"Mama said we must call Aunt Grace *Your* Grace," Teddy said, directing a steady and seemingly unimpressed gaze at his new uncle. "Is it because she belongs to you now?"

"She does not belong to me," amended the duke with a happy smile. "I belong to her."

"Oh," said the little boy in confused tones.

"She is still your Aunt Grace," said the duke. "Your mama was referring to her new title. Grace is my duchess now."

"Because you are a duke and all those other things?"

"Yes," said Standen. "Not the least of which is your uncle."

"Shall I call you Uncle Duke then?"

"Horrors! That makes me sound like a mastiff." Standen set Teddy on a chair in the hallway and pulled thoughtfully at his lip. "I thought we were friends."

"Well, we were," Teddy replied, throwing his arms about his Aunt Grace. "What should I call Perry now?" he demanded.

"At home you may call him Perry or Uncle if you like," she said, saving her veil from his clutching fingers. "But in public, Teddy, you must call him 'Your Grace' if you do not wish to be thought impertinent."

"And you must remember to address your aunt in the same manner," said Amity, taking her youngest child in hand and shooing him toward his father. "Oh, dearest Grace," she said, shedding many tears as she embraced her sister. "You have surprised us all most delightfully." Then, setting her apart a little, she gasped, "And frightened us most dreadfully. We are afraid to speak to anyone, suspecting even our best friends of collecting evidence against you."

"None of that," said Standen in quelling tones as he perceived his bride's sudden pallor. Taking Grace's hand in his warm one, he extricated her from her sister's apprehensive grasp and said, "I'll have a blushing bride, not one quaking in her slippers over rumors and hearsay. Come, my Grace," he said, drawing her toward the receiving room, "Our guests await."

Giving a nod to his footman, who opened the door with a flourish, Standen guided his new wife into a lavishly appointed chamber wherein a cluster of guests turned as one to salute "Their Graces, the Duke and Duchess of Standen" with a burst of affectionate applause and heartily voiced huzzahs.

After most of the well-wishers had passed before the couple to wish them happy, then had moved into the state dining room to find their places at the table, Grace looked in awe upon her husband. How on earth had he managed to arrange such a lavish bridal breakfast in such short order?

To her mortification, she realized she had voiced these sentiments to the lady just now passing before her. Mrs. Ramsey stumbled in her curtsey and laughingly replied, "Why don't you know, Your Grace, that where love is concerned a gentleman is able to work miracles?"

Smiling on the embarrassed lady, Grace raised her from her deep curtsey and said, "That is what he must have done, ma'am," adding incautiously, "And I must have faith that he can repeat further miracles on my behalf."

Mrs. Ramsey patted Grace's hand in an endearing, confident manner. "Do not despair, Your Grace," she said emphatically. "Standen will do battle for you as faithfully as St. George ever did against the dragon. And is that not what gossip is, a serpent who twists the truth to suit his own ends?"

Forgetting herself and her lofty estate, Grace embraced the wife of her husband's childhood friend. "You are too kind, too good," she said in the startled lady's ear. "I do not deserve such consideration. Thank you!"

Then she was hurried into the state dining room, where the guests immediately leapt to their feet and initiated a series of toasts to the happy couple that raised a self-conscious, but happy blush to her face.

Her embarrassment had scarcely faded when a pair of King's Messengers strode unannounced into the banquet hall. In view of all the guests they made their way toward the dais. One of them demanded, "Grace Penworth?"

The duke, arising from his chair, towered over the guards in an intimidating manner. Looking down his nose at the pair, he snapped, "You wish to speak with my wife, Her Grace, the Duchess of Standen?"

"Aye, Your Grace," said the spokesman of the pair without apology. "We have a warrant for her arrest. The duchess must come with us."

Father Penworth came to his feet in an uncharacteristic burst of energy. "But this is preposterous. We are celebrating a wedding. Surely you can wait until tomorrow."

"When the bride and her duke have flown the country?" retorted the guard. "I think not, sir." He turned a stern eye on Grace, who was not able to suppress a shudder from passing down her spine. "Ma'am? If you please."

"Yes, if you are sure it is me you want," she said, her voice breathless with fear as she came shakily to her feet. "I am ready to attend you."

Standen placed a steadying hand at her slender waist and turned her to face him. Raising her eyes to meet his resolute gaze, he uttered fervently, yet quietly, "I shall move heaven and earth to win your freedom." Then, he charged the guards, "Protect my lady wife, gentlemen. She has only lately been given to me, and I shall not take it at all kindly if she is taken from me so soon."

The King's Messengers frowned as if weighing the duke's concern for his bride against the gravity of his threat. Then nodding, the leader said, "We will protect Her Grace from all threats while she is our custody, Your Grace."

At the guard's assurance, Standen guided Grace down the steps and held her arm while they walked between the officers into the grand foyer. Shaking as she moved toward the doors, Grace felt every eye in the dining room on her as she was taken away, and feared she would disgrace her husband by falling into strong hysterics or into a dead faint before they reached the relative privacy of their hallway.

"Likely they will take you to the Horse Guards before admitting you to the Tower," Standen said as he took from a footman a midnight blue velvet cloak and wrapped it about her trembling shoulders. "I shall be with you, my dearest," he said, pressing a kiss to her forehead.

"Yes," she said, clinging to him. "I know we shall be together in heaven."

"Do not martyr yourself," he warned, clasping her forearms and bestowing a piercing look upon her. "Do you trust me, Grace?"

"With my life, Alan," she said wholeheartedly.

"Then answer the Councillors' questions honestly, but know when to be silent," he said, giving her an urgent shake when she did not at first nod understandingly.

"Yes," she said at last.

"I cannot come with you," he said, clasping her to him and kissing her one last time before giving her into the keeping of the King's Messengers. "But I shall summon my solicitor for your defense. And we will see you in the Tower."

Seventeen

Grace was taken in a closed hackney coach to White-hall and placed for what seemed like hours in a dark, hot, windowless room that was little more than an air-less closet. From the first, she felt the room fill with such a choking presence of doom that she feared she must suffocate on its stench. Fear and darkness seemed to penetrate her soul until she could not rest on the hope of love and abide in faith in her husband's promise.

But while she waited—for what she did not know—her father's admonition to pray in all circumstances came to mind. For the first time in her life, she didn't know what to pray for, doubted even that she had a right to petition the Almighty. Freedom seemed too grand a hope to lay hold of, especially if she were guilty of inciting people to mutiny against their government. And so she asked simply for help, mercy, courage, and for justice.

Of a sudden she was cloaked with a peace she could not understand. She was not alone in this dark pit, she knew it. Whatever happened, she would never be alone.

When the door was opened and she was summoned into the blinding light of the council room, she astounded her inquisitors, who seemed to have expected to find a weeping female begging for mercy. Striding into the austere chamber, Grace stood unbowed before a stern council, one of whom said in sneering tones, "I have been told felicitations are the order of the day."

Clasping her hands loosely at her waist, she said, "Thank you, my lord," without taking offense at his arch tone.

The gentleman sputtered angrily, "You are awfully brazen for one facing such serious charges." He then shuffled a stack of papers on the table before him.

"I am confident you will find me innocent according to English law," she replied. Then, in an open display of fearless curiosity, she enquired, "Will you kindly tell me what it is I am supposed to have done?"

"That is why we are convened," said another Councillor in a kinder tone. "To determine whether a crime has been committed." Holding up a book, he enquired, "Do you recognize this volume of essays entitled *Cock and Bull Stories?*"

Holding out her hand, Grace perused the book for several moments. It contained nothing additional to what she had already written, essays expounding on the revolutionary life of a true Christian believer. To her way of thinking, it was not seditious or libelous except where it touched on the nobility's casual acceptance of adulterous affairs. But every word was her own, and so she said, "Yes, my lord."

After a pause, the second man said, "And can you tell us who wrote them?"

"I did, my lord."

"You did?"

"Yes, my lord. Every word."

"You expect me to believe that a woman could instruct men?"

"You flatter me, sir, if you found something of value in the essays."

"You mistake me, Your Grace. I remind you of St. Paul's admonition to women to learn in silence and submission."

Against her will, Grace frowned. That verse had been used at one time or another by every man whose authority had been threatened by a thinking woman. "I rather think," she said, "that he was warning against those women who used their feminine wiles as lures cast out to susceptible men."

"That is a dangerous philosophy, Your Grace," said her first inquisitor in quelling tones.

Incredulously she stared at him and enquired, "Is a woman not allowed to think for herself?"

"You would be safer to abide by your father's teachings and now, your husband's," said the kinder Councillor.

"I hope you will not call my father to account for my writings," Grace said, fighting the sudden fear that the Council also meant for Mr. Penworth to suffer. "He was too busy with parish work to question my doings. And I can only hope you will allow me to go home to learn from my excellent husband."

"That remains to be seen," said her Enemy. "How did you, with your unorthodox views of aristocracy, manage to snare His Grace, the Duke of Standen, into marrying you? By using your 'feminine wiles'?"

"I do not presume to understand that mystery," Grace said in all innocence. "You must ask that of the duke."

"We will, madam," he said in menacing tones that had her quaking in her slippers.

How she wished she had not embroiled Alan in her troubles. A society that held the husband solely responsible for a wife's conduct would not allow even the Duke of Standen to go unpunished if she were found guilty of seditious libel. The Council must understand that she alone was responsible for her philosophy. "I beg you to remember that the outspoken views I expressed in my essays were formed long before I met my husband."

"Hmph," was the only reply forthcoming. Everyone at the table was either consulting notes or scribbling on parchment.

Leaning forward on her toes, Grace said, "I cannot rest easy until you assure me he is not to be held accountable for my folly."

"Folly?" The man she had come to call her enemy rose from his chair and regarded her through a quizzing glass. "Do you mean to recant, then?"

Swallowing a lump of fear that threatened to throttle her fragile calm, Grace said, "I cannot easily renounce my beliefs, my lord."

"Can you tell us why not?"

"If God in his wisdom chooses to bestow upon any individual an exalted rank, I believe that person must accept a certain responsibility."

Her accuser bestowed upon her a thin-lipped, bloodless smile that reminded Grace of a serpent's grin. Unable to look away from the nobly disapproving stare, she could only nod when he said, "And so you take full responsibility for your seditious writings?"

He glared at her when she did not reply aloud. "We cannot hear you, Your Grace." His sneering inflection on her title left no doubt as to the council's contempt of her.

"Yes, my lord," she replied. "I wrote what I believed to be true and just, as God is my witness."

"Do not presume on the Almighty," said her accuser in frosty tones. "He is not your advocate, but your judge." Then, directing a cursory glance at the guards who stood at either of Grace's elbows, he said, "Take her to the Tower."

Grace looked at each of the men who were seated around the council table. Not one of them returned her questioning gaze, and so she knew she had been given up.

"Come with us, Your Grace," said a now-familiar voice at her ear.

Turning toward her guard, she smiled tremulously at him. "Thank you for standing with me," she said, allowing him and his comrade to take her arms and guide her away.

"It's our job, Your Grace," said the Messenger not unkindly as he escorted her into the hallway. "Here now," he said, waving away a group of journalists who were circling around them like carrion crows. "Stand aside."

"A moment of your time, Your Grace," shouted the most persistent of the journalists, his pencil poised over a notebook. "How is it possible that one of the most noble men in the country could have been so deceived in his bride as to wed a traitoress?"

Grace turned a look of shock and dismay upon the

heartless reporter, seemingly forgetting the others, whose pencils hovered just as viciously over their notebooks. "I hope my lord is not deceived in me," she said in a voice barely stronger than a whisper before her guardians hurried her into the relative safety of the closed coach and slammed the door behind them.

Shouted queries battered her ears in the seconds before the guard driving the hackney coach sprung his team. Echoes of "When did you mean to call the people to revolt?" and "Does the duke believe in your innocence?" badgered her all along the drive to the Tower.

As she was ushered into a drafty chamber overlooking the Thames, she asked of the governor, "Will I be allowed to see my husband?"

"That's up to the Council," he said kindly. "Not to worry, Your Grace. No lady's blood has ever been on my hands. And to be sure you 'ave the best of care, my wife has consented to be your maid until such time as the Council authorizes you to have your own."

Privately Grace was of the opinion that the governor's wife was to attend her as a spy for the prosecution, but she was not so lacking in good sense as to admit such doubts to her jailer. Thanking him for his kindness, she merely said she would be glad of his wife's assistance, then sat on the edge of the hard bench provided for her bed until he took himself away.

Immediately she was possessed of a frigid certainty that she was going to spend the rest of her days within these walls. So pervasive was this numbing feeling of dread that a gray, cold ache seeped into her very bones despite the heat and brilliance of the summer day outside. Shivering, she clutched her velvet cloak tightly about her, glad to have this tangible evidence of her husband's concern to comfort her.

For the longest time she sat undisturbed in her apartment. Outside could be heard the noise of a drilling garrison and the applause of appreciative spectators. Grace found herself wondering if someone—a soldier or sightseer, it did not matter who—was imagining anyone unhappily housed within the gray stone fortress, or if everyone thought it was now simply the home of several miserable creatures contained in the menagerie, as well as the repository of the Royal Jewels and Armor.

It was frightening to be locked away as a state prisoner without any clue as to how she was to defend herself. How she wished she had a copy of her foolish essays, so that she might reread them and discover why, after gathering dust on various bookshop shelves, her little book should have stirred up that same dust as made the World choke on it.

Hadn't she adjured the people to obey those in authority over them?

Perhaps it was because she had exhorted those fortunate individuals in high-ranking places not to lord it over their inferiors. Or perhaps it was because certain gentlemen loathed intelligent women. But that, she reminded herself, as she chewed the corner of her lower lip anxiously, was such a defense as would lead directly to the gallows. And that was not the sort of ending Hugh and Teddy and Kate had prayed for her. Their childlike faith must sustain her in her dark hour where, within her heart, all was gray.

Despite her gloomy thoughts, a sunbeam bravely illuminated a corner of her chamber. Turning on her hard seat, she looked upward at the window that was set high in the wall above her bed. Climbing onto the sturdy wooden frame, she stood on tiptoe and peered outside. The sun shone brightly on the green where the garrison was drilling, reminding Grace that life continued apace whether or not she was a part of the current.

Of a sudden the door to her chamber swung open. Turning on her perch, she watched as a gray-haired matron bearing a tray on which tea was laid entered. "She is in here, Your Grace," she said, curtseying as the Duke of Standen filled the doorway.

"Alan!" Grace cried in relief and pure joy. Bounding off the wooden bench, she flung herself into her husband's arms. "I feared I should never see you again."

"Why is that, my love?" he enquired, allowing her to cling to him while the governor's wife set the tea tray on the wooden table set against the far wall. "Am I so faint-hearted as to abandon you in your trouble?"

"No," Grace said. She was ashamed to look at him, for she was the faint-hearted one, weeping the way she was. "Only the governor said you must have the Privy Council's permission to come." Ashamed of the way she lost control of her emotions, she swiped at her eyes with the kerchief the duke pressed into her hands. "Surely it is a good sign that I shall be home soon?"

Then she was made aware that her husband had not come alone. "Grace," he said, drawing her onto the bench. "I should like to make known to you my counsel, Lloyd Kenyon and his associate, Mr. Erskine."

Both gentlemen bowed and acknowledged her with a reverent, "Your Grace," then stood silent while the duke pressed home to her the desperation of her case.

"The prosecution is calling for your head," he said urgently. Twining his fingers amongst hers as she flinched at his words, he went on without pity, "DuBarry has incited them to a fever pitch with his accusations against you. They insist on an early trial."

"Then I shall be home soon," she said, clinging to his hands. "Alan, I have gone over in my mind everything I might have written in that accursed book. None of it is treasonous. I might have written the essays directly from some of Papa's sermons."

"I pray you will not confess that in court," said Mr. Kenyon, a cold-hearted businessman. "Or your poor father will suffer the consequences."

"Oh, no," she gasped. "I will not. Only tell me, Alan, what must I say?"

He was gripping her hands tightly as to compel her to meet his flintlike gaze. He stared at her as if testing her mettle, and she forced herself to wait patiently on his advice. Finally, he said slowly and firmly, "You can say nothing, but must appear at all times to depend on counsel to win an acquittal."

"But Alan," she began, panic rendering her stupid for the moment.

The duke pressed her hands together as if demanding silence. "Ladies are not permitted to speak in court, either to offer testimony or to speak in their own defense. Trust me, Grace."

"I do, my love. When may I go home?"

"I want nothing more than to carry you out of this place now," he said. "But that is an impossibility. You must stay here in this good woman's care."

"I will," Grace said, lowering her head to their clasped hands. "I'm so sorry, Alan."

"What? Do you lack the courage of your convictions?" he enquired. "That does not sound like the Grace Penworth I came to love."

"No," she said. "Only I am sorry to be more trouble for you."

"I wouldn't suffer it for anyone but you," he said, smiling when she raised her red eyes quizzically. "No more apologies now. Come, Mr. Kenyon, Mr. Erskine, I imagine you want to interview my lady wife and discover for yourself how she came to express such shocking ideas."

Eighteen

Mr. Kenyon's terse queries did not ease Grace's troubled mind but rather served to increase her anxiety. He gave every evidence of believing her guilty of inciting the people to revolt against the King, by informing her that her essays had been found in the possession of admitted revolutionaries who claimed to have been influenced in no small way by her inflammatory writings. "Do not think your lofty marriage will save you from the hangman's noose," he said as he paced the length of her chamber. "If anything, it will irritate the prosecution and infuriate your former allies."

Grace bestowed a frightened look upon the duke. Standen gave her hand a reassuring squeeze as if to say not to worry. But he was not being tried for a capital crime and could scarcely understand the agonies of fear to which she had fallen prey. Turning back to the councillor who seemed to have turned persecutor, she said, "I do not know what you want me to say, Mr. Kenyon. I did write the essays. But not with any evil intent. Certainly not to cause riots in manufactories."

"I did not say they caused riots," Mr. Kenyon said in cagey tones. "When is this riot supposed to take place?"

"Standen," she said, clinging to her husband's fingers. "Tell him he mistakes me."

"Leave off, Kenyon," said the duke, unconsciously scratching a spot on his jaw. Then, recalling his dignity and the cause of the irritation, he explained, "Grace has been rather occupied at sickbeds lately and cannot have planned to overthrow any government."

"How long have you known her?" demanded the lawyer.

"Long enough to know she hasn't a rebellious bone in her body," Standen replied, ignoring their discussions about independence.

"And if you commanded her to cease writing, would she obey you?"

Grace felt her husband's eye on her as if he were measuring how far he could claim her complaisance. She tilted her face upward, offered a contrite smile, and was rewarded with a firm declaration of support. "I would not ask her to hide her light beneath a bushel, Mr. Kenyon. Don't defend her on the probability that marriage has silenced her. Defend her on the truth: that she has written nothing scandalous, libelous, or seditious, and cannot be held responsible for others' erroneous interpretation of her innocent work."

"Truth, Your Grace?" Mr. Kenyon enquired. "What is truth?" He paused, as if for dramatic effect, then said, "Truth is whatever the jurors believe."

In what seemed like an uncharacteristic about-face of manner, he grinned and said, "It is my job, and Mr. Erskine's, ma'am, to convince the jury that the Truth is what *we* say it is. Never fear, Your Grace," he said, directing a benign glance upon the duchess, "We shall bring you about. But you must repose absolute trust in us."

"Oh, I do," she said fervently. "I should jump through hoops did you think such acrobatics would improve my chances."

The elder counselor frowned, as if he believed after all his priming, she still did not fully appreciate the seriousness of the case against her. But Standen clasped her hand affectionately and said, "I do not think we need to make you appear ridiculous before the court to win acquittal, my dear."

"No doubt they will think me ridiculous enough to hang," she returned as her fears threatened to overset her nerves.

She was caught in a firm grip and fairly shaken. "Stop that," Standen commanded, so that she was compelled to stare at him. "Don't give doubt a foothold, Grace. Remember, you are the Duchess of Standen. I did not marry a wild-eyed revolutionary, but a delightful woman I cannot wait to carry over the threshold."

Mr. Kenyon cleared his throat as if the intimate tenor of the conversation struck a raw nerve. "We shall leave you now, Your Grace," he said as his assistant bundled a stack of papers into a leather case. Touching his forelock in a valedictory salute, he said, "Courage, madam."

When the councillors had gone, Grace lay her cheek on Alan's smooth, hard shoulder and felt the ripple of powerful muscles as she spread her hands across his back.

"This isn't how I envisioned our wedding night," he said, dropping a kiss on the top of her head.

Shame constricted Grace's throat until she could neither swallow her fears nor breathe in her husband's strong and confident air. "I wouldn't blame you if you no longer want me," she said at last in a voice that was pinched and frightened.

"Oh, I want you," he assured her, and he began to show her how much. Raising her face from its hiding place on his shoulder, he covered her lips with his.

As he kissed her, every niggling fear fled before the warm assurance that he did love her and would cherish and protect her against every foe. Grace clung to him, kissing him back with all her heart.

"Ah, Grace," said the duke, cradling her tenderly at last, as if he was content just to hold her. But then his arms tensed around her as if he was warring with an unfamiliar emotion. Finally, he exhaled a long, sibilant breath that seemed to deflate him a little, and he said, " 'Twill be a lonely bed I seek tonight, my dear. But I take consolation that in the nights to come we—"

"Begging your pardon, Your Grace."

Her heart pounding in a panicked rhythm, Grace would have fled her husband's arms at the governor's wife's untimely interruption had Standen not been holding her in a commanding but gentle grip. Turning a frigid stare on the grim-faced female, he enquired in regal tones what was so important as to cause her to forget to scratch at the door before gaining entrance.

She dipped a curtsey that was in no way servile and met his frosty glare with a knowing one of her own as she said, "You must leave now, Your Grace. Rules do not permit . . ."

"Not until you have seen to my wife's comfort," Alan

said. "And brought the clothing, food, bedding, coal, books, and paper that I have provided her."

"They must be inspected," said the clever woman. She crossed her arms over her broad stomach and said suspiciously, "For weapons and gunpowder."

"Good God, woman," Standen exclaimed. "Do you believe my wife, the Duchess of Standen, capable of inciting a rebellion by blowing up the Tower?"

The woman's narrow-eyed glare told him she thought that very thing. "We cannot be too careful," she said, holding wide the door as if the gaping aperture would lure the duke into the hallway.

He did not take the bait, for which Grace was exceedingly glad. The governor's wife kept looking on her with such hostility, she felt she was being placed under an evil eye. It was all she could do not to cling dependently to her husband's side. Clinging instead to the shreds of her courage, she compelled herself to breathe in a normal rhythm so that her jailer could not see how frightened she was.

When it became apparent that Standen had no intention of leaving of his own volition, the matron said in more conciliatory tones, "If you will come with me, Your Grace, you may assure yourself that your wife's property is delivered to her. And we can discuss terms of payment for services rendered during her . . . confinement."

Raising a cynical eyebrow, Standen said, "Of course," and clutched Grace to him for one more brief, intense moment. Then, caressing the fine line of her jaw, he said, "Do not give up hope, my dearest Grace," in tender accents that buoyed her flagging courage. "Put your imagination to good use; remember the knight and his lady."

"And their happy ending," Grace murmured. She raised a shy, budding smile to her husband. "Sleep well, my lord," she said, tucking a hand within his to walk with him toward the door as if she was bidding farewell to a gentleman come to pay his compliments over tea. She had to make him think she was confident in their future together, even if she feared she was to have no future. And so she kissed him and waved goodbye, smiling as he accompanied the governor's wife through the door.

When he had gone, the door clanged shut, locking her inside with her thoughts. Grace could hear his boot heels striking the stone floor with a purposeful rhythm as he strode toward freedom. Each footfall seemed to reverberate within her until she was possessed of the choking terror that she would never see her husband again.

She leaned her forehead on the heavy wooden panel that barred her escape and breathed slowly, not letting herself give into her nauseating fears.

That it was no use arguing with the part of her mind that was possessed of fear, she knew from long experience. Like a barrister, Fear refuted even the most convincing arguments. Rather than cower like a craven-hearted fool, she placed herself on a straight-backed chair and began to occupy her thoughts with the more pleasing tale that Standen wanted to see complete.

When the governor's wife and two servants returned to her cell bearing the comforts Standen had delivered, she surprised them so with her serenity that the matron offered to make up her bed.

Self-discipline had enabled Grace to complete the story in her mind. Rather than put words to paper immediately, she thanked the matron for her kind offer but declined the assistance, saying that she needed to keep her hands busy. Then, before the guards quit the room, she began to make her bed and set her things in order, so that they would have no complaints against her.

These domestic tasks relieved her anxiety a great deal, for she had long taken comfort in attending to routine matters, and she knew her confinement would not weigh as heavily on her soul if she kept up a semblance of normalcy. And the most normal thing she could do after setting up housekeeping was to write. As soon as she could, she sat down and committed the knight's story to paper.

Her optimism continued until the next morning, when Standen burst into her chamber, waving a copy of the *Morning Post* and demanding to know if he had married the Queen of Fools.

Grace looked up from her writing to gaze at him in puzzlement. His normally well-styled Wind Blown looked as if he had taken hold of the sides of his head and pulled, and the veins in his neck were pulsing furiously. All in all, his appearance and demeanor were not very loverlike. But she was flushed with the fever of writing and said the first thing that came to mind. "If I am Queen, then you must surely be the King. Or did a bee get into your bonnet?"

"No, madam," Standen said frigidly. "But I can only surmise one must have set up housekeeping between your curls. What did you mean by granting the *Post* an 'exclusive interview'?"

Grace shot to her feet and snatched the broadsheet from Alan's hands. "I did not! Some one asked me a question as I was leaving the Privy Council, and I—God help me!" She crumpled the sheet in her fists as the huge black banner DOXIE DUPES DUKE shouted at her.

"You did not ignore the query," Standen said, clutching the hair above his ears in a convulsive movement. Then, directing a furious glare at her, he said, "Do not stop with the headline, Grace. Read the story. Not only does he paint me a fool, he gloats over your 'confession.' "

"I did not," Grace said as she scanned the page which virtually condemned her as a traitor. "I promise I did *not* tell any reporter that I wrote seditious lies. And in the next breath I am supposed to have said I cannot easily renounce my beliefs? He makes me sound like a woman who does not know her own mind. And look at this." She turned the paper so Alan could peer over her shoulder and see the caricaturist's rendering of the duke playing cat's paw to the new Duchess of Standen, who was teaching roosters to lay eggs and bulls to give milk.

It was the second time Standen had seen the cartoon, and now he realized what an awful likeness of Grace the caricaturist had rendered. She looked more like an ecclesiastical nightmare than a duchess, and was saying, "Death to all Tyrants." It was a most un-Grace sentiment and sank the report to a level of absurdity that was not to be believed. If Grace's circumstances weren't so desperate, he would have found the article and accompanying etching laughable. As it was, he could scarcely find the words to reassure her. He was forced to exhale several breaths to clear his mind.

Mistaking the sounds he was emitting as inarticulate fury, Grace turned and threw her arms about his neck, crying, "Oh, my poor darling, can you forgive me?"

He suffered her to hug him for several moments while he strove to master himself, then grasped her wrists and drew her arms off his neck and down to her sides. "Grace," he said, bestowing a loving, but solemn look on her, "I understand you perfectly. But the rest of the world does not. It cannot understand you. That is why the Councillors released this story to the press."

"How could they do such a thing? It's not fair!" she gasped. "And it isn't true, at least the way it's written."

He knew her perplexing, earnest justification was perfectly logical and completely guiltless. But he also knew the unrestrained candor of an innocent would fail to convince the cynical jurists who must decide her case. "Regardless," he reasoned, "the people will believe what they read in the *Post*." He gave her a gentle but urgent shake and said, "Promise me you will say nothing more in your own defense to anyone who enquires about your circumstances."

Grace's pale gaze was captured in a potent, deep blue stare that did not for once appear either affectionate or indulgent. It was, instead, imperious, as if he were not merely requesting her cooperation but commanding obedience. It was precisely the kind of self-important, aristocratic stare that infuriated her, because it looked down on others as if they were a lower form of life.

How could he look at her, his wife, in that ominous,

forbidding manner? Had he suddenly come to believe he had married beneath himself?

A sickening fear heated the pit of her stomach as a roiling suspicion assailed her that the man she loved doubted her innocence.

He dragged a finger lightly across her lips. Grace closed her eyes against the trembling caress and was taken unawares as his mouth covered hers.

The kiss lasted only a moment, but when he released her lips, she felt as if an eternity had passed. Once more, she recognized the spark in his eyes and felt relief rush over her like a shower of warm water. Smiling giddily, she said in a quivering, compliant voice, "My lips are sealed."

The corner of his mouth turned up in a forgiving grin that made her heart leap joyfully. "Pray you do not confess that to your jailers," he said carelessly.

Her pulse, at first so light, thudded painfully in her ears as she considered the threat he had left unsaid. "I don't understand, Alan," she said in breathless, frightened tones. "Surely they would not 'make' me talk. I have nothing to confess."

He clutched her to him fiercely. "I did not mean to terrify you, Grace," he said. "But perhaps now you understand the danger you are in."

"I begin to," she replied, pressing against him as if she could vanquish in his arms the fears that battered at her. And as long as he remained with her, the tormenting thoughts were held at bay.

But Standen necessarily went away, taking the shreds of her courage with him. That night, as she huddled under the satin coverlet he had brought her, finally submerging her ever-present fears in the oblivion of sleep, she battled one nightmare after another, and started awake as the sound of a tortured cry penetrated her uneasy repose. For a long time, she sat clutching the coverlet to her breast, listening for a repetition of the eerie sound.

It was raining. Water sluiced down a copper drainspout, its hollow metallic sound the only disturbance in the night. But Grace could not go back to the sleep where nightmares lurked. Nor could she face the doubts and recriminations that reared their ugly heads in the dark. Shaking, she struck a flint and blew on the lint in the tinderbox until she could light a candle.

When she sat huddled at last within the dim circle of light, cutting a new pen and willing her imagination to cease its wild conjectures or at least confine itself to rendering the happy ending for her knight and Standen's lady, she heard slow footsteps making their way toward her and then the clank of a key in the lock of her door. As it swung open, admitting the yellow glow of lantern light, Grace's overset nerves expected to find that guards had come to wring a reluctant confession from her lips. Not wishing anyone to find her cowering in fear, she drew her comforter more securely around her shoulders, gazing calmly, she hoped, at the intruder.

It was only the governor's wife and a servant bearing a tray on which sat a pot and two cups. "I heard you cry out," said the matron, setting the lantern on a hook in the wall. "This is a horrible place, Your Grace. Sometimes in the night, I hear ghosts, and none of them happy." She poured out a cup and pressed it into Grace's

hand. "A cup of tea is just what you need right now."
Then she directed a questioning look at the second cup.

Holding the warming bowl in her fingers, Grace said,
"By all means, ma'am. I would welcome company for
awhile. Will you sit?" She offered the matron the companion chair.

The woman sat on the edge of the straight-backed
chair and seemed determined to make small talk. After
uttering the obligatory comments about the dismal
weather and the sad state of affairs when government
thought it had something to fear from a woman, she
said, "Trial's set for Monday."

"That soon?" Grace enquired, wondering inwardly
whether the prosecution thought her so dangerous as to
push for such an early trial. It had not been a week
since she had been charged. Chills beset her until she
trembled so violently she was compelled to set the cup
aside or risk burning herself.

"Not that I wouldn't welcome the company, Your
Grace," said the governor's wife in what seemed like
the warily open manner of one starved for companion-
ship and not sure how her overtures would be received.
"For it gets that lonely tending to empty chambers. But
I cannot help but think you don't belong here. Certainly
you don't act like a traitor."

Clutching her inadequate coverlet around her as she
recalled how suspiciously the matron had looked on her
at the beginning of her incarceration, Grace reminded
herself of her husband's warning against trusting others
unwittingly, then said, "Perhaps I should have my councillors call you as a character witness."

"Yes, well, the proper word from me in my husband's

ear could only help you," the governor's wife said, smoothing her mobcap and the folds of her shawl.

She looked to Grace like a cat preening itself after making a meal of a mouse. Determined not to be that mouse, Grace folded her lips together before she confessed her desire to be well thought of.

"Good opinions do not come cheap," said the matron in unmistakable tones as she leaned over the rim of her cup in the confidential manner of one who meant to relay the most tantalizing tidbits of gossip.

Directing a steady gaze upon the matron, Grace smiled understandingly, but she was not so desperate as to buy her jailer's favor, even if doing so might prolong her life or win her freedom. A few moments of silence gained her the presence of mind and courage to reply calmly, "I have nothing of value with which to purchase your good opinion, ma'am, and so I must rely on your good heart."

The woman seemed so taken aback that she fumbled with her cup, spilling some, but quickly salvaged her customary air of self-importance. Brushing off the drops of tea which she had inadvertently poured on her wrapper, she turned on Grace a smile that did not reach her eyes and said, "And to be sure I am not mistaken in your character, Your Grace, I feel certain you will not object if I borrow your writings." As if sensing Grace's hesitation, she added, "Or are they too private?"

"They are private, ma'am," Grace said. "But nothing you cannot see." Coming to her feet, she swept her papers into a tidy pile, then glanced at the final, unfinished page. "I was writing down a story for my niece and nephews."

"Children's story, eh?" said the matron, snatching the

per out of Grace's fingers and looking over several
heets. "Don't look like traitorous stuff."

"No," Grace said, controlling a sigh before it escaped.
: was nothing high-minded or lofty; only a silly story
f adventure and chivalry. "I fear it is not quite finished,
1a'am. Would you be so kind as to read while I scribble
1e ending?"

The governor's wife seemed to believe a supreme
ompliment had been paid her. Setting herself at one
ide of the table, she set to reading at once. Grace fin-
shed cutting her pen to her satisfaction, then quickly
rapped up the knight and lady's happy ending the way
he and Standen had planned in the garden.

She finished writing long before the matron com-
leted reading the previous pages. But she did not call
ttention to that lady's lingering perusal, only apologized
or her own wretched hand when the governor's wife
eached for the finale.

"Is there no more?" she demanded, her eyes shining
1 appreciation when she looked up from the last page.

"You have read the end," Grace reminded her. "Did
. not satisfy?"

"Perfectly," responded her jailer, unconsciously re-
arning the manuscript. "What I meant was, have you
o other stories?"

Grace knew that to answer in the affirmative would
nsure a search of her home. Unwilling to subject her
amily and especially her husband to such an indignity,
upposing it had not already occurred, she said, "None
1at would please you so well, ma'am." As she expected,
er jailer's eyes narrowed suspiciously, and she added
1 what she hoped was an honest tone, "I expect the

authorities have already confiscated everything else. S⟨
you see, I have nothing to hide."

"Be that as it may," said the governor's wife. "I mus⟨
read everything you put to paper from now on."

Nineteen

Grace was glad for her jailer's interest, for it distracted her from the relentless pressure of the coming trial. Mr. Kenyon or his assistant Mr. Erskine seemed to dog her days as they completed her defense at a breakneck pace. Neither they nor her husband, who they assured her was taking an active part in planning her defense, would share their strategy with her, but only reminded her in maddening tones of confidence that she must trust them.

Realizing there was nothing else for her to do, Grace tried not to let their constant exhortation that she not worry distress her.

Even though she reminded herself of Standen's belief that he had been "sent" to help her, she could only wonder why the Almighty should trouble Himself on her account. But when she remembered how much she loved Alan and that he loved her enough to fight so that they might make a life together, she gave up questioning Divine Plans and offered up heartfelt thanks for their swift completion.

When the trial opened, she knew she could use all the Help she could get. The weather was stiflingly hot, and the crowd before Westminster Hall was enormous.

Within a minute of the doors being opened, the court-room was filled with spectators, none of whom looked sympathetically at Grace as she entered the prisoner's box.

She clutched the bar as an ominous hissing rose from among ranks of the spectators. "Traitoress," they chanted, pointing fingers and raising children on their shoulders as if they had brought them to a Punch and Judy show. Grace swept a frightened glance around the airless room, then found her gaze locked onto Alan's reassuring stare.

They might have been alone in that moment. Even though she could not touch him or hear the words of encouragement he was mouthing, she felt strength coursing through her veins, fortifying her against every-thing that might come against them. She straightened her shoulders and tipped up her chin confidently, be-stowing a radiant smile on her husband.

Standen returned the smile, nodding as if he approved her courageous stance before the rabble that crowded the courtroom. Even they seemed to recognize her quiet assurance, for the assemblage settled down to an expec-tant quiet before the jurors and the Lord Chief Justice took their places.

The Attorney General glared at Grace as if he ex-pected to see horns sprout from her hair, then asked if any of the jurors had read the scurrilous volume of es-says by the defendant. Those who admitted to having done so and confessed to some sympathy toward the writer or her "questionable ideals" the prosecutor in-structed to "stand down," with a sweeping look of tri-umph toward his prisoner.

Grace smiled as three gentlemen shuffled out of the

ury box, relieved to see that even so few were willing
to admit sympathy to ideals which had conveyed her to
prison.

Mr. Kenyon, answering his opponent's challenge,
gruffly dismissed those jurors who "having read the
Duchess of Standen's excellent treatise, strongly objected to the charitable attitudes so nobly expressed
therein." Five stood down, every one of them scowling
as if he considered the Councillor's challenge an af-
front to justice.

Grace could not suppress the sigh of relief which escaped her lips as she watched those good men depart.
Nor could she refrain from feeling as if the burden on
her shoulders lightened each time a potential juror was
excused for prejudice against her, even if the predisposi-
tion was due to the fact that the gentleman was a caricaturist, "and therefore," as Mr. Kenyon intoned ironically,
"prejudiced by nature for or against everything," or the
gentleman "prejudiced by extreme interest" on account
of his trade—ropemaking.

A burst of appreciative laughter ushered that worthy
man out the door, where he might ply his trade regardless of its effects on the defendant, and he bowed toward
Grace as if to say he bore her no ill will. She smiled
at him, even though she was glad to see him go. She
knew very well that a guilty verdict could only profit
him.

When at last the jury had been pared to twelve good
men, the Attorney General stated the Crown's case
against "Grace Penworth Faulkner—the Duchess of
Standen." He said her name and new rank as if the
sound of it tasted like mildewed wheat.

Grace's grip on the bar tightened when she saw Alan's countenance darken in fury. He looked as if he would like to pummel the man threatening her peace.

Throughout the reading of the indictment, Grace gazed serenely upon her husband, willing him to master his temper. If he were compelled to leave the court due to an angry outburst, she knew she could not stand against the charges the chief counsel for the State was so venomously spitting out—"that Her Grace, the Duchess of Standen, not having the fear of God before her eyes, but being seduced by the instigation of the devil, did maliciously write and traitorously cause to be published certain vile essays which intended to raise and levy war against our Lord the King." He directed a scathing and lingering look upon her, as if by staring at her he could cause her to burst into flames or at the very least cower before his authority.

Grace stiffened her spine against his malevolent stare and compelled herself not to flinch as he droned loudly on, "To be guilty of treason, it is not necessary to prove that the duchess meant to levy war against the person of the King. If it can be shown, and I intend to show, that the prisoner levied war against the 'Majesty' of the King, so that she might Incite the Rabble to Force an Alteration of the Established Law, that is enough. For *that* is also high treason."

Grace paled under the chief prosecutor's gloating grimace and swayed against the charges that he had leveled against her. War against the King. Never, never had that been her intention. Dumbfounded, she forced herself to honor Alan's command that she remain silent. It took all her strength and courage not to cry out in confusion and fear.

Anxious perspiration chilled her. It was so hot. She felt as if she was getting a foretaste of Hell. But she refrained from fanning herself with the plain white silk fan Alan had given her to complement the elegant blue and white silk gown that he said made her look like an angel.

Though the compliment had warmed her at the time he had spoken it, Grace was not sure now how well that comparison served her. The prosecution was capitalizing its portrayal of her as a "Fallen Angel in League with the Devil, and a Daughter of Eve, deceived by her own Pride into leading devoted followers down a thorny path of civil disobedience and even violent rebellion."

When the prosecutor finished his opening remarks, Grace realized her chances for acquittal were so remote as to be impossible. If she had been so misguided as to dupe the public into committing crimes against the King by her writings, then she deserved no less than the punishment worthy of a traitor.

She ought to accept her sentence gladly, except that her gaze was once again captured in her husband's embracing stare. He loved her. She could not give up as long as Alan believed in her and loved her.

When the prosecution called its first witness—William DuBarry—she felt the blood drain from her countenance. With him she had discussed topics that might, indeed, *must* be considered treasonous. If her publisher had enlisted with the opposition, she was doomed.

And the Solicitor General played DuBarry as if he were a violin, leading the publisher to recall the minutest detail of every conversation or correspondence he had shared with the defendant. That the details omitted the fact that the political sentiments expressed had most often been DuBarry's was overlooked. Coached by the prosecutor, DuBarry eagerly depicted Grace as an opinionated female who would stoop to any level to achieve what she called "true equality and liberty."

Those inflammatory words seemed to incite a riot within the courtroom. The Lord Chief Justice loudly called for order, warning the spectators he would clear the court if they could not contain themselves against the fatal words that had ushered in the French Terror.

The judicial statement raised eyebrows among the jury and made Grace tremble violently. True equality and liberty *before God,* she wanted to cry out. Why had Mr. DuBarry left out those two crucial words? Did he *want* her to hang?

Standen saw his wife sway on her feet as if DuBarry's testimony had slapped her across the face. She was blinking back tears and shaking her head in such a manner as wrung his heart. Every manly instinct demanded he go to her comfort and demand satisfaction from the scoundrel who had made her suffer such indignities as she had suffered in the past weeks.

Only by the strongest measure of self-control was the duke able to command himself to remain in his chair so that he would not throttle the witness. Such an outburst would evict him from the trial, and he knew Grace needed him here. But he felt like less of a man for allowing such calumny to be heaped on his wife's slender shoulders even in search of justice.

"Now it's our turn," said Mr. Kenyon into Standen's

right ear as the Solicitor General was concluding Du-Barry's examination. "I know you'd like to be the one to strike the first blow, Your Grace, but if you will allow me?"

"With my compliments," Alan said, knowing Kenyon would let no opportunity to batter DuBarry's testimony go untouched. He compelled his jaw to unlock as the councillor rose and began his attack.

"Pray, what are you, Mr. DuBarry?" asked Mr. Kenyon in conversational tones.

"By trade, a publisher."

"Did you publish the duchess's essays?"

"Yes," said Mr. DuBarry. "She had a very convincing manner of—"

"Pray, just answer my questions," said the councillor in a somewhat irritated tone as if DuBarry's overeager explanation distracted him from his own thoughts. Then immediately, he asked, "Do writers pay you to publish their work, or do you pay them?"

DuBarry ran a finger around his high collar and swallowed nervously. "They receive royalties based on the sales of their work."

Mr. Kenyon spread his thick hands wide and presented the appearance of a benign fool. "Pray, enlighten a confused man, sir. Who pays whom?"

DuBarry's neck turned purple as he said, "If sales permit, I pay the writer."

"I see." Mr. Kenyon fell silent for several moments, staring at the floor as he paced before the witness box.

Grace leaned forward in her box, wondering what royalties had to do with the crime she was supposed to have committed. She had as yet received no monies from her book.

Of a sudden, Mr. Kenyon turned on the witness and said, "Publishing must be a rather uncertain business."

"That it is," agreed Mr. DuBarry with a sigh.

Kenyon wasted no time. "I believe you were a bankrupt?"

DuBarry seemed taken aback by counsel's brisk rejoinder. He swallowed several times and scratched the top of his head as if wondering where this line of questioning might next lead, then said hesitantly, "Yes."

He looked as if he might like to justify himself, but Kenyon gave him no opportunity. "You were desperate to sell books."

"It is my business," said DuBarry.

"Yes, well, it appears you weren't very good at your business," Kenyon shot back. "Or at managing your writer's opinions."

"I tried, but she would not listen to me, she would not have me—"

"For her husband?" demanded Kenyon.

"Yes. That is, *No!*"

"Did you ask the Duchess of Standen to be your wife?"

Grace was very uncomfortable with the tack Kenyon was taking, but she clenched her hands behind the bar and gazed steadily at her husband in hopes that he could reassure her. Alan was still looking at her. Against all reason, she smiled radiantly, eliciting a startled gasp from several of the jurors.

"I thought I could guide her . . ." said DuBarry, his

gaze sliding toward the duchess. When he saw the bea-
tific smile on her face, his own purpled in fury.

Kenyon pressed doggedly on. "Did you propose to
Grace Penworth?"

DuBarry pushed his spectacles against the bridge of
his nose belligerently, saying, "Yes, I did. But she
wouldn't have me. But I knew why, even *then* I did."

"And when she refused to accept your guidance and
your hand," Kenyon went on, seemingly ignoring
DuBarry's disgruntled commentary, "you devised the
perfect revenge—to promote her little book in a way
guaranteed to call attention to it *and* her?"

"I only wanted the thing to sell," said DuBarry.
"Make my investment back. It was purely business."

"Is that all?"

"Of course." DuBarry glared at Grace, but she was
still gazing on her husband. *"No!"* he shouted. "I
wanted her to pay attention to me and knew the book
was the perfect way to—"

"Win her heart?" Kenyon chuckled, then immediately
said, "I ask you, why should you wish to marry a lady
in whom you say you were so deceived?"

"I cannot explain myself," DuBarry said. "Anymore
than I can explain love."

"I am not asking you to explain love, but you must
explain yourself," said Mr. Kenyon. "Were you not
rather more intent on having your own way?"

"I will not answer that question," DuBarry said angrily.

"As you wish," said Counsel, as if the question mattered nothing to him. But he was not finished. "Tell
me, Mr. DuBarry, how has the duchess's little book
sold?"

"Very well," DuBarry confessed, his voice betraying pride. "It has sold out everywhere."

"Are you very proud of your part in its success?"

"Yes," DuBarry said without hesitation. "I could not foresee all the effects of my campaign, of course, but it has made my fortune."

"And how is that, when the Duchess of Standen stands penniless and accused of treason?" demanded Kenyon, ordering DuBarry in a disgusted voice to stand down in the next breath.

The publisher stood, pursing his lips together as if he had only belatedly realized he had spoken too long. As he passed beyond the bar, he glared at Grace, who had the misfortune to meet his gaze. Dropping her lids, she stared at her feet, feeling very much as if she had been burned.

The prosecution's next witness was a laborer from Cherhill who had been fired for inciting Mr. Davies's weavers to smash their looms. He had been arrested carrying a copy of Grace's book, and under the Solicitor General's direction was quick to condemn her for her interfering manner and prosy ways. Mr. Kenyon was hard-pressed to redirect the witness, who was stolid and unshakable, stirring him up only when he asked whether the duchess had taught his wife to read.

"She weren't no duchess then, and I don't hold with folks gettin' above themselves. Especially women: they need to be ruled with an iron hand," said the worker named Tom Flint. Grace knew him as a tyrant in his own home, laying down the law and his fist at any sign of hesitation or defiance. His wife Ellie and their six children had the bruises to show for his iron hand.

"Did the defendant teach your wife to read?"

"Aye, she did. I caught Ellie readin' that piece o' trash and fillin' her head with its nonsense. Men and women equal in God's eyes. I never heard the like. Why then did He command wives to keep silent and obey their men?"

"That is a point to think over," Mr. Kenyon said in seeming absorption to the witness's angry rambling. "However, more to the point, why then did you take to reading Cock and Bull Stories?"

"To find out what other lies she be fillin' her head with."

There seemed to be nothing to say to Tom's reply. Grace felt the noose tighten around her neck.

"How long had you known Miss Penworth before she married?"

"Since she were a little girl. Always interferin' in me business."

"Your business?"

"That's right. A man's got a right to live 'is life as 'e sees fit. But she uz allus tellin' me to come to church and see how God loves me. Bah. If He loves ever' one equal like she says, I'd be a duke like 'er man."

"And did you find any 'other lies' in her book?"

"Must be," Tom said, turning toward Grace with a wicked gleam in his eye. In the heat and hostility that was directed toward her, she felt a sick knot twist her stomach. "Didn't understand the half of it. An' the half I did understand, I didn't like."

"Is that when you began smashing looms, Mr. Flint?"

"Who d'ye think I am?" Flint growled. "I don't take nothin' from a woman who don't know her place. Even

'Er Grace'll tell you I been smashin' looms ever' since Davies brought 'em into our homes."

Grace wasn't sure such a belligerent confession could help her, but Mr. Kenyon simply told Tom Flint to stand down.

As her counsel lowered himself onto his hard chair, Grace leaned the heel of her hand on her forehead, fighting a vertiginous wave of heat that threatened to knock her down.

Twenty

Her guards caught her as she swooned. The Lord Chief Justice called for a chair.

Immediately Standen arose and carried his own chair to Grace, placing her on it with great care and then dabbing at her face with his handkerchief. "Courage, my love," he said under the cover of the speculative rumble that swept the courtroom. "Kenyon knows what he is doing."

"But I do not," she whispered, clinging to his hand.

"That is so," he said. "But *I* do."

"That is comforting," she said, her voice and courage very faint. "At least *you* will know why I am to hang."

Squeezing her fingers, he came to his feet and asked in a commanding voice, "Could my wife have a glass of water, my lord Justice?"

Immediately, though it was not customary to see to a prisoner's comfort, a glass was brought forth and placed in the duke's outstretched hand. While she sipped, the duke held it to her lips and said, "I promise you as I love you, we will come through this fire together."

She looked on him adoringly as he drew a gentle finger down the curve of her cheek. "If you give your word, Alan, I will believe you."

"Your Grace?" intoned the Lord Chief Justice in frosty tones that drew the couple's attention toward the bench. "Is your wife recovered? May we continue?"

"By all means," Standen said, taking his former place next to Mr. Erskine who had foreseen the necessity of replacing the duke's chair.

After three more witnesses, the prosecution rested its case. Standen's promise bolstered Grace through the discouraging testimony of another of her father's discontented parishioners, who claimed she had always been too prosy and high-minded for her own good. She prayed for strength when a man, calling himself Villiers, stood before the court to malign her as a thinking woman who had beguiled his wife at a meeting this summer in Charing Cross, and felt her confidence collapse when the final witness claimed he saw her assignation with the duke at the Swan and Bell last May. "She threw 'erself at him she did, shriekin' like a demon possessed. An' he carried her off, like he was right pleased." Not even Mr. Kenyon's skillful handling could erase the image of Grace flinging herself at a duke's head. For some reason, the bee didn't now seem to her to have been an adequate excuse.

It was late in the afternoon when Mr. Erskine arose to examine the first witness for the defense, Mr. Edmund Davies, the cloth merchant and the Penworths' wealthy neighbor. The stolid, likable merchant and his mild, rather indolent manner came as a surprise to those who thought of the middle-class as having pinchpenny, overindustrious ways. He assured the court that "Miss Grace was ever about the parish, doing good works as if she expected the Second Coming hourly. Tireless, she was. Took my breath away." And when the prosecution tried to shake the merchant's story by making it appear she was a meddler who was not satisfied with her lot in life, he skewered the Attorney General with a look that had put down more than one strike in his district and said, "Don't put words in my mouth, my lord. I don't criticize Miss Grace. She did what most of us only talk about—feeding the hungry, clothing the poor, and such like. And didn't make anyone feel guilty while she did it. She'll make her duke a good wife if you let her go home." Before he could damage the prosecution's case further, Mr. Davies was ordered to stand down.

Grace could have hugged her neighbor as he returned to the public arena, had she not been compelled by the force of law to stay in her box. That and shock in hearing the name of the next witness—her own father—kept her on the chair.

The Reverend Mr. Penworth answered Mr. Erskine's queries forthrightly but in a somewhat embarrassed, apologetic manner. He confessed that she had followed him on his rounds of the parish and that perhaps she had seen things young ladies ought not to see—unspeakable poverty, mothers and children abandoned by ablebodied men who preferred to chase bottle dreams than earn an honest wage, workers too old or infirm to be productive turned out with no pension. "But she was always a good girl, learned her catechism and helped her mother without complaint. We reared her to be a good Christian and a loyal Englishwoman," he vowed.

"God and King," he concluded stoutly, adding, "If I'd known she must marry a duke, Letitia and I might have brought the girl up differently."

The Solicitor General pounced on the vicar's justification. "How would her upbringing have been different, sir?"

"Why, we should have insisted she be finished. You know, my lord: learn a song, paint a picture, embroider—ladylike occupations. Other than being useful, her only talent is telling stories."

Grace raised herself from her chair and stared at her father. He had known all the time, and he had not forbidden her to exercise her pen or her ideas.

"Like these *Cock and Bull Stories?*" said the Solicitor General.

"They are not in her usual style," said the vicar. "But more like sermons."

"Really, Mr. Penworth. Sermons?"

"She was, I believe, very affected by the poverty in our parish and could not stand idly by as a pretty ornament while others starved. Her ability to relieve suffering would have served her very well had she become a nurse."

The court officer's brow lowered, giving him the look of a spider considering an unwary fly. "Do you admit your daughter is no lady then?"

Mr. Penworth looked on his inquisitor as one filled with the Wrath of God. "My daughter is a duchess."

The counselor clenched a fist and angrily dismissed the witness who had not fallen into his trap.

As Penworth passed the bar, Standen leaned toward him and said, "If you had brought her up differently, Father Penworth, I doubt she'd *be* my duchess."

Then Peter Ramsey witnessed to Grace's good character and kindness to people, especially to those newly arrived to their circle. Colin Spencer swore that Grace was too busy doing charitable works to foment rebellion. Several tenants from Bon Chance added high praise for their new duchess's unfailing kindness and willingness to nurse them through sickness and injury. Even the jailer's wife testified that "Her Grace was a quiet and obedient prisoner and wrote the most amusing stories." Finally Standen was called.

"Your Grace," said Mr. Erskine, when the duke had disposed himself in the box. "How long had you been acquainted with Miss Penworth before your marriage?"

"Since May," Standen said.

"Did she ever express revolutionary sentiments to you?"

The duke chuckled as if enjoying a memory. Grace wondered what could amuse him in such surroundings. He then looked at her and said, "She did say that my dining room would serve adequately as a banquet hall for beggars and the infirm."

Laughter rumbled around the courtroom until the Lord Chief Justice quelled it. Mr. Erskine did not share the spectator's mirth, but only said, "This is a serious matter, Your Grace. Can you recall any other incidents?"

"Yes, she once said I was too proud."

"When was this, Your Grace?"

"When I did not come to visit her in Harley Street after standing up with her during a dance. But I could not help doing so when I rescued Teddy—her nephew—in Hyde Park."

"How long have you known of Miss Penworth's charitable sympathies?"

"That very day, when her nephews and niece spoke

of her. No," Standen recalled, smiling on Grace as memory unfolded. She felt as if she was aglow in his regard and smiled back. "It was on the day we met. Her coachman wrecked my curricle at the Swan and Bell. At first she offered in such an innocent manner to take me to Town with her, I knew she could have no understanding of the damage it could do to her reputation. Then she offered to pay for the repairs to my equipage."

"Had she earned enough money from her writing to pay such an expensive debt?" Mr. Erskine enquired.

"I think not. She gave me her entire fortune: five shillings three pence. A widow's mite."

"Did you marry Grace Penworth to exact payment for the debt she owed you?"

"I did not," Standen said in emphatic tones. "I married her because I love her."

"How touching, Your Grace," said the Solicitor General in a tight-lipped manner as Mr. Erskine retired. Arising to his feet, the prosecutor came around the table and said, "All this proves is that the defendant has deceived you also. A pretty face and a shapely figure has fooled many a man into making a match. How came you, a War Hero, to fall for the oldest trick in the book?"

Standen regarded the Solicitor General as if he were the Enemy and inwardly berated himself for foolishly speaking of his feelings. "I understand trickery, my lord. Grace did not trick my heart. She won it by her unfailing honesty."

"Honesty? How can she be 'unfailingly honest' when by her father's own admission and that of the jailer's wife, the defendant was in the way of telling stories?

alsehoods. Bald-faced lies. Am I making myself clear? your wife a liar as well as a traitor?"

Standen glared at the prosecutor, willing himself to answer the insulting query in a calm, straightforward manner. It was of no use to mask the rage he felt, although his voice trembled with the effort at control when at last he spoke. "My wife is no liar, sir. As to the latter charge, these good men," sweeping an arm toward the jurors, "will decide that matter. I will not condemn my wife for entertaining children and impatient patients with harmless tales of derring-do and romance."

Offering his thin-lipped smile, the Solicitor General said, "But then we could not expect *you* to condemn a woman you profess to 'love,' could we, Your Grace? I have no further questions." And he spun on his heel and strode to his table as if he had wasted his time in questioning this witness.

Grace clasped her hands together, wondering what had so angered the Solicitor General. Alan had confessed before the Lord Chief Justice and twelve good men that he loved her. She knew it, of course, but it made her spirit soar to think it would be part of the court record. Not many wives had official documentation of their husband's affection.

But though she rejoiced in his unimpeachable declaration, she trembled at what was to come. Mr. Erskine had once again risen to his feet and was asking the Duke a final question. "Where was your wife, Your Grace, if she was not at this meeting at which Mr. Villiers claims she spoke?"

"She was at Bon Chance with my grandmother and me," Standen said without hesitation. "Telling stories to

a sick little boy and a sicker duke to keep us quiet so
we might recover."

"Was she with you at all times?"

"Not always. But she could not have traveled into
London and back in the time she was not with me."

Mr. Erskine directed his gaze toward the bench. "We
are prepared, if the Court thinks it material to go into
evidence to show where Her Grace was every hour and
every minute of that day Mr. Villiers claims she was at
a meeting in Charing Cross."

It sounded like a threat, and it was intended to be
one. It was already midnight, and Court had been in
session nearly sixteen hours. The Lord Chief Justice did
not think it material.

Glancing at the jurors in the flickering candlelight,
Grace was more than grateful for the judge's decision.
Several of them were yawning, and about the room
could be heard the sound of shuffling feet and restless
coughing. She herself could scarcely keep her eyes open
in spite of the grave consequence that faced her.

As her husband left the witness box, he caught her
faltering gaze in his resolute one. She felt as if he were
telling her to lean on him. Oh, if only she could. She
was so tired, she was shaking with the effort not to give
in to panic.

But she depended on Alan's steady gaze, longing to
soothe his dear, tired eyes with her own hands, and hoping the Lord would restore her to him. He had given
everything to her—his name, title, wealth, affection, and
the protection of his position in society—and she had
given nothing. She was his wife, but she was his wife
in name only, and as Mr. Erskine began an impassioned

summation for the defense, she wondered whether she must suffer death without giving Alan the full measure of her love.

Her hopes began to rise as the young councillor pled for her life, refreshing the tired jurors' recollection of the testimony to the strength of character and depth of emotion that compelled her not only to serve those in need, but cry out their need to a world intent on serving only itself. "The fact that so many citizens are not behaving well is surely no fault of the duchess," he said. "She did not call for 'revolution,' but an individual change of heart—to regard others more highly than one regards himself. That is no crime. The most serious crime of which she might be thought guilty is a lack of foresight." He added in a hoarse voice that was no less moving, "But, gentlemen, we are not trying whether she might or ought to have foreseen the mischief others might do, but whether she maliciously or traitorously preconceived and designed it."

Grace heard his appeal and was grateful for it, but she depended more on her husband's calm, loving regard. She had eyes for no one but Alan, and she rested in the security of his steady gaze.

While the duke and duchess were absorbed in one another, Mr. Erskine wound up his emotional speech. "Grace Penworth Faulkner stands clear of every hostile act or purpose against the Legislature of her country, since the whole substance of her conduct denies the traitorous purpose charged by the indictment. My task is done. I shall not address your passions. I will not remind you that she was taken from her husband on her wedding day. I will not speak of her youth, her beauty, her goodness, and purity of heart.

"Such topics might be useful in the balance of a doubtful case, yet even then I should trust to the honest hearts of Englishmen to have felt them without inspiration. The rules of justice are plain and rigid and sufficient to entitle me to your verdict; and may God fill your mind with their deepest impressions and allow you with virtue to follow those impressions. You will then restore my innocent client to liberty and to the arms of her faithful husband."

For several moments, no one seemed even to breathe, but to hear the dying echoes of an inspired plea that assured Grace of her freedom. But when the Solicitor General arose to recite his closing arguments, the joy of certain acquittal burst like a soap bubble.

He restricted himself to the facts as his witnesses had presented them. He referred to Mr. DuBarry's claims that Grace Penworth had used her charm to excite his own more moderate views, Mr. Villiers's assertion that she had spoken at an inflammatory meeting, and made great use of Tom Flint's happy home which the duchess had purposely sabotaged, saying it was "a brief step from subverting the home to the country." He reminded the jurors, who were now frowning deeply, of the dissatisfied laborers who had responded to her traitorous appeal, and made a point of questioning that "pure love" between husband and wife by reminding them of her prior "loose behavior at a public inn."

The prosecution's summation was not inspiring, but it was coldly effective. Grace was no longer confident of acquittal. Worse, she did not believe she was worthy of her husband, as much as she loved him. Standen did not deserve to have as his wife an accused felon. She was not even worthy to look on him.

Tears of exhausted hope fell onto hands that had been clasped tightly together most of the day. She did not look up as the Lord Chief Justice summed up the case and dismissed the jury with the usual admonition, "If the scale should hang doubtful and you are not fully satisfied that she is guilty, you ought to lean on the favorable side and acquit her."

Grace did not look up as the jury retired. She did not look up until a strong hand covered hers and she saw her husband kneel at her side.

"Alan," she whispered, her voice hoarse and weak from emotion. She could not help the spark of happiness that he ignited in her gaze, but asked anxiously, "Ought you to be here?"

"I have every right, my love," he assured her. "But *you* ought not be here. You ought to be safe at home, and I shall see that you are."

She shook her head. "No, Alan, you deserve a wife who—"

"Pray do not tell me again what I deserve," he said, smoothing a hand alongside her wet cheek. "I want you. Now hush. The jury returns."

Grace knew that they must have decided she was guilty to have reached a verdict so quickly. She clung to her husband's hand and willed herself not to give way to her fears.

She was even more convinced she had been found guilty when Mr. Erskine fell into a dead faint. Her heart was pounding so hard, she could scarcely hear the bailiff's command, "Grace, Duchess of Standen, hold up your hand." Alan held it aloft while the court official said, "Gentlemen of the jury, look upon the Prisoner. How say you? Is she guilty of the indictment wherewith she stands charged, or not guilty?"

The foreman of the jury stood up and looked at Grace. She could not read his expression, but found that she was no longer frightened.

He grinned and said, "Not guilty."

Birds were greeting the dawn with rapturous songs that proclaimed their own joy as a footman let Alan and his Grace into Standen House a little after five o'clock.

At the doorstep, the duke swept her up in his arms and carried her over the threshold. "Welcome home," he said, ignoring the startled footman as he pressed a kiss on her parted lips.

"Ought we tell our families?" she asked.

"Your father and brother-in-law will proclaim our good news when everyone arises," Standen laughed as he strode up the stairs. "I have a mind to keep you to myself and out of trouble for the time being."

"I'd like that," she said, reclining in the cradle of his arms. She could scarcely believe she had been acquitted and was home. Placing her hand over his heart, she said, "Alan?"

"Yes, my love?"

She looked, smiling, into his adoring gaze. "Could I trouble you to take me to our room?"

"Oh, my Grace," he said, carrying her at last to their bed. "I promise t'will be no trouble."

ZEBRA REGENCIES
ARE
THE TALK OF THE TON!

A REFORMED RAKE (4499, $3.99)
by Jeanne Savery

After governess Harriet Cole helped her young charge flee to France — and the designs of a despicable suitor, more trouble soon arrived in the person of a London rake. Sir Frederick Carrington insisted on providing safe escort back to England. Harriet deemed Carrington more dangerous than any band of brigands, but secretly relished matching wits with him. But after being taken in his arms for a tender kiss, she found herself wondering — *could* a lady find love with an irresistible rogue?

A SCANDALOUS PROPOSAL (4504, $4.99)
by Teresa DesJardien

After only two weeks into the London season, Lady Pamela Premington has already received her first offer of marriage. If only it hadn't come from the *ton's* most notorious rake, Lord Marchmont. Pamela had already set her sights on the distinguished Lieutenant Penford, who had the heroism and honor that made him the ideal match. Now she had to keep from falling under the spell of the seductive Lord so she could pursue the man more worthy of her love. Or was he?

A LADY'S CHAMPION (4535, $3.99)
by Janice Bennett

Miss Daphne, art mistress of the Selwood Academy for Young Ladies, greeted the notion of ghosts haunting the academy with skepticism. However, to avoid rumors frightening off students, she found herself turning to Mr. Adrian Carstairs, sent by her uncle to be her "protector" against the "ghosts." Although, Daphne would accept no interference in her life, she *would* accept aid in exposing any spectral spirits. What she never expected was for Adrian to expose the secret wishes of her hidden heart . . .

CHARITY'S GAMBIT (4537, $3.99)
by Marcy Stewart

Charity Abercrombie reluctantly embarks on a London season in hopes of making a suitable match. However she cannot forget the mysterious Dominic Castille — and the kiss they shared — when he fell from a tree as she strolled through the woods. Charity does not know that the dark and dashing captain harbors a dangerous secret that will ensnare them both in its web — leaving Charity to risk certain ruin and losing the man she so passionately loves . . .

ELEGANT LOVE STILL FLOURISHES —
Wrap yourself in a Zebra Regency Romance.

A MATCHMAKER'S MATCH   (3783, $3.50/$4.50)
by Nina Porter
To save herself from a loveless marriage, Lady Psyche Veringham pretends to be a bluestocking. Resigned to spinsterhood at twenty-three, Psyche sets her keen mind to snaring a husband for her young charge, Amanda. She sets her cap for long-time bachelor, Justin St. James. This man of the world has had his fill of frothy-headed debutantes and turns the tables on Psyche. Can a bluestocking and a man about town find true love?

FIRES IN THE SNOW   (3809, $3.99/$4.99)
by Janis Laden
Because of an unhappy occurrence, Diana Ruskin knew that a secure marriage was not in her future. She was content to assist her physician father and follow in his footsteps . . . until now. After meeting Adam, Duke of Marchmaine, Diana's precise world is shattered. She would simply have to avoid the temptation of his gentle touch and stunning physique — and by doing so break her own heart!

FIRST SEASON   (3810, $3.50/$4.50)
by Anne Baldwin
When country heiress Laetitia Biddle arrives in London for the Season, she harbors dreams of triumph and applause. Instead, she becomes the laughingstock of drawing rooms and ballrooms, alike. This headstrong miss blames the rakish Lord Wakeford for her miserable debut, and she vows to rise above her many faux pas. Vowing to become an Original, Letty proves that she's more than a match for this eligible, seasoned Lord.

AN UNCOMMON INTRIGUE   (3701, $3.99/$4.99)
by Georgina Devon
Miss Mary Elizabeth Sinclair was rather startled when the British Home Office employed her as a spy. Posing as "Tasha," an exotic fortune-teller, she expected to encounter unforeseen dangers. However, nothing could have prepared her for Lord Eric Stewart, her dashing and infuriating partner. Giving her heart to this haughty rogue would be the most reckless hazard of all.

A MADDENING MINX   (3702, $3.50/$4.50)
by Mary Kingsley
After a curricle accident, Miss Sarah Chadwick is literally thrust into the arms of Philip Thornton. While other women shy away from Thornton's eyepatch and aloof exterior, Sarah finds herself drawn to discover why this man is physically and emotionally scarred.

Available wherever paperbacks are sold, or order direct from the Publisher. Send cover price plus 50¢ per copy for mailing and handling to Penguin USA, P.O. Box 999, c/o Dept. 17109, Bergenfield, NJ 07621.Residents of New York and Tennessee must include sales tax. DO NOT SEND CASH.